SPACE
TRIPPING

SPACE TRIPPING

PATRICK EDWARDS

INKSHARES

Published by Inkshares, Inc., San Francisco, California
www.inkshares.com

Edited and designed by Girl Friday Productions
www.girlfridayproductions.com

Cover design by Edward Bettison

ISBN: 9781942645214
e-ISBN: 9781942645221
Library of Congress Control Number: 2016937658

First edition

Printed in the United States of America

For Gabriella Rose
aka Gabitron
aka Gabzilla
If you're reading this, it's past your bed-time. Go to sleep, sweetie.
And don't give me any of that "That makes no sense, because reading a book has nothing to with the time of day. Have you lost your mind?" back talk.
Love,
Dad

TEXT UNIT 0001

Inebriated space travel is ill-advised . . .

. . . is what it said on the first page of the Sentient Coalition's official intergalactic travel manual, which happened to be conveniently wedged under the seat of an incredibly intoxicated alien who just crashed on Earth.

The ship in question careened into an abandoned city lot with all the grace of an anvil. After extracting himself from the impact crater, the alien, hereinafter known as Jopp, staggered his way through the gathering crowd, all the while shouting an unintelligible string of curses. None of the Earthlings could tell that Jopp was an alien, mind you. In his final moment of lucidity, Jopp made the shrewd decision to trigger his holoskin, making him appear to be no more than a disheveled human vagrant. The fact that his downed ship disintegrated into a pile of ash was due less to shrewd decision-making and more to the blind luck of him bumping the self-destruct button on the remote in his pocket when he stumbled into a parking meter. He looked up to berate the inconsiderate meter and spotted what he believed to be a Class 3 Danowitcz model space cruiser. Jopp scrambled over as fast as his stubby legs would let him and hopped in with the intention of piloting to the nearest liquor dispensary. After Jopp spent a minute fumbling with what he thought was the primary thrust converter, the alcohol in Jopp's system decided it was time to turn out the lights. His unconscious form slumped against the vehicle door.

It was then that the driver of what was in reality a semi-trailer truck jumped into the front cab to kick out the belligerent drifter. The driver, hereinafter known as Chuck, pulled himself into the cab just in time to see Jopp's holoskin generator start to malfunction.

Chuck gaped in horror as Jopp's apparently human flesh flickered like an old TV with bad reception, removing the last vestiges of human appearance. The individual sitting next to him was barely over five feet, with a stocky yet firm build, pale yellow skin, and a wide nose. No ears, but rather a pair of antenna-like nodes, each about three inches long. There were no visible seams, lines, or buttons adorning his blue uniform. He wore a thick black bracelet on his left wrist.

Chuck was at a loss for words. He'd already had a long day and just wanted to finish his route in time to make it to the bar for their fifty-cent wing deal. He had just decided to kick the unwanted passenger out and chalk up the odd appearance to his own exhaustion when the truck was suddenly enveloped in a cone of fluorescent red light. Then, either surprisingly or totally predictably, depending on who you ask, the truck began to rise up into the sky. Chuck sat frozen with shock as they continued to fly higher. In a matter of minutes, they were exiting Earth's atmosphere. Looming above the ever-ascending semitrailer, on the edge of space, was a massive metallic-blue structure. The red light came from an opening on the underside of the ship, which stretched well over a mile. As the truck passed through the opening, the red light ceased, and the truck dropped about two feet back down to the now-closed floor panels. This drop simultaneously jolted Chuck out of his shock and woke Jopp from his blackout. Jopp vigorously shook his round yellow head in an attempt to kick loose the alcohol-soaked cobwebs. Chuck couldn't tell where they were, as the only light came from the interior of the truck cab.

Jopp looked over at Chuck and blurted out, "⏀⌇⌾ ⬧⌇⼦⬧⬧ ◆⬧◻◻◻⬧⌾ ◌⏁◼⬧ ✋ ◆⬧◻◆⽁⬧◆ ◆⬧⼦◆ ◆⏁◆ ◻⌇ ⬧⼦◻⬧ ✳⬧⏁◆⸓ ⏁ ⽁◻◻⸫ ⬧◻●◻⬧◆⬥⼦⼦ ⽟⌇ ◆⬧⛧ ◆⏁⌇."

Chuck's expression remained frozen in place, while Jopp's became annoyed.

"⏀⬧⏁◆⌧ ◆◻◻◼⽁ ◆⼦◆⬧ ⌇◆◆⬧ ⬩◻◆ ◻ ◌◻◆⬧⏁◼ ◻◻ ◆◻◻⛧◆⬧⼦◼⽁?"

Again, Chuck just sat there and stared. Jopp then sighed and said, "☺◆◆ ◻⌇ ●◆⛧⬥ ✋◻⸫ ⽁⛧◆ ◆◆◆⬥ ◆⼦◆⬧ ◻ ◆⼦◻●⛧◆◻◼."

Finally, Chuck managed to utter, "What?"

Jopp's eyes bugged out in what Chuck assumed was shock. He dug his hand into a pocket of his blue uniform, and after rooting around for about ten seconds, pulled something out and held it aloft. It appeared to be nothing more than a small silver oval, about half a thumb long. Jopp pointed at Chuck, and then mimed the act of placing this item on the back of his neck. It took a good three or four goes before Chuck fully understood what he was being asked to do.

"No way." Chuck turned to open the door and felt a prick as something small and metal was jammed into the back of his neck. It felt as if countless tiny needlelike legs were digging through his skin. Chuck cried out and tried to rip the device off with his left hand, all while trying to throttle Jopp with his right. His left hand failed, as the device had now gone fully under his skin. He could actually feel it attaching itself to his spinal cord. His right hand wasn't making much progress either, seeing as Jopp's neck was barely an inch long, and as wide around as a coffee can. Jopp swatted Chuck's hand away and said, "All right! All right! Calm down, would you?! I didn't know you were human!"

Chuck halted his attack when it hit him that he could actually understand the alien's words. Jopp continued, "I know. I know. The TellAll hurts like a bitch when it's implanting itself, but hey, at least you can understand me now, right?"

Chuck remained still, eyes blinking, mouth hanging open.

Jopp continued, "Hello? Dude, say something. You're freaking me out."

Chuck broke his silence. "I'm freaking *you* out?! Are you fucking kidding me?! How the fuck do you think I feel right now?! Where the fuck am I?! Who the fuck are you?! *What* the fuck are you?!"

"And I thought *I* cursed a lot. . . . *What the fuck are you?* That hurts, man. I have a name, you know. I'm sentient. . . . A lot more sentient than you Earth apes."

"You're an alien?"

"No, *you're* the alien."

Chuck opened his mouth to reply, but a loud buzzing noise cut him off. The space around them became illuminated in a soft white light. The truck was sitting in a massive rectangular room, about the same dimensions as a football field. He wasn't able to see the ceiling. The room was the same shade of blue metal as the outside of the ship. Chuck's eyes were caught by a line of what could only be described as spaceships parked across the room. There were two that looked like futuristic jet fighters, one that looked like a Rubik's Cube, an honest-to-goodness flying saucer, one that resembled a jagged chunk of crystalized rocks, and one that looked surprisingly similar to his own truck.

A door opened on the opposite wall, and in walked four tall slender figures. Other than varying heights, there was no way to distinguish one from the other. They were clad in what appeared to be tactical body armor. From the neck down, their suits reminded Chuck of a SWAT team's, except rather than the typical drab gray coloring, these uniforms were khaki with pink trim. Their helmets looked very much like armored gas masks. He wasn't exactly sure about the function of the objects they were carrying, but he was pretty sure he could recognize a gun when he saw one. His hypothesis was confirmed when, after the figures had walked up to the truck, the objects were pointed at the windshield.

Jopp grumbled, "Oh, shit. . . . Tahls."

The Tahl standing second from the right spoke in a voice that sounded like it was being fed through an intercom. *"Step out of the Class 3 Danowitcz immediately. Keep all hands, tentacles, and other prehensile appendages out in the open."*

They stepped out of the truck with hands held out, and the four beings surrounded them. Chuck couldn't hold in his panic any longer. He panted heavily, wide eyes shifting rapidly from Jopp to the others.

"Listen, I don't know what the fuck is going on here! I'm not with this fucking guy! He just jumped into my tru—"

He was interrupted by one of the Tahls stepping forward and ramming the butt of the gun into his gut. As he crumpled to the floor, coughing and wheezing, the guard spoke. *"Please refrain from wanton use of verbal obscenities. You will conduct yourself with proper decorum, or else be met with additional retribution."*

After Chuck regained his wind, he cautiously pulled himself to his feet. He noticed that two more Tahls had joined the group, holding the nozzles of what appeared to be giant hoses. The hoses stretched back to cylindrical tanks that were strapped to their backs. Jopp quickly whispered, "Close your eyes and hold your breath! Oh, and keep your mouth shut!"

The Tahl who had struck Chuck spoke. *"Douse them."*

The hoses spewed out a stream of thick blue foam, completely coating the two prisoners. Chuck slipped on a patch of the foam and fell onto his back. Ignoring Jopp's advice, he tried to take a breath and almost passed out. The antiseptic fumes were overwhelming. He looked up angrily and said, "Motherfu—" but caught himself as the guard took one step forward, arm raised to deliver another blow in the name of good manners.

Again, Chuck pulled himself to his feet. The Tahl guard spoke. *"Please move toward the hall."*

"This is a b—big . . . *big* mistake! I don't belong here! Please just . . . let me *go."*

"Please move toward the hall."

"Now wait a minute, here! You've kidnapped and assaulted me. I deserve an explanation."

"Please move toward the hall."

Chuck put his hands on his hips. "That's it! I'm not moving another inch until someone explains to me what the he—*heck* is going on!"

The armored Tahl guards looked back and forth between themselves. Jopp smirked and shook his head.

***

Chuck and Jopp were led through the hallway. More accurately, Jopp was led through the hallway while Chuck was carried over the shoulder of a guard. Chuck's view was that of a grinning yellow face.

"You happy now?" asked Jopp.

"Thanks a lot," grumbled Chuck.

"Hey, I didn't tell you to get all fussy with the well-armed security personnel."

"*Please cease communication during transit,*" ordered a guard behind Jopp.

Chuck tried looking around the hallway. From what he could tell, the ceiling was at least thirty feet above them, and its entire surface area glowed with a white light. The wide-set walls were the same khaki as the guards' uniforms. A pink carpet ran down the center of the floor. The tapestries along the walls gave Chuck a peek into what the Tahls looked like under their armor. Tahl skin tones apparently ranged from deep purple to light pink. Their heads were long and narrow, and two small oval-shaped eyes were set about three-quarters of the way up their faces. A thin nose ran from between their eyes to a place just above their wide, thin mouths. Despite their physical appearance and the unfamiliar settings, the tapestries reminded Chuck of those stock photos you see in corporate brochures. One depicted a Tahl giving a presentation to a full boardroom. Another showed a pair gazing lovingly at the skeletal structure of what would, presumably, become a gigantic tower. It was difficult for Chuck to gauge how long they'd been walking, as the hallway had no real turns, but rather barely perceptible curves.

Chuck's mind began to race, as he thought about the people who would be wondering what had happened to him. His dad wouldn't be too concerned, considering their last conversation had been at Chuck's mother's funeral and had consisted mostly of four-letter words. Chuck's dispatch manager would certainly be pissed. He wondered if "alien abduction" was an acceptable excuse for missing a delivery. Probably not. Then there was Chuck's ex-girlfriend, Amy, who had broken up with him because his life just "wasn't exciting enough." He wasn't sure if the irony was more comedic or tragic. His roommates would definitely come looking for him. Chuck knew he could count on Paul and Ryan. A sudden stop shook Chuck out of his thoughts. He guessed they'd been at it for about five minutes when the hall ended abruptly.

The group stood in front of a seamless wall at the end of the hallway. One of the guards placed his palm in the center of the wall. A door-shaped panel pulsed green and slid open, revealing a simple circular room with no portholes . . . or ocular apertures . . . or whatever the hell aliens called windows. The group stepped inside, and the guard set Chuck down on his own feet. There was a low humming noise, and Chuck felt the slight pull of an elevator rising. During the ascent Chuck noticed that the blue foam had completely evaporated, leaving his clothes bone dry.

The doors opened again, and the guard reached for Chuck, who jumped back and blurted out, "I'll walk! I'll walk, okay?"

The group left the elevator and entered a vast room. The ceiling was completely transparent, revealing the bespeckled canvas of outer space. A long, oval-shaped table spanned the length of the room. It was obviously one solid piece of rock, yet its surface was moving. Uncountable shapes, swirls, and colors writhed, as if a thousand hurricanes were raging silently across the table. Chuck's study of the table was cut short when one of the guards pushed him and Jopp forward. Three figures sat at the opposite end of the table. They were all built long and lean, like the guards. Unlike the guards, however, they were wearing neither the body armor nor the helmets. The one on the left's skin tone was pale lavender, the one on the right's was fuchsia, and the center individual's skin was deep purple.

Jopp spoke first, "Kek! Quo! Loq! It's great to see you three again. Look, I know you're all really pis—I mean, upset with me, and that's totally reasonable. I totally get it, but—"

The individual on the left, presumably Kek, bellowed, "Silence!" Jopp closed his mouth, and in that moment looked very much like a scolded child (a stout yellow alien child, but a child, nonetheless).

Quo spoke in a deep, melodic voice, "Joppenslik Wenslode, you were contracted by Prime Partners Intergalactic Consortium. This contract involved the transport of some incredibly valuable goods, and as of today, it has not been completed. Prime Partners' efforts to locate both our transport craft and its contents have not yielded results. Where is our product?"

Jopp was looking quite wobbly at the moment. He steadied himself and then exclaimed, "Marauders! I got hijacked in the Dayukon System! I just came out of the jump, and there they were! I tried to jump away, but they were on top of me too fast. Real bad guys . . . probably defectors from the Vashnii Armada! One of 'em had mandibles the size of—"

Quo cut him off. "Mr. Wenslode, why doesn't your companion introduce himself? Furthermore, why does he continue to use an illegal holoskin in my presence?"

Chuck squeaked out, "Holoskin? What's a hol—"

Joppenslik interjected, "Ah, Quo . . . um . . . well . . . actually . . . he's not exactly wearing a holoskin, per se. . . ."

Quo raised what might have been his eyebrows. "Are you telling me that this is an actual Earth human being?"

This revelation made the other two Tahls gasp, and Quo continued, "Mr. Wenslode, this is not only disappointing, but highly unprofessional. Why in the world would you ever think this would be an acceptable course of action? Now we are left with no option but to put it down."

"What?! *Put it down?!* You mean kill me?! You can't do that! I am a human being! With like . . . rights and stuff!"

"He's actually got a point. For a bunch of gluttonous drunken apes, they're surprisingly sentient. And if I might add in my own defense, it really wasn't my decision to bring him up here. . . . Also I just want to point out that I am neither drunk nor hungover. I was drugged by the marauders."

"Mr. Wenslode! Cease your prattling this instant!" Quo motioned for his two companions to lean in closer. The three of them conferred in whispers.

Quo drummed his fingers on the table. "Mr. Wenslode, you owe our company restitution for our lost product, and let me stop you before you continue to lie. There are no marauders in the Dayukon System, and I can smell the Flanisi Ale in your perspiration from over here. You have a choice to make: you can choose to work off your debt, or you can choose to spend the next twenty standard annuals in the Helon Penitentiary System."

"I can't go to Helon! I'm not built for prison! And it'll take forever to work off that debt!"

"You're being dramatic. We estimate it will take roughly twenty standard annuals for you to pay off the debt, plus the interest. Very fitting, wouldn't you say?"

"What'll I tell my family?"

"Do you wish me to send word to your father's estate?"

Jopp reared back. "Nope!" He hesitated for a minute and then asked, "Do I still get my quarter-span bonuses?"

The condescending smirk from Quo answered that question well enough.

Jopp buried his head in his hands. "This is the worst thing that's ever happened to anyone ever!"

"Worse than Helon, Mr. Wenslode?"

Jopp sighed, and his shoulders sagged.

"What about him?" He gestured toward Chuck.

"He will also have a choice." Quo turned to Chuck. "What is your name, Earth human?"

"My name is Charles Higgins. People call me Chuck . . . and can't you all just, like, 'neuralize' me or something? Wipe my memory and drop me back on Earth?"

The three Tahls were visibly holding back laughter. Joppenslik cocked one eyebrow in disbelief. "Dude, seriously, you're embarrassing me. There's no such thing as a neuralizer."

Quo composed himself. "I am afraid that Mr. Wenslode is correct. That is not an option. What is an option, however, is that we will allow you to assist Mr. Wenslode in his continued service to our great organization. I doubt your limited cognitive skills will be of much use, but I'm told your kind can at least follow orders. We calculate this will dramatically reduce the amount of time it takes for us to recoup our investment."

"What if I say no?"

Quo casually replied, "If you refuse, we go with my original plan and you become tomorrow's lunch special."

Chuck nodded. "Your choices aren't ever really choices, are they?"

Quo smirked.

Chuck sighed and said, "Well, I guess you're looking at the first being from Earth to be employed by the . . . what was it, again?"

Quo tilted his chin up. "Prime Partners Intergalactic Consortium, the universe's oldest corporation."

Chuck sighed. "Thrilled to be a part of the team."

TEXT UNIT 0002

The newly joined partners in indentured servitude were led down another long corridor by a pair of armed escorts. Jopp was the first to break the silence since their dismissal from the conference room. "So what kind of name is Charles Higgins, anyway? It just sounds like gibberish."

"Call me Chuck, all right? And for your information, Charles Higgins is a very normal name on Earth. Why don't you go back there and tell everyone *your* name? See the kind of reaction *Joppenslik Wenslode* gets."

"Hey! Watch yourself, pal. Wenslode happens to be a very respected galactic family line, okay? And *you* can call *me* Jopp. Okay, *Chuck?*"

"Don't get feisty with me, man. You started it."

"Given the situation, I think I'm allowed to be a bit on edge!"

"Seriously? You're on edge? I'm the one who just got pulled into the damn Twilight Zone! My entire reality was just shattered in the span of a few minutes! Yesterday, I didn't think aliens existed. Now I'm apparently going to be spending the rest of my life slaving for the Procter & Gamble of the universe. Honestly, I'm surprised I haven't passed out from the shock!"

Jopp opened his mouth to retort, then hesitated, and after a moment of thought said, "You *are* handling this relatively well. I would've totally expected you to have soiled yourself by now."

They walked in silence for another minute before Jopp asked, "Hey, what's a *Twy Lite Zohn?*"

"Never mind. Where are they taking us?"

"We're going to the SBR department for processing."

"SBR?"

"Sentient Being Resources. It's where they handle all the basic employee details. You know: hirings, firings, airlock ejections . . . that type of stuff."

One of their armed escorts turned his head. "*We have one stop to make prior to the SBR office: med bay.*"

"Why would we need to go . . . ohhhhhhh, shiiiiiiiiit. . . ." He glanced at Chuck. "Comprehensive Sanitization."

"What?"

"Well, that blue foam they doused us with was Initial Sanitization. It's standard for when you're coming in from the not-so-civilized regions. Seeing as you hail from one such region, they're going to want to give you a more extensive 'cleaning.'" Jopp headed after the guard, calling back over his shoulder, "It's, uh, not *not* unpleasant."

"Wait, what?"

Five minutes later they were standing in a stark white cylindrical room. In the center was a large circular wraparound desk. There were three Tahl females seated within it. At least Chuck assumed they were female. They looked like the executives, except their eyes were slightly larger, the noses smaller, and their lips poutier. They also had long purple growths stemming from their scalps, which fell around their shoulders like hair. The necklines of their uniforms revealed what Chuck could guess was violet-tinted cleavage.

A dozen identical doors surrounded them. The nearest Tahl woman looked up. "What do we have here?"

"*New hire processing. We need sanitization and immunization.*"

"What level?"

"*Earth.*"

She made no attempt to hide her revulsion as she pointed to the door directly to her right. "Head through there."

The guard nearest Chuck put a hand on his shoulder to lead him on. Jopp gave him an impish grin and a little wave. "Have fun, pal. Hope you're not too ticklish." At that moment, the processing clerk let out a noise not unlike humans make when clearing their throats. Jopp turned back to her to see her arm outstretched to the other side, pointing to the door directly to her left. "And *you* will be having *your* exam through there."

Jopp's grin dropped. "Excuse me? I don't need sanitization. I was just in and out. Didn't spend any real time or—"

He felt the other guard's hand on his arm. The force of the grip indicated this wasn't a negotiable situation.

Forty minutes later, Jopp was seated on a bench in the central med bay room, fidgeting with his newly pressed uniform. He didn't mind the pink trim but had always felt the khaki clashed terribly with his natural yellow glow. He had to wait an additional twenty minutes before an uncomfortable-looking Chuck finally came in through the opposite door. He, too, was fidgeting with a uniform identical to Jopp's.

"So, how was it?" called Jopp.

"Um, well, they are definitely thorough. . . ."

The guards herded them back out into the hallway.

"I don't know about you, but for me the worst part is the whole body cavity thing. . . ."

Chuck shuddered and changed the subject. "I wanted to ask earlier, but we were a bit preoccupied at the time. What the hell is this thing in my neck?"

Jopp gave him a sidelong look. "You mean the TellAll? I forgot about that. It's Prime Partners' bestselling product. Basically it fuses to your nervous system and then translates whatever is said to you into a language you can understand. There's something like eleven thousand languages in the database. The one downside is that you get some real nasty headaches whenever they transmit an update patch."

Chuck nodded, then changed the subject again. "I gotta ask, what's with all the khaki and pink?"

Jopp gave him a baffled look. "I guess I'm just going to have to get used to answering these questions. Tan is a symbol of wealth and prominence on the Tahl home world, and the pink? Well, pink is just damn beautiful, wouldn't you say?"

They almost ran into the back of their security escorts, who had stopped abruptly in front of a large door. The door was emblazoned with three distinct characters. Chuck thought they looked like stylized versions of the pi symbol rotated at different angles.

Jopp saw him studying the door. "Oh, yeah. We gotta get you some of those . . . oh, hell, what are they called?" He snapped his fingers. "ReadAlls! We gotta get you fitted for ReadAlls."

"Really? You just explained the TellAll to me two minutes ago, and you couldn't think of the name ReadAll?"

"Shut up. Anyway, what they do is—"

"I got it. They translate words I see into a language I can understand. I can't wait to shove alien contacts into my *eyes*."

"Look at you, catching on so fast."

With that, the doors slid open, and they stepped into a massive office pool. There had to be at least a hundred desks arranged in a perfect grid. The guard directed them toward a white bench built into the wall. The black bracelet on Jopp's wrist beeped and projected one of the unrecognizable symbols in the air in front of them.

"Looks like we're number forty-two."

Jopp put his hands behind his head and leaned back against the wall. The image disappeared, and Chuck took a moment to study the room. The Tahl at each desk was surrounded by a hovering array of holographic icons. Then a sobering realization hit him: his roommates, Paul and Ryan, would not be looking for him. That would require actually getting off the couch. Combining that with Chuck's penchant for joking about disappearing one day to go be a bartender in the Virgin Islands, it all added up to Chuck being all alone, with no one coming to get him. Chuck fought back the rising anxiety the only way he knew how, by making inane small talk.

"So, why was it such a big deal that I'm a real Earth human? Like, what would've been the harm in putting me back? No one on Earth would believe me if I told them the truth."

"Yeah, well, Earth falls under the jurisdiction of the WPS."

"What's that?"

"The Wildlife Preservation Service. So, anyway, they get really upset when—"

"Hold on. Earth is monitored by park rangers?!"

"Well, yeah. Hate to break it to you, dude, but to most of the intergalactic community, your planet is little more than a nature preserve."

With that, they heard an amplified voice projected from speakers on the ceiling. *"Number forty-two, please proceed to desk twenty-two."*

Jopp rose. "Let's go"

They walked to the second row of desks and then down to the last one in the line. Seated behind the desk in question was a female Tahl. Jopp gave Chuck a slight nudge in the ribs, which he guessed was meant to imply that Jopp found the Tahl female attractive. Chuck could tell she wasn't quite as tall as her male counterparts, but was still easily in the six six, six seven range. She had what looked like a full head of hair. It was pulled back and fell behind her head right down the middle. When they got closer, Chuck noticed that this "hair" was comprised of a single strand, wide enough to cover her scalp. She gestured for them to sit in the two backless chairs in front of her desk. Once they had situated themselves, she said, "Hello. My name is Lavla, and I will be facilitating your employment transition."

Jopp leaned forward with a wide grin. "Well, I must say, Lavla, that it is a true pleasure to meet you. My name is Jopp, and I can't tell you how thrilled I am that we are going to be working together. Say, you wouldn't happen to hail from the Saline region of Tasa Major, would you?"

Chuck rolled his eyes.

Lavla gave Jopp a tired look. "Nice try, but I don't date drunken Yoblons. Why doesn't your friend deactivate his holoskin?"

Chuck sighed. "I'm not wearing a holoskin. I'm an actual Earth human."

Lavla's eyes got wide, and she leaned back. "Oh, my! And you've been employed by Prime Partners?! This is highly irregular! What is your name?"

"Charles Higgins." He turned to Jopp. "I should just get used to that type of reaction, shouldn't I?"

Jopp shrugged.

Lavla spent the next few minutes waving her hands through the holographic interface. Chuck noticed her make the same motion, each time a little more slowly and deliberately than before. He assumed that was her way of triple checking the system.

She turned to face him. "Well, I guess congratulations are in order. You are the first being from your solar system to be employed by Prime Partners Intergalactic Consortium. It has been quite a while since our department has had to create a new species profile. There are some questions I will need to ask you."

"Uh, okay. . . . Shoot."

"Oh, that won't be necessary unless you violate company policy. Anyway, let's get on with those questions, shall we? How old are you in Earth orbits, and what is the average life span of your species?"

"I'm twenty-three years old . . . and, uh, I guess the average life span on Earth is around eighty years?"

"Oh, good. I was worried you were near the end of your life cycle. I guess that's just how your kind looks. Let's see how that converts." She made a few quick keystrokes. "It looks like you have another 45.6 standard annuals left to be of service. Now, moving on, are you male, female, zemale, or asexual?"

Chuck again turned to Jopp. "What the hell is a zemale?"

Jopp leaned over and whispered something in Chuck's ear. His eyes bugged out and he almost fell out of his seat. "They do *what* with *what*?!" To Lavla he answered, "Male. I'm definitely a male."

She gave Chuck a skeptical look, shrugged, and went on. "I take it you are having no trouble breathing right now?"

"I'm good."

"Okay . . . carbon based. . . . at least that's normal. Do you have any notable natural defenses?"

"What do you mean?"

"Do you have armored skin?"

"No."

"Venomous glands?"

"No."

"Claws or any sharpened appendages?"

"No."

"Self-camouflaging abilities?"

"No."

"Flight capabilities?"

"No."

"Extrasensory abilities such as ESP or telekinesis?"

"No."

"I see. . . . Classification 'Squishy' it is." She then reached below her desk and handed him an object. "Please fill out this cognitive assessment."

It was a thin, translucent oval that lit up with a blue light revealing some unrecognizable script. Chuck looked up at her. "I can't read this."

"He doesn't have ReadAlls," Jopp explained.

Lavla was no longer attempting to hide her annoyance. Her eyes narrowed, and she studied Chuck. "You know, your eyes don't appear to be all that different from ours. Let's try a Tahl set." She reached back under the desk and retrieved a container the size of a jewelry box. She slid the object across the desk. "Try those on."

Chuck leaned back. "You know, I'm not too comfortable with this. I could really hurt myself or—"

Lavla's patience was spent. "Put those in your eyes, or I buzz management and explain how uncooperative you are being."

Jopp leaned over and whispered, "Lunch special, dude! Just do it!"

He let out a deep sigh, reached out, and grabbed the box. He opened it, and sitting there were two clear ovals that looked quite similar to normal contacts. He delicately lifted out the first contact. After one more pause, he gently placed it on his right eye. It slid into place effortlessly. He repeated the process with his left eye and commented, "Oh, that wasn't bad at all!" He blinked a couple of times, looked back down at the tablet, and was amazed to see that he could understand the writing. Lavla turned to Jopp. "While he works through that assessment, let's get you processed. What is your full name?"

"It's Joppenslik Wenslode. I'm already in the system."

"Yes, apparently you are. Well, this is a surprisingly impressive yet checkered track record. And of course, there's this most recent contract . . ."

"Yeah, uh, there were some complications. . . . You know, hazards of the trade. Not that it's a big deal, but I was actually attacked by marauders. A lesser professional wouldn't have made it out of there alive."

"Mr. Wenslode, unless this story is going to help me process you faster, you can cease talking."

Jopp sulked in silence as Lavla continued working. He glanced over at Chuck, who seemed to be actually enjoying himself. His hands were flying across the tablet.

Lavla stopped working and looked up. "Okay, we are just about done here. I have a number of available contracts that fit Mr. Wenslode's abilities." She produced a black plastic ring and slid it across the desk to Jopp. "Here is your standard issue data bracelet. Before I can transmit your order specs, I'll need to see how Mr. Higgins's profile aligns with yours."

Chuck raised a finger but didn't look up. "One minute. I think I'm just about done here . . . aaaaaannnnnd . . . finished!" He cheerfully handed the tablet back to Lavla, who slid the tablet into a vertical slot in the desk.

"You seem pleased with yourself," quipped Jopp as he clasped the data bracelet around his right wrist.

"That was fun."

"*Fun*, huh? You're determining how we'll be spending the foreseeable future. If you got us put on waste transport . . ."

"I don't think that will be a problem."

They both turned back to Lavla, who was looking quite surprised. "I must say, Mr. Higgins, that your assessment results are much better than expected. I had always heard your species was little more than a bunch of gluttonous, drunken apes."

"Um, thank you?"

"You're welcome! Let's just do a cross-reference of your assessment and Mr. Wenslode's profile. . . . Okay, we have a match." The tablet popped back up from the slot. Lavla pulled it out, read it, and then slid it across the desk. "You two will be running a series of contracts out of our Forssa 6 distribution center."

Jopp cocked an eyebrow incredulously. "They trust me and this ape with running Forssa 6 contracts?"

Lavla let the slightest hint of a laugh slip out. "Your skills are more than adequate for these contracts. Regarding your reliability, well, I don't think that is something we'll have to worry about."

Jopp's forehead crinkled as he glanced sideways at Chuck, who simply shrugged as he had no idea what the exchange implied. Lavla reached under her desk and came back up with what could only be described as a glowing yellow pistol. Chuck's instincts kicked in, and he screamed as he dove from his seat, "Jopp! Look out!"

Chuck covered his face and waited for the sting of a laser blast. It never came. After a few seconds, he peeked through his fingers to see Lavla and Jopp staring down at him with looks of utter disbelief.

Jopp held a hand out toward Lavla and quipped, "You sure you don't want to quadruple-check his test results?"

She could only shake her head as she pressed the "yellow gun" to the black bracelet on Jopp's outstretched wrist. She pulled the trigger, resulting in a pleasant ping sound. Jopp then turned his wrist so Chuck could better see the bracelet; rows of numbers scrolled across a small rectangular screen.

"It's just the order stamp, dude," he explained. "It makes sure we don't get the wrong shipment."

Lavla spoke up. "Yes, about that. We happen to have a small shipment of cyclo gears that needs to be delivered to Forssa 6. Technically, this will be your first assignment." She gestured behind them to a Tahl security guard, who had materialized next to them. "This individual will escort you to the next stage of your employment processing. I wish you success in your endeavors with Prime Partners."

The guard yanked Chuck up off the floor. They all turned to leave and had taken two steps when Jopp looked back. "We should get a drink the next time I pass through."

Lavla rolled her eyes. "I'll get a drink with you the day a Gorthan wins the Huelly Award."

The guard stifled a laugh, and Jopp's face fell. Chuck figured that must've been a good dig. Part of him felt bad for his new comrade, but the other part of him appreciated clever quips, regardless of whether he could actually understand the reference.

TEXT UNIT 0003

They were standing in a large hangar, virtually identical to the one they'd ended up in after being lifted off the Earth's surface. The big difference was that this hangar was very much alive with activity. Chuck looked to the far end, apparently the airlock, as there was a constant flux of newly arriving and departing spaceships.

A flurry of beings rushing to and fro surrounded them. Most appeared to be Tahl, but Chuck noticed four or five new races. There was one individual whom Chuck felt looked very much human, minus the giant eyes, wings, and tail, of course. It appeared to be having a conversation with a sparkling pink cloud. Another that caught his eye was a short, round being, coated completely in silky white hair. Its facial features were aligned extremely close together. The next one that passed by was built like a steroid-infused bodybuilder. Chuck was convinced its arms were thicker than his own thighs; however, its head was somewhat small in proportion, and its complexion reminiscent of red brick. The one thing they had in common was that they were all openly staring at Chuck. He cocked his head to say something to Jopp, only to discover that his yellow associate had wandered off. Chuck turned back to find his field of vision engulfed in crimson. The "bodybuilder" was standing a mere foot in front of him. Chuck jumped back in surprise. The being just stared at him. Chuck gawked back nervously. The being started smiling. Chuck smiled back. The being continued smiling. Chuck's smile disappeared.

The being stretched out his hand, his fingers spread wide, like an exaggerated miming of an Earth handshake. Chuck ran some quick mental calculations and decided that his fear of having his hand crushed was outweighed by his fear of offending the being, and subsequently having more of him crushed. He held out his own hand in similar fashion. The being's fingers closed gingerly around the offered hand, and he led Chuck though three slow, deliberate up-and-down movements before releasing his hand.

"Hello. My name is Bhanakhana Bhen Bhindo. What is your name?"

"Um . . . Chuck."

"Umchuck! It is nice to meet you."

"Uh . . . thank you. It is nice to meet you, too."

Bhanakhana Bhen Bhindo leaned in. "How was my greeting? Was it Earth authentic?"

"Oh, uh, yes. It was very authentic."

He leaned back, beaming. "Splendid! Studying Earth has been my little hobby as of late. I find your species to be utterly fascinating, especially your one tribe called *Ah-mair-icka*. In my studies, I've seen some elaborate societal performance pieces, but that Ahmairicka group is hands down the most eccentric. Now, Umchuck, you absolutely must tell me how it is you came to be aboard this vessel. I would assume you are quite brilliant. The consensus in the zoological community is that your species is still a good two hundred standard annuals away from achieving contact with the Sentient Coalition."

Chuck began to relay the events of the past few hours. As he heard the words come out of his mouth, the reality of his situation finally started to sink in. He felt his chest tighten and his breathing become shallow. Beads of sweat formed on his forehead. He wavered a bit and felt as if he was going to pass out. Before that could happen, Bhanakhana Bhen Bhindo rested his massive hands on Chuck's shoulders to steady him. "Are you all right? I apologize if I have upset you."

Chuck took a deep breath and wiped his forehead. "No, no, no. It's not your fault. I think I'm just now realizing the magnitude of what's happened to me."

Bhanakhana Bhen Bhindo nodded. "I am sure this is indeed quite overwhelming." He then offered, "It is likely a small consolation, but you should take solace knowing that you are going to be working for one of the universe's most respected organizations. You will find an affiliation with Prime Partners to be very valuable."

A beeping noise began to sound from a device attached to Bhanakhana Bhen Bhindo's belt. It was black, metallic, and reminiscent of an Earth smartphone. He pressed a button to shut off the noise and then looked back at Chuck. "Well, my new friend, I must be off. I thoroughly enjoyed meeting you. I wish you the best in your endeavors. Good-bye, Umchuck."

"Oh, well, it was nice meeting you as well, Bhana . . ." He couldn't remember the full name. He looked up, afraid that he had caused offense.

"Do not be alarmed. The proper pronunciation is 'Bah-nah-kah-na Ben Bin-doh.' Now you try."

"Bah-nah-kah-nah Ben Bin-doh."

Bhanakhana Bhen Bhindo smiled. "That was perfect, Umchuck!"

"Thanks, and actually, my name is just Chuck."

"Oh. Okay, Juschuck."

"No . . . I mean. My name is Chuck. You can call me Chuck."

He smiled again. "Chuck. Splendid. And you can call me Bhanakhana Bhen Bhindo."

Chuck nodded. "Sure thing."

As Chuck watched his new friend walk away, he felt a sting as something smacked him right in the center of his back. He sucked in air and whipped around to see Jopp standing there with a mischievous grin. "Hey, look at you! Making friends already . . . and with a Dronla, no less." He then leaned in. "He didn't get all preachy and philosophical on you, did he?"

Chuck was trying to rub the spot on his back where he was certain a fat handprint had started forming. "He was a nice guy. Where the hell did you go, anyway?"

Jopp held up an oval-shaped tablet device. "I was getting the specs for our first delivery run. You know, that thing we have to do to keep me from going to prison and you from getting eaten." He gestured to the far side of the hangar. "Our ship is down that way. Let's go check her out."

A few minutes later, they were looking up at the craft that would be their home for the foreseeable future. Jopp explained it was a Class 4 Longstrider. Not particularly luxurious, but not bare bones either. It wasn't new but wasn't exactly old. It was perfectly average. Chuck wondered how he would describe the appearance to someone back home. He guessed he'd start by having them envision a bullet the size of an ocean tanker, then add about dozen engine-looking contraptions situated on the bottom, the top, and the back end. Then paint the whole thing a shade of dark blue, and have the khaki-and-pink PPIC logo emblazoned across the sides.

Toward the front, about halfway up the side, a door slid open and a ramp extended to the floor. Out stepped two Tahls.

One was holding a tablet device identical to the one in Jopp's hand and seemed to be lost in whatever was currently illuminating the screen. The other, Chuck noted, was unmistakably one of the three Tahl executives from earlier. He was pretty sure it was the middle one, the boss. He couldn't remember the name. . . . It was something like Cro, or was it Plo?

"Quo!" exclaimed Jopp with a forced smile. "What an honor it is that you would take the time to come see us off."

The two Tahls had descended the ramp, and Quo approached, his expression cold, hands clasped behind his back. He bent down to Jopp's eye level, his almond-shaped eyes narrowing. In a calm, measured tone he spoke. "Mr. Wenslode, your recent blunder has cost me dearly. I no longer care how or why it happened. Personally, I would like to see you thrown in prison. My colleagues, however, feel there is an opportunity for us to recoup our loss, so that is what you will do. If this means I have to personally oversee every single run you make for the next twenty standard annuals, then so be it. You will not eat. You will not sleep. You will not rest. You *will* earn back what is owed. But understand this: should your incompetence cost me so much as one additional Tahlian, I will cut my losses and see that you spend the rest of your life as the bunk buddy of some gabber on Helon. Have I made myself clear?"

Jopp swallowed and nodded. Quo stepped back, gave Chuck a dismissive glance, and walked away. The other Tahl was still standing at the base of the ramp, looking impatient. Jopp approached and handed him his tablet. The Tahl took it and held it up alongside his own.

"Okay. Everything looks to be in order. Your identification number for this delivery is 00019733. You will be delivering this shipment of eleven thousand cyclo gears to our distribution center on Forssa 6. Your flight plan is cued up on the main control panel. We are currently orbiting Hyok 3. You will need to take the Pio-path to the Hyok 27 anomaly. From there, it's a straight shot across the Forssa system. This shouldn't take you longer than two days."

He finished speaking and looked at Chuck expectantly. All Chuck could muster was, "I know some of those words. . . ."

The Tahl's right eyebrow rose, and he looked to Jopp, who sighed and rolled his eyes. "Don't worry about him. I got it. It's an easy run. Piece of jubla."

The Tahl shrugged and began walking away. Over his shoulder he called back, "You are scheduled to depart in fifteen minutes. Make sure you are ready."

Chuck watched him leave, then felt another slap on his back. He really hoped this wasn't the beginning of a trend.

"Let's go, Earth man. Time to check out this glorified mobile jail cell."

He scurried up the ramp, and Chuck plodded after. As soon as they stepped through the doorway, the ramp retracted and the door closed. They were standing in what appeared to be some sort of common area. There was a circular pedestal in the center of the room, and couches situated around the walls. There were four doors: one directly across, one to the right, one to the left, and the one behind them, through which they had entered. Jopp led the way through the door on their left, toward the front of the ship. They walked down a short hall-way with two doors on either side and another at the end. Jopp pushed a button next to the last door, and it slid open to reveal the control room. There was a large windshield spanning the width of the room. There were three chairs situated in front of what appeared to be a long glass panel, which was tilted up toward the chairs at a forty-five-degree angle. Jopp jumped into the middle chair and lightly touched his hand to the glass. The whole panel lit up with a yellow-green tint. Jopp's thick fingers moved across the display with surprising dexterity. Chuck heard a soft humming noise and felt a faint vibrating sensation as the ship came to life. He wondered if he should sit down.

Jopp looked back. "You should sit down."

Chuck sat himself in the chair to Jopp's right. He gazed across the illuminated panel at the dozens of control icons. Jopp noticed his stare. "Do I need to explain why you probably shouldn't touch anything?"

Chuck rolled his eyes.

Jopp touched an icon, which then began pulsing red. He spoke to seemingly no one, "Prime One Dispatch, this is Transporter Wenslode, transporting cargo load number 00019733. We are ready for departure."

A speaker-filtered voice suddenly sounded all around them. "*Affirmative, Transporter Wenslode. This is Prime One Dispatch clearing you for departure. Please make your way to the airlock.*"

The red icon stopped pulsing, and Jopp tapped through another series of commands. The vibrations intensified as they were lifted off the deck. Their ship was hovering about six feet above the hangar floor. Chuck noticed that the display in front of Jopp had changed. There was a large space to his right that now looked like the mixing board in a music studio. There were ten vertical lines or scales, each with a—oh, Chuck didn't know what to call them—*node* displayed at various locations along the line. Jopp placed his fingers on the nodes of the three left-most scales. He slowly slid them forward, about halfway up the line. The ship shuddered and began to move forward. They traveled down a long open lane toward the end of the hangar, stopping about fifty feet from the wall. Jopp tapped the pulsing red icon again. "Prime One Dispatch, this is ship number 00019733. We are at the airlock."

"*Affirmative. Opening airlock now.*"

Chuck stared as the wall in front of him split down the middle. The two halves then began sliding open, revealing nothing but stars and blackness. He looked over to the right and saw about a dozen individuals milling about on the ground just a few feet from the retracting wall. They didn't seem to be taking notice of this, and Chuck felt panic set in. "Jopp! We have to stop them! Tell them to close the doors! Those people are going to get sucked out into space!"

He hopped up and ran to the windshield. He started frantically waving his arms, while trying to yell through the glass, "Hey! Look out!"

They couldn't hear him, but even if they could, it was too late. The hangar doors had fully opened. There was now nothing between the individuals and the vast expanse of deep space. He was too late to save them. He could do nothing now but watch as those poor forsaken souls . . .

. . . went on about their business as usual. Behind him, Chuck heard a slow deliberate clapping. He turned around to see Jopp dramatically exaggerating the clapping motion, a stunned look plastered across his face. "Wow. Just . . . wow."

Chuck could only mumble, "But space . . ."

"Yes, Earth man, *space*. The electromagnetic field acts as an airlock between the inside of the ship and the terrifying blackness. And it expends quite a bit of energy, so why don't you sit back down, so we can take off and not get in any more trouble, okay?"

Dejected and embarrassed, Chuck plopped back down into his chair and hung his head.

Jopp shook his head and tapped one more control icon. The ship lurched, and a moment later they were hurtling through the void.

TEXT UNIT 0004

"Man, I haven't eaten anything in like forever! We have any food on the ship?"

Jopp nodded. "These models come equipped with full galleys, and the company always keeps the rigs stocked. Why don't you head on back and find us something? It should be the first door on the left. Think of this as your first official duty."

Chuck left the control room and walked to the first door on his left. It hissed as it slid open, revealing what Chuck hoped was not the kitchen. The entire top half of the wall across from him was a mirror. Just below it was a trough that ran from wall to wall. Both the right and left walls were comprised entirely of frosted glass. It had a very sterile vibe. Chuck stepped back into the hallway and said to no one in particular, "Probably the bathroom . . . I hope. . . ."

He turned to face the door directly across the hall, and said, again to no one in particular, "Maybe he meant his other left." He allowed himself a slight chuckle as he pressed the next button. The door slid open to reveal what was clearly the kitchen . . . or galley. Rows of metal cabinets lined the walls.

Chuck strolled over and started casually flinging the doors open, finding a colorful array of neatly stacked boxes. As he started perusing the selection, he realized he had no idea what any of the items were. Apparently his ReadAll eye implants had no English equivalents, as his dining selections were *Galia*, *Rzackio*, and *Wsentigs*. He thought Rzackio sounded like it might be tasty and pulled down an orange box. He pried it open to find a dozen individually wrapped rectangles. They were each about the size of a king-size candy bar, which Chuck took to be a good sign. He snagged two and stuffed them in his pocket. He figured he might as well bring back a selection, so he popped open one of the green Galia boxes to find a similar assortment of bars. Again, he grabbed two and shoved them in another pocket. He put the boxes back where he found them, and as he closed the cabinet, he spied a tall metal cupboard. He walked up and pulled on the handle. The door made a dry sucking *shup* as it opened and unleashed a rush of cool air. Just like the cabinets, each shelf was perfectly organized into rows of color-coordinated containers, and just like before, Chuck couldn't understand any of the words. His eyes were caught by a row of white labeled bottles near the top. Well, it wasn't the bottles that caught his eye, but rather the fact that he could actually read the label. It read, in big block letters, "WATER." Chuck shrugged, figured that would be good enough, and grabbed two bottles.

As Chuck reentered the control room, Jopp pointed to a small table that had materialized between their seats. "Let's see what you found us, Earth man." He watched as Chuck set the two bottles and the four packaged bars down.

"You some kind of health freak?"

"Hey, man, I don't know what any of this stuff is. . . . I mean . . . I know what water is . . . but the food? No clue. Couldn't understand any of the labels."

"Ah, I'm just giving you a hard time. Sit down and let's eat. Besides, I could stand to lose a few kilos."

Chuck plopped down and picked up one of the orange wrapped bars.

"Rzackio," explained Jopp. "It's a protein booster bar. Actually tastes halfway decent. The green ones, Galia, are a made from a bunch of plants or something. . . ."

Chuck ripped open the Rzackio and took a small bite, chewed a few times, and swallowed. His face lit up, and he tore a second, much larger, bite off the bar.

"Dhish ibs sho guhd!"

Jopp shot him a sidelong glance. "What the hell did you just say?"

Chuck held up a finger, chewed a few more times, and swallowed. "This is so good! It takes like bacon!"

"Great. What's *bay*—wait, you know what, never mind." Jopp saw that Chuck had taken another mouthful and quickly added, "Just try not to choke, okay?"

Chuck nodded and continued to enjoy. When the first bar was finished, he tore into the green wrapper of a Galia bar and took a big bite . . . and found the taste to be reminiscent of grass . . . grass and dirt. It definitely reminded Chuck of dirt. He took a swig of the water to wash it down.

"I'm getting more Rzackio! You want anything?"

Jopp tossed Chuck his unopened water bottle. "Put this back and grab me a Friznitz. I need to stay alert."

Two more Rzackio bars and a Friznitz later, and the two were respectively satiated. Jopp glanced over. "You holding up okay?"

"I think so. I keep waiting to wake up. . . ."

"Well, you're going to be waiting a long time, Earth man. Might as well get settled in. We're going to be spending a lot of time in this rig. This room in particular."

"Great, I'm a truck driver all over again." He tapped his foot a few times. "So, you going to teach me how to fly this thing, or what?"

Jopp scoffed. "Oh, yeah, sure. We're sitting on a thousand tons of metal, electronics, and fuel, with more computing and propulsion power than exists on your entire planet, crossing half a galaxy. I'm sure it's exactly like driving that land crawler thing of yours from one city to another. Hell, why don't you take over right now?"

Chuck sulked in his chair.

Jopp rolled his eyes. "Okay, okay. You see these scales? Each one controls the power to one of the turbines. And this window over here is calculating the level where each scale needs to be to ensure we're on the right track."

"That's it? Just make sure these numbers match those numbers? And that'll take us to . . . what was it called? Fort Something? The distribution center . . ."

"Forssa 6. The distribution center is called Forssa 6. And no, that's not where we're headed right now. We're headed to the anomaly at Hyok 27. Then Forssa 6."

"The anomaly?"

"Yeah, how do I explain this. . . . So, sentient planets are often multiple light years away from each other. You know what light years are, right?"

Chuck nodded. Jopp continued, "Obviously, that makes it tough to sustain an intergalactic economy. Well, there just so happen to be these . . . *spots* situated throughout the universe. And if you so happen to fly through one of these spots at the right speed, you pop out the other end in a completely different section of the galaxy. Those are the anomalies. Now, where you actually end up is determined by the angle at which you enter the anomaly. That's why it's important we hit the Hyok

27 anomaly at these coordinates. Otherwise there's no telling where we might end up."

"So they're like wormholes?"

"Um, what?"

"I don't mean literal holes for worms. . . . It's an expression. I mean, like, they're rips in space."

"Yeah, I guess that's a good way to explain it."

"So where did they come from?"

"The anomalies? Don't know."

"How many are there?"

"Don't know."

"So, what, we just make sure the numbers line up, hit the anomaly at, like, light speed or something and"—Chuck snapped his fingers—"bam! We show up millions of miles away?"

"It's actually 91.67% of light speed. Science has yet to come up with an engine that can hit the full one hundred. And most ships, this one included, can only sustain that pace for four to five seconds. The trick is to time our acceleration just right, so we don't burn out before hitting the jump. And then"—Jopp imitated Chuck's snap—"*we show up millions of miles away.*"

"What's it feel like?"

"The jump?"

"Yeah."

"You ever been touching something fuzzy or furry, and you feel a tiny little zap?"

"Static electricity."

"Yeah. So, imagine that feeling . . . only all over your entire body . . . and like, ten times more intense."

"And you do this on a regular basis?!"

"Relax. It lasts less than a second. You'll be fine."

"Are there any lasting side effects?"

"Well, my natural skin tone is blue, and I used to have five fingers on each hand . . . but I'm not convinced it's the jumping that's responsible."

Chuck's jaw dropped. His eyes shifted back and forth between Jopp's hands and his own. His chest was pounding, and his breath started quickening. Jopp caught Chuck's expression in the corner of his eye and burst out laughing. "Oh, c'mon, man! Are you serious?! I'm messing with you! The jump is perfectly safe. Holy Bjordax, you're more gullible than a Gorthan!"

Chuck's brow furrowed. "Well . . . when I woke up this morning, I had no idea that aliens, intergalactic societies, anomalies, or any of this shit even existed. So I'd guess you could say I'm pretty open to suggestion right now."

Jopp nodded. "Fair enough. I can try to keep the jokes to a minimum while you're still adjusting to all this, but there are going to be some times when I just can't help myself."

A few moments passed silently before Jopp couldn't help himself anymore. "That was really funny. I mean, your face was hilarious. I wish you could have seen it."

"Glad you enjoyed it. Let's hope every alien we meet finds me so amusing. That can be my big contribution to this endeavor: Chuck: the Sideshow Freak."

"Cute. That reminds me. You're going to want to put a lid on the *alien* word. It carries a rather insulting connotation in a lot of circles. I'm not joking around on this one. Best to simply not use it at all."

"Okay, okay. Don't use the a word. Got it."

A few moments passed silently. Then Chuck turned to Jopp and spoke in a calm, even tone. "So . . . when are we going to have sex?"

This time it was Jopp's eyes that bugged out as he whipped his head around. "What?!"

Chuck looked him dead in the eye. "Sex. When are you and I going to have sex? On Earth, it's considered incredibly bad luck, not to mention rude, for two individuals to embark on a long trip together without having sex."

Jopp reared back. "Uh . . . um . . . uh . . . well . . . yeah . . . you see I'm not . . . you know . . . not that there's anything wrong with . . . but . . . still . . . I mean . . . it's just . . ." A bead of sweat slid down his forehead.

Chuck could not contain the smile that had been fighting to emerge across his face. He tilted his head back and let out a howl of laughter. "Oh, man! If you think *my* face was funny earlier, you should have seen yours just now! I don't want to have sex with you, dude! I don't even know how we'd do it in the first place!"

Jopp's expression returned to normal, and he wiped his sleeve across his forehead. He wanted to be upset but couldn't prevent the hint of a smirk from appearing in the corner of his mouth. "Well played, Earth man, well played. Maybe this whole experience won't be such a pain—"

Jopp suddenly sat upright, his eyes wide with terror, as the console began flashing red lights. His stubby yellow fingers pounded the controls.

"What's wrong?!"

"We're about to—"

Jopp never finished his sentence as the explosion threw the pair violently from their seats.

TEXT UNIT 0005

Haaga Viim stood on the bridge of his ship, the *Pfraza*. At six and a half feet, he was tall for his species. Rough orange skin lay over thick knots of muscle. A square jaw sat below angular cheekbones. His left eye was bright yellow and oval shaped. His right eye was a thin vertical line, about two inches long. His ears resembled the three-pronged fin of a fish. He had no nose, as his respiratory system fed through his ears. He was an Ochrean from the planet Gralt.

"Fire," he commanded.

The ship's viewscreen zoomed in as two red blasts hurtled toward the Class 4 Longstrider. The right blast connected with the target's primary turbine, while the left came dangerously close to puncturing the living quarters' hull.

Haaga quickly stomped over to his gunners, also known as the Twins; a pair of short, round beings coated completely in silky white hair. Their humanoid facial features sat about two-thirds of the way up their spherical forms and were the only part of their bodies not covered in hair. To be honest, no one in the crew knew whether they were actually twins, or were even related at all. They earned the nickname because nobody could tell them apart; that and they always seemed to be bickering over something, as siblings are wont to do. He heard the chitter of a disagreement brewing as he approached. He wasn't sure if it was their species as a whole or just these two in particular, but they had a way of communicating with each other through a series of grunts, hums, and whistles that the TellAll implants could simply not translate. Luckily, they also spoke a somewhat broken version of the generic tongue. They hadn't noticed Haaga's arrival and jumped at the sound of him clearing his throat. Haaga glared at the one on the left. "What the phoob are you doing, Rigu? I said to concentrate on the turbines."

The one on his right scrunched up his face. "Rigu me." He pointed at his counterpart. "Pilu he."

Haaga growled, "Well, stop switching seats."

This time Pilu, the one on the left, scrunched his face up and pointed down to his chair. "Seat lucky. Pilu win gridspar match. Pilu seat lucky."

"Obviously not," countered Haaga.

Pilu pointed accusingly at the *Pfraza*'s pilot, Vaatu. "Flyboy shaky!"

"What the hell you call me?" shot Vaatu, a young Ochrean man who looked like a shorter, skinnier version of Haaga.

"Enough!" bellowed Haaga. "Vaatu will keep us steady. You two just take out the turbines without damaging the life support or cargo."

"Yes, boss!" they replied in unison.

Haaga marched back to the command post and spoke to his first mate. "Shai, get the crew up here now."

Shai, a reptilian Soreshi with a humanoid body and python-like head, spoke through the intership commline. "Jorwei, get your team to the bridge."

Haaga felt the ship vibrate as the Twins unleashed another barrage. He was pleased to see the blasts connect with one of the target's primary thrust turbines. Haaga heard the bridge door open and turned back to see four beings enter. The first two were Ochreans like Haaga and Vaatu, albeit half a foot shorter and much wider. The third to enter was a titanic, bloodred Dronla who bore a collection of crescent-shaped scars that ran from his right cheek to his neck, across his wide shoulder, and down his arm, ending at the back of his hand. The fourth was a lean Puzuru, whose jigsaw-patterned skin varied from dark blue to white. He ran a hand through his thick shock of blue hair.

"Did someone here place an order for the best-damn-looking thug this side of the nebula?"

Haaga ignored the comment. "We all understand what needs to happen?"

They nodded in unison. Haaga continued, "After the Twins disable the turbines, we board. The transporter crew is to be put down immediately."

The Puzuru arched an eyebrow. "No interrogation?"

Haaga shook his head. "Not necessary, Jorwei."

"Doesn't have to be *necessary* to be fun," quipped the large Dronla.

"While I appreciate the enthusiasm, Ghono, we already have the ship's access codes. We need to be quick and efficient. Our contact has supplied us with a time frame where no one should cross our path, but this is still protected space and that window won't last for long."

The crew nodded again. Haaga continued, "Head to the boarding bay and get suited up."

Once they exited, Haaga turned back to the viewscreen in time to see a blast glance off the outer casing of one of the target's turbines.

"Hmm," he grumbled to himself, "must have upgraded the armor plating." Then to Shai he said, "Can our cannons crack it?"

"It will require a few extra hits," Shai answered, "but it should not be a problem."

Haaga folded his arms across his chest. "Open a commline."

TEXT UNIT 0006

Chuck lay on the floor of the control room looking up at the ceiling, his vision hazy. He blinked several times, trying to get his eyes to focus. He turned his head in time to see Jopp scrambling up off the floor and back into his seat. Chuck saw him slam the console a few times, and what appeared to be two analog joysticks materialized in front of him. Jopp grabbed ahold and yanked them to his left. Chuck felt the ship lurch and felt the Rzackio in his stomach attempt a comeback. It looked like Jopp was silently mouthing a message to him. After a few seconds, he realized that Jopp was not silently mouthing anything but was, in fact, shouting at him, and it only seemed silent because Chuck's hearing was currently being monopolized by an intense internal ringing. The ringing began to subside, and the pained rasp of Jopp's shouting was more than eager to take the ringing's place. "Get up! Get up now! Get over here or we're going to die!"

Chuck felt his whole body give an ache-filled protest as he pulled himself up off the floor. He staggered over and fell into his chair. The entire console screen was flashing with a rainbow of various alarms. Before Chuck could even ask, Jopp spat out, "Somebody is fucking shooting at us!"

He then pointed at a pulsing icon in front of Chuck. "Hit that! It'll pull up the rear viewscreen!" Chuck slapped the icon, and a rectangular window popped up in the upper-right corner of their viewport. Half of the screen was obscured by a spider web of cracks, but the other half clearly showed a ship bearing down on them. It was black and menacing. Chuck thought it resembled a six-winged pterodactyl.

"Oh, shit," gasped Jopp.

"Wha—what is it?" stuttered Chuck.

"Marauders."

Chuck's head whipped around. "Marauders? As in pirates? As in *space* pirates? Are you shitting me? That's a real thing?"

"Countless quantities of valuables are transported across the galaxy every single day! You're surprised there are yok-heads out there willing to steal it?!"

"Well, no . . . it just seems so cliché, is all."

"What the phoob are you talking about?! Listen! Our ship has scrambler pods. They should screw with their targeting systems. I need you to fire them off when I tell you to. It's that button right there."

Chuck looked to see an orange icon that displayed a circle with what appeared to be lightning bolts shooting out in different directions.

"You hit that exactly when I tell you to, and *only* when I tell you to."

Chuck nodded. Just then he noticed a green flashing icon shaped like a speaker and heard a high-pitched beeping.

"They want to talk," grumbled Jopp. "Press that blinking button."

Chuck pressed the icon and another window opened in the center of their viewport. They were looking at the face of an alien species Chuck had yet to encounter. Its rough skin was dark orange, and it had no nose. Its left eye was bright yellow and oval shaped. A thin vertical scar covered the spot where his right eye should've been. The being sized Jopp up and then shifted its gaze to Chuck. Chuck thought he noticed a wave of shock cross the being's face. It opened its mouth and a gravelly voice sounded around them. "I am Haaga Viim, captain of the *Pfraza*. If you wish to live beyond the next thirty seconds, power down your turbines and prepare to be boarded. Do I need to explain what will happen should you refuse?"

Jopp and Chuck slowly shook their heads in unison. The pirate captain's eye once again appeared to focus on Chuck. "What exactly are you?"

Jopp jumped in. "Oh, he's nobody. Just a harmless, hairless Earth ape. It's kind of like having a novelty pet on board, you know? Supposed to bring good luck."

The yellow eye looked back to Jopp. "Obviously the wrong kind of luck for you, Yoblon."

During this exchange, Chuck had been racking his brain, trying to think of a way out of this situation. Suddenly he had it. All those hours spent watching movies were finally about to pay off. He just needed to tell Jopp before it was too late. His eyes scoured the console until they fell on a particular icon. It was red and "Power Down" was printed below it. The picture was similar to the one he'd pressed to open the communication line. He decided this was no time to think, but rather a time to act. He leapt across the console, pressed the icon, and everything went dark. He grabbed Jopp's collar and pulled him in close. "Quick! Orange roughy back there thinks we just lost power. This ship has got to have some kind of hidden panels or storage compartments or something. Let's go hide in there! They'll come aboard, take what they want, and leave. They'll think we, like, jettisoned or something. It'll be just like when

Han Solo hid on the *Millennium Falcon* when they were captured by the Death Star." He started creeping toward the door. "And by the way, a space pirate captain with only one eye? Seriously? I mean, c'mon! How cheesy can you get?"

A good five seconds passed silently. Chuck had almost reached the door before he noticed that Jopp wasn't following him. Then there was the sound of gravelly throat clearing. "*Ahem.*"

Chuck heard Jopp's palm slap the console, and the lights came back on. Chuck looked up to see the orange pirate captain's image still displayed on the viewport. Chuck looked from him to Jopp, who was staring back at him, mouth hanging open. Chuck felt his face flush. The pirate spoke. "I'm sorry to disappoint you, Earth ape, but simply turning the lights off doesn't prevent me from hearing. . . . And this"—he pointed to the right side of his face—"is not a scar. It is my eye. My right eye looks this way because it allows for perfect sight in complete darkness. So, by all means, feel free to turn the lights back off. It won't bother me."

Chuck trudged to his seat, sat down, and stared dejectedly at the floor. The pirate captain turned his head and spoke to someone outside their view. "Shai, make a note. We are never to carry a hairless Earth ape aboard this ship. They are apparently very bad luck."

While the pirate's head was still turned, Jopp poked Chuck in the leg and whispered, "Remember that button I mentioned earlier?"

Chuck glanced at the console and saw the orange circle with the lightning bolts. He looked to Jopp and nodded. Jopp slowly wrapped his hands around the steering columns and exhaled deeply. "Hit it."

Jopp slammed the yokes, and the ship rocketed forward. The momentum threw Chuck against the back of his seat. It might have been the shock or perhaps the force of the acceleration, but Chuck felt frozen to the seat. Everything felt fast and slow at the same time. Chuck wondered if this is what dying felt like. A piercing siren snapped him back to the present just in time to hear Jopp yell, "They've fired again! Hit the damn button! Hit it now!"

Chuck lunged forward and slammed his hand down on the orange icon. Jopp yanked the ship left, and they felt the shudder of another explosion vibrate through their seats. Panic crept into Chuck's expression. Jopp glanced over. "It's okay. That was their shot hitting the scrambler pod. If that had been us, we'd be swimming through space right now. Get ready to fire off another when I tell you."

Chuck's hand hovered tensely above the panel. A bead of sweat traced a path down his forehead. He could see a purple vein bulging from Jopp's neck.

"Hit it!"

Chuck slapped the console, and Jopp yanked them to the right. Another explosive shudder ran through the room.

"Hit it!"

Chuck slapped the console. Jopp yanked them back to the left. Another familiar shudder.

"I assume we can't just do this until they get bored!"

Jopp kept eyes forward but retorted, "Wow. You actually got something right for once!"

"Well, what the hell are we going to do?!"

"I'm trying to—*hit it!*" Slap. Yank. Shudder. "I'm trying to figure that out!"

Another beeping alert. This was a new one to Chuck.

"Holy Gorthan piss! I don't believe it!" exclaimed Jopp.

"What? What is it?!"

"It's an anomaly . . . an actual uncharted anomaly!"

"So what does that mean?!"

"It means our status just went from certain death to only probable death."

"So what are you—*you're going to fly us into it?!*"

"Two correct guesses in a row, Earth man!"

"But without coordinates we could end up anywhere!"

"Thanks for telling me the thing I told you a few minutes ago, and *anywhere* sounds a shitload better than *here* right now, don't you think?"

As if to illustrate the point, they were thrown from their seats and slammed against the console by another explosion in the rear of the ship.

"Well, what are you waiting for?" hollered Chuck. "Get us out of here!"

"You're something else, Earth man," retorted Jopp. He resituated himself at the controls. "Sit back and hit that blue icon."

Chuck complied, and two seat belts extended from his chair above his shoulders and crisscrossed his chest. They tightened themselves to a comfortably snug fit.

Jopp brought the ship around, and the anomaly came into view. *Black* did not come close to describing the image that rose up before them. This was not black. This was the pure and utter absence of light. This was a gap on a canvas, as if the universe had forgotten to paint that spot.

"Hold on to your yub nubs!"

Chuck leaned forward. "What's a yub—" But before he could finish the question, his head slammed against the back of his chair by the force of sudden acceleration. The ship hurtled forward at a speed greater than anything Chuck could fathom. The white dots of the stars around them appeared to stretch into shining streaks of light. Ahead of them, the gaping black maw of the anomaly grew and grew until it encompassed their entire field of vision. Chuck became aware of a new sound filling the flight deck. It was a solid, unwavering tone, very loud and very shrill.

He suddenly realized what it was.

It was the sound of his own voice.

He was screaming.

Then his vision went blank.

TEXT UNIT 0007

Chuck could see again. A starscape filled the viewscreen, and for all he could tell, they hadn't gone anywhere.

"Did it work?" he asked.

Jopp didn't look up from the console. "Yeah, I think so. I've got the Galactic Positioning System working to find our coordinates."

"Ha! GPS!"

"Huh?"

"Nothing. Never mind. So, where are we?"

"It looks like we're orbiting some planet I don't recognize. Other than that, I'm not sure. The ship's acting a bit—" A wailing siren cut him off.

Chuck pressed his hands to his ears. "Again? Seriously? Can this ship actually do anything besides sound alarms?"

The ship shuddered and jerked to the right, and then they started to free-fall. Chuck's stomach jumped into his chest. Jopp wrestled furiously with the controls. "They must've taken out both primary turbines before we hit the jump! We don't have enough juice to escape this planet's orbit!"

"So what the hell does that mean?"

"It means we're going to crash, Earth man."

"Don't we have, like, escape pods or something?"

"Nothing stronger than a planet's gravity. They're meant for deep space."

"So what? We just crash and die?!"

"That's one option, yes. Now please shut up so I can try to make that not happen!"

Chuck sat back and buried his head in his hands. The ship's shuddering intensified to the point that he swore he felt every molecule in his body vibrating. A series of violent lurches pried Chuck's fingers away from his eyes. He looked through the viewscreen to see a grayish-blue landscape rushing up at them. Jopp braced his feet up against the front of the control panel and used the full weight of his body to pull back on the yokes. The front of the ship began slowly tilting upward. Inch by inch, their trajectory lessened.

"Minus ten!" shouted Jopp.

"What?!"

"Watch that dial! We need to get our angle of approach to minus ten degrees!"

Chuck found the dial Jopp was referring to: a half circle, sliced vertically. A red dash showed they were currently heading downward at a forty-degree angle, or "-40" as per the dial's display. Chuck relayed this to Jopp, who strained even harder against the controls. Purple veins were bulging out all over his yellow hands, neck, and forehead. Chuck felt the familiar trickle of sweat stream down his face.

The ship tilted up. "Minus thirty!" called Chuck.

A bit more. "Minus twenty!"

Just a bit more. "Minus fifteen!"

Jopp grunted in agony and gave the yokes a final determined pull.

"Plus three!" cried Chuck, "that's too much! Pull it ba—" The rear end of the ship hit the planet's surface. Chuck's teeth slammed together as the front end quickly followed the back end's example, smashing into the ground. He felt a molar crack. He wasn't worried so much about that as he saw the giant cliff face currently getting closer and closer. The ship skidded along the dusty ground, careening head-on toward the rocky wall. Chuck looked over to see what Jopp was doing about that and was dismayed to learn that it was apparently nothing. His yellow companion looked practically catatonic, wide eyes staring blankly ahead.

"Jopp!"

There was no acknowledgment.

"JOPP!"

Still nothing.

Once again, Chuck acted on instinct. He prayed he was in the right for once. He slapped the icon that released their safety restraints and hopped up. He grabbed Jopp's right arm and leg, and with a determined howl, hoisted Jopp across his shoulders. He turned for the door and ran. He made it two steps into the hallway before the front of the ship collided with the cliff face. The collision sent them both careening across the floor. The shriek of rending metal pierced the air.

Then, for the first time since Chuck could remember, everything was silent. There were no explosions, no sirens, no alarms, no beeps. He felt as if he'd forgotten what silence sounded like. He decided it was his new favorite thing in the universe. He lay still for a few seconds, unwilling to move for fear that it might make the silence go away. Finally, he rolled over onto his back. He looked up at the ceiling and saw a flashing red light. He turned his head to see Jopp, sitting up, blinking, staring back at the control room. Chuck winced as he pulled himself up to a sitting position. His whole body ached. He wiggled his toes, flexed his fingers, bent his arms a few times; he was going to be hurting tomorrow, but nothing appeared to be broken. Chuck noticed Jopp was still staring straight ahead, and he followed the stout yellow alien's gaze toward the control room, or what used to be the control room. Now it was simply a tangled mess of twisted metal and wires. Denim-colored rock filled what used to be the viewport.

"Holy shit," the pair uttered in unison.

Jopp looked at Chuck. "You saved my life. . . . Holy shit, *you* saved my life."

Chuck raised his eyebrows. "Uh, yeah, I guess I did."

"Thank you . . . Chuck."

"Don't mention it, Lemonhead. Besides I think that makes us even."

"What was that you called me? A *lemon*?"

Chuck groaned as he climbed to his feet. "It's just a type of plant back on Earth." He smirked as he held out his hand. "And its fruit is sour, round, and yellow. Remind you of anyone we know?"

Jopp cocked an eyebrow and looked up at Chuck. "I'll give you that one. Pretty funny"—he grabbed Chuck's hand and pulled himself up—"for a hairless Earth ape."

Chuck gestured toward the remains of the control room. "So, what do we do now?"

Jopp looked down the hall toward the back of the ship. "We go see what it is we're actually carrying."

"What do you mean?"

Jopp stomped down the corridor. "No damn way those guys attack us for just a load of cyclo gears. They had to have thought we were carrying something else."

Chuck scurried after him. "Shouldn't we, like, check for a hull breach or something?"

"Nah, the emergency stasis field has us covered, and besides"—Jopp glanced at his data bracelet—"the atmosphere is breathable."

They entered the circular lounge area and Jopp pointed to the door on the opposite end of the room. "Storage is through there."

Chuck followed hesitantly, contemplating what could be hiding on the other side of the door. He felt goose bumps rise as his imagination took hold; were they carrying some kind of treasure? Maybe they were unknowingly smuggling illegal weapons? Or could it be drugs? Do aliens have illegal drugs? And if so, what would they do to a human? Chuck shook himself out of his reverie just in time to stop himself from walking right into Jopp, who had stopped in front of the door. He was peering skeptically at the numerical control panel.

"What's wrong?" asked Chuck.

"My code isn't opening the door," replied Jopp.

"Maybe it got busted during the crash?"

"No, it's working just fine. It's just not accepting my code."

"Sounds like someone didn't want you getting into the shipment."

"Oh, you think so? Good intuition, ape."

"Hey, just saying . . ." And after a pause: "You know, no offense or anything, but from what I gathered about your last job, maybe it's not so surprising that they'd want to restrict your access a bit."

Jopp wheeled around. "Listen good, Earth man. You don't know shit about shit about my last job, okay? And besides that"—he gestured to the door—"it's supposed to be a load of cyclo gears; not exactly a big-ticket item. I'm telling you there is something else going on here."

Chuck held his hands up defensively. "Okay, okay . . . sorry. So what do we do now?"

Jopp turned back to the panel, reached into his pocket, and pulled out a small black rectangle. It reminded Chuck of a flash drive. "What's that?"

Jopp popped the panel off the wall, revealing a matrix of wiring and circuitry. "Eh, you spend a long enough time in this line of work, you pick up a trick or two to help get around some of the more annoying bureaucracies."

He plugged the black device into an open socket. "Here we go."

Chuck held his breath as the door slid open. The two stepped into the ship's massive containment center. Chuck and Jopp gawked around the space in stunned silence. They couldn't believe what they were seeing. It wasn't anything like Chuck had imagined. The entire storage space was completely . . .

. . . utterly . . .

. . . empty.

"Uh, that's not exactly what I was expecting," said Chuck.

"No shit," muttered Jopp.

They took a few more cautious steps to confirm what they already knew to be true. They had been transporting ten thousand square feet of nothing.

Chuck broke the silence. "Okay, I didn't know it was possible, but I'm actually more confused now."

Jopp placed his hands behind his head. "You and me both, Earth man. Now give me a minute to try and figure this out."

Chuck stood quietly. His eyes followed as Jopp paced back and forth. After a minute, he could no longer help himself. "Just what the hell is going on here, Jopp?"

Jopp threw his hands up. "I don't know, okay? Are you happy? I don't know why the ship is empty! I don't know why we were attacked! I don't know why they stuck you here with me! I don't even know why they rehired me in the first—*what the shit is that*?!"

Jopp's eyes were fixed on something behind Chuck, back toward the doorway. Chuck followed his gaze and turned around to see what Jopp was staring at. Just inside and to the right of the door was a case. It was rectangular, with a handle on the top. It looked to be just a bit larger than a standard Earth briefcase. A polished black finish coated its seamless surface. In any other setting, there would be nothing remarkable about this case. But against the contrast that was the stark vacantness of the storage facility, it shone like a beacon. The point was driven home by the four heavy straps stretched across its surface. Someone had obviously taken great care in affixing it to the wall. Chuck stood still while Jopp approached the case. He flinched as Jopp ran his fingers across its surface. Jopp noticed this. "Relax. It's not going to explode. You think those yokheads would've been shooting at us like that if this thing was some ultrasensitive bomb?"

Despite the merits of his logic, Chuck couldn't help but cringe as Jopp indelicately removed the straps. He gripped the handle and lifted the case away from the wall. "Not very heavy," he commented to himself, then called over his shoulder to Chuck, "Let's go into the other room and check this out."

Chuck hung back as Jopp headed into the lounge. After a few seconds he heard Jopp's voice echo back through the door. "Man, would you quit being a Preeloin, and get in here?"

Chuck took a deep breath and headed through the doorway. The case was sitting on the circular table in the center of the lounge. Jopp was dragging two chairs over. "Hey, there he is."

"What's a Preeloin?"

Jopp dropped himself into one of the chairs. "Huh?"

"What's a Preeloin?"

Jopp was studying the case. "Oh, they're this sentient species from the Reeb System. An amazingly cowardly group of people. Their home world has been conquered something like a thousand times. I think they're currently being occupied by the Vashnii Armada. Not a bad gig. The Vashnii are an efficient bunch. Probably have the society humming with productivity."

"That's messed up, man."

Jopp kept his eyes on the case as he responded, "What is?"

"I thought you were supposed to be this superadvanced society. No one's doing anything to help these people?"

Jopp continued eyeing the latch. "They tried that once a while back. The Preeloins almost went extinct."

"Wait, what?"

Jopp finally looked up. "Okay, imagine that for thousands of years your entire civilization has been existing under some form of subjugation. We're talking a hundred generations here. A hundred generations of having your society's every decision made for you. What do you think happens when you're suddenly left to your own devices? It took less than a year for the planet's entire infrastructure to collapse. Half the population died due to starvation, sickness, and various accidents. They actually submitted an official request to the Sentient Coalition begging to be conquered by someone."

"Oh."

"Yeah, *oh*. Now we can either continue this riveting sociopolitical discussion"—Jopp rummaged around in his pocket, pulled something out, and tossed it to Chuck—"or you can head back to the galley and grab us a couple of Flanisi Ales."

Chuck caught the object. It was a key card, or at least it looked just like one. Jopp continued, "They're in the cooler box, in the locked drawer at the bottom."

"They let you have alcohol onboard during a job?"

Jopp scoffed. "Ha! No! That's why I left you alone in the hangar. First I needed to get a line on some chuz. Then I needed to figure out which ship would be ours. Then I had to pay off one of the prelaunch techs to stash it."

Chuck turned to leave, took a step, stalled, and turned back. "So you didn't think to check to make sure everything was cool with the ship? Like our payload, for instance? But you went to all that trouble to make sure there was alcohol on board?"

"Yeah, so?"

"I'm just sayin' . . . you might have a problem."

"And *I'm* just saying you can keep your opinions to yourself." Jopp allowed the hint of a smirk to creep onto his face. "Now fetch them ales, Earth ape."

Chuck rolled his eyes. "Sure thing, Lemonhead."

TEXT UNIT 0008

Haaga Viim stood on the bridge of his ship. He ground his teeth as he glared out into the empty blackness, where just moments ago his quarry had vanished. Shai was sitting back, scaly arms folded across his chest, his narrow eyes watching the captain cautiously. Vaatu, the pilot, was also staring out into the blackness, his mouth hanging open in stunned silence. The only sounds came from the front of the deck, where Pilu and Rigu where loudly bickering in unintelligible gibberish, likely in reference to who was at fault for their prey escaping them.

Haaga grumbled through a clenched jaw, "What. Just. Happened?" His gaze fell on Vaatu, who was frozen in place. He turned back to his right. "Shai?"

"It's an uncharted anomaly."

"So they could be . . ."

"Anywhere."

"We are not losing this target. You send word to every informant, dispatcher, smuggler, dealer . . . *everyone* in our network. Tell them the first person to get us information about that ship's location gets fifty thousand Tahlians."

Shai said, "Fifty thousand? That will clear out our reserve account."

"Fifty thousand is nothing compared to what we are getting paid for this. Do it."

Shai nodded. Haaga continued, "And set a course to get us back to Pa Tahae as fast as possible. We need to activate the auxiliary crews. I want a team situated at each of the major waypoints, ready to respond once word comes in about their location."

"I can follow them!"

Haaga and Shai spun around to stare at Vaatu. Shai looked as if he was about to speak, but the Twins' disagreement up at the front had devolved to a more physical nature. A few slaps and pokes quickly turned into two giant cotton balls rolling across the floor. Haaga gestured to them. "Shai, handle that."

As Shai moved quickly to break up the kerfuffle, Haaga approached Vaatu, arms crossed. "Care to explain?"

"I had us in a perfect Ripsin strafe maneuver."

"So?"

Vaatu continued nervously, "So the Ripsin strafe maneuver dictates approaching your target from a very specific angle. Our logs will have recorded our exact trajectory when they hit the jump. If I adjust that trajectory by the Ripsin strafe angle, that gives us their exact flight path. We hit the anomaly with that same trajectory, we end up right where they did."

Haaga's expression was unmoving. "That's all presuming we were in absolute perfect position."

Vaatu's voice was resolute as he said, "We *were* in perfect position. I can do this."

Shai walked up behind Haaga and added, "It's not impossible."

Haaga glanced over his shoulder to Shai, then back at Vaatu. "Okay. Make a note of the anomaly's coordinates. We can't stay here while you work it out. A ULE patrol will be coming through this sector before long. Shai, find the nearest safe-house location. We should refuel. And after that, I still want you putting out the bounty. Even if Vaatu's idea works, it's unlikely they'll be sitting at the exit point."

A shrill voice piped up. "Nuh-uh!"

The three of them turned to see the Twins standing there. One had a dark bruise forming under his left eye, and the other had two or three tufts of hair missing from his chest. The one with the black eye spoke. "No go."

Haaga's eye narrowed. "And why do you say that?"

This time the one with the missing hair answered, "Turbine boom!"

Shai chimed in. "If they actually hit it, the strain of the jump would've been too much for their engines. They wouldn't be capable of getting very far from the exit point."

The Twins glared at Shai, and in unison barked, "*IF?*"

Haaga replied, "If you say you shot them, I believe you. Now get back to your posts."

Their expressions lit up, and they puffed their chests out, and then gave their best attempt at a sprint back to their seats, chattering as they went.

Haaga spoke to Shai and Vaatu. "You two know what you need to do. I need to go update the rest of the crew."

Vaatu and Shai went about busying themselves at their posts, and Haaga made to leave the bridge. Just as he was getting to the door, he heard Shai's voice calling, "Captain, there's an incoming commline. They're asking for you, saying it's 'absolutely crucial' that you pick up."

"Who is it?"

"They won't give me a name. They're telling me to tell you that it's an 'old friend.'"

Haaga's face darkened. "I'll take the call in my quarters."

Haaga poured himself a glass of cloudy liquid and sat down at his desk. The console lit up, and one icon started flashing. He sighed, pressed the icon, and spoke. "This is Haaga Viim."

A robotic synthesized voice said in response, *"What's your status?"*

Haaga took a pull from his glass before answering. "We have an issue."

A pause and then: *"What kind of issue?"*

"A they-got-away kind of issue."

Another pause and then: *"Not exactly what I'd hoped to hear. I thought I'd mentioned how little room for error there was on this contract."*

"You did. And it would have gone perfectly had you not selected a staging area with an uncharted anomaly."

"What?"

"You heard me."

"That system is fully mapped."

"That's how it's classified, yes. But the fact that I just witnessed the target ship disappear through a giant black spot leaves me slightly skeptical as to the map's accuracy."

Another, much longer pause, and then: *"This is not good."*

"How observant of you. I knew there was a reason you were calling the shots."

"Sarcasm. How uncharacteristically unproductive of you, Haaga. You remember how much is at stake here?"

"My pilot believes he can duplicate the path they took through the anomaly."

"Do you believe he can?"

"I trust my crew. If he says he can do it, he can do it."

"How nice. I'm sorry I don't share your sentiment. I'll get you their exact location within a few hours."

Haaga sat up. "And how exactly would you manage that?"

"*I guess that's why I call the shots, isn't it? Now get your ship somewhere out of sight, and don't do anything until you hear from me.*"

The source of the robotic voice terminated the connection. Haaga downed what was left of his drink, resisting the urge to throw the glass against the wall.

TEXT UNIT 0009

Jopp's eyes narrowed as he stared Chuck down. "Well, go ahead, Earth man. Make your move."

Chuck returned the glare and growled, "You've left me no choice."

Jopp's stare was unflinching. "You do what you gotta do."

Chuck looked down, then quickly back up. "If I don't do this, you'll kill me."

Jopp arched an eyebrow. "Maybe."

Chuck held his breath as his hand slowly reached forward . . .

. . . and moved his gridspar piece across the holographic game board. Jopp's menacing glare melted into a wide grin. "Ha! You fell for it!"

He then moved his own game piece, causing the holographic display to morph into a brief animation, culminating with the destruction of Chuck's game piece. Jopp threw his hands up in triumph. "That's three matches in a row! Finish your drink, winklinker!"

The pair sat across from each other on the roof of the ship. The black case rested next to Jopp. Chuck groaned as he lifted the bottle of Flanisi Ale to his lips, seeing it was still at least half full. He drained it, let out a violent belch, and tossed the bottle over his shoulder. It bounced a few times and then rolled over the edge of the ship. The next two seconds passed silently as the bottle fell fifty feet to the ground, where it promptly shattered amid a dozen of its brethren.

It had been fifty-four minutes since the crash. Three of those minutes had been spent on trying to open the case. Jopp determined it had some form of advanced DNA lock.

You see this square red light? he had said. *That's the lock. Only the bio-signature of the dick who originally locked it can turn this lock green, thus allowing it to open.*

The next four minutes had been spent climbing up to the ship's roof to get a look at their surroundings. The cliff face stretched farther than they could see, and the landscape behind them consisted of blue sand. Lots of blue sand. After determining their landing location to be precisely in the center of the middle of nowhere, they spent the next forty-seven minutes drinking and playing the game of gridspar. There was nothing to do but wait for the company salvage crew that Jopp was "positively sure" was on its way.

Jopp grabbed two more bottles, handed one to Chuck, and asked, "You wanna play again?"

Chuck wavered a bit before finally nodding through a series of hiccups. Flanisi Ale, it turns out, is much more potent than anything he'd had back on Earth, and things were starting to get a tad hazy. He peered at Jopp quizzically as he busied himself with resetting the gridspar board.

Chuck couldn't help himself, "So—*hic*—what's your deal?"

Jopp looked up. "Huh?"

"Like . . . what's your—*hic*—deal?"

Jopp reached for the deck of gridspar cards.

"No!" protested Chuck. "Not *deal* . . . I mean, what's your story?"

"What do you mean?"

"So, I know I don't know a lot about a lot of—*hic*—this space galaxy stuff . . . but I know an underachiever when I—*hic*—see one."

"Oh, yeah?"

Chuck nodded lazily. "For sure. That flying was ri—*hic*—diculous."

"So? I'm a good pilot."

Chuck shook his head. "You're a *great* pilot. Those pirates had us. . . . I mean, they *had* us. You got us out of there"—he reached down and slapped the ship's hull—"and with our ship and cargo intact—*hic*—more or less."

"What's your point?"

"My point is—Hey! My hiccups are gone! My point is . . . like . . . what . . . what are you even doing in this job? And another thing! What happened on your last run? I mean, whatever actually happened, there's no way it was crazier than this shit, right? But somehow you lost an entire ship?"

Jopp sat back and folded his arms and peered skeptically at the Earth man. Chuck took advantage of the lull in conversation to attack his next drink. You see, the other thing about Flanisi Ale is, it tastes better the more you drink, or at least it seemed that way to Chuck. After a few moments of silence, Jopp leaned forward. "You're right."

Chuck pulled the bottle away from his face, a bit of purple liquid trickling down his chin. "Huh?"

Jopp took a big pull from his own bottle before repeating, "I said, 'you're right.'"

A quizzical look crossed Chuck's face. "I'm right about what?" A third quality of Flanisi Ale was that it could rapidly affect short-term memory.

Jopp sighed. Chuck furrowed his brow and fought hard to remember. He suddenly jumped up, pointed a finger at Jopp, and exclaimed, "Oh! Yeah! Pilot stuff! Missing ships and whatnot!"

Jopp nodded. "I started working for Prime Partners because . . . well, because my father was a dick . . . probably still *is* a dick, for that matter."

"Huh?"

Jopp breathed another heavy sigh and continued, "I wasn't exaggerating earlier when I told you the name Wenslode was a big deal."

Chuck sat back down, cross-legged. His eyes fixed on Jopp, while his mouth nursed his bottle, as if he were a child getting ready to hear a bedtime story.

"Every male in my family takes a particular career path: military service followed by politics. Every single one of my brothers, cousins, and uncles is either currently active in the military or has parlayed that into a diplomatic career. And of course, my father is the chief asshole of them all. He's the governor of one of the larger provinces."

Chuck tossed aside the now-empty bottle and looked pleadingly at Jopp, who interrupted himself. "Dude, you're going to pass out if you have another. So anyway, of course, I was put on the same path as everyone else in the family. I basically spent every day of my adolescence at one type of academy or another, doing the bare minimum to not flunk out. It turns out I have a natural talent for flying. So, I get to the third cycle of Flight Seminary, on pace to finish top of the class and . . ."

He had noticed that Chuck's eyes had fallen about two-thirds closed. "Are you shitting me? Chuck . . . CHUCK!"

Chuck's eyes shot open, and he blurted out, "Flight class! Dad's an asshole! Got it!"

Jopp chugged the rest of his drink, all while glaring at Chuck. He finished and said, "To sum it all up, I decided one day that the family plan was bullshit. I told my father I had no intention of seeing it through, and he promptly disowned me. I needed money, and this was the best-paying job I could find. It's given me the chance to see a shitload of the galaxy, and with the exception of the last three weeks, it's been pretty fun."

Chuck's head lolled in a manner that could have almost been described as a nod.

"So what about you, Earth man? What's *your deal*?"

Chuck burped. "It's not too different from yours, honestly."

"Oh, really? You travel around the universe because your politician father cut you off?"

"No, smartass, I mean . . . Dad's a doctor. Grandpa's a doctor. . . . I didn't want to be a doctor. So Dad says he's not paying for college anymore. I can't afford tuition. I drop out and take the first job I find."

Jopp snorted. "Dads, huh?"

Chuck raised his drink. "Dads."

They each took a long swig from their respective bottles. A few moments passed silently.

Chuck let loose another burp, and then mumbled, "Ship."

"What?"

"What happened to the other ship?"

Jopp gave him a sidelong glance as he reached for another ale. Chuck pointed at him and shouted, "Don't pass out!" Jopp popped the top and took a long pull, all while holding up his middle finger.

Chuck squealed. "Ha! We do that on Earth, too!"

Jopp set the bottle down and wiped his mouth. "Oh, screw it. You're not going to remember this later, anyway. . . . So, there I was—*what the hell is that?!*"

Jopp was staring over Chuck's shoulder, into the arid blue-gray landscape. Chuck's head felt heavy. *Must be the gravity,* he thought, as he swung it around to see what Jopp was looking at. There was a billowing dust cloud growing on the horizon. Chuck wore a glazed expression as he watched the cloud grow larger. His face turned pensive when he realized the dust cloud wasn't actually growing, just getting closer, which was making it appear larger. His eyes widened with shock when it hit him that this meant whatever was causing the dust cloud was rapidly heading in their direction. He glanced to the right to see that Jopp had moved next to him, and had witnessed that roller coaster of emotion wash over Chuck's face. "Wow, Earth man. I would love to get a glimpse inside your head sometime."

Chuck ignored the comment and swung his head back toward the oncoming dust cloud. It was close enough now that they could make out a dark mass at the center, and a barely audible humming noise was growing in their ears. Chuck swung his head back to Jopp. "Ish it the shalvage team?" *Apparently the gravity is making my tongue heavy, too,* he thought.

Jopp shook his head. "Nope. They wouldn't show up in a land crawler. They'd send a ship."

"Should we be worry?"

"Why should we be worried? I've now botched two jobs in a row for the universe's most powerful corporation, we're being hunted by marauders, and it's a toss-up whether these beings"—he gestured at the dust cloud—"are going to help us or eat us."

The humming noise at the center of the dust cloud gained a few more decibels.

"So . . . should we, like, get weapons or somethin' . . . jus' in case?"

Jopp shrugged. "I doubt the ship has any weapons. The regulations on that are always changing. First, you have unarmed transporters . . . then you see a rise in hijackings. So, you issue them all weapons . . . then you see a rise in transporters shooting each other. So, it swings back around, and the cycle starts over. . . ."

"Why would the transhporters shoot each other?"

Jopp shrugged again. "Anomaly right-of-way disputes . . . gridspar matches . . . the usual stuff. If you ask me, most of 'em have seen too many Noha Sol films."

"Too many what?"

"Noha Sol films."

"Um, what?"

"You don't know who Noha Sol is?"

Chuck pointed at himself. "Dumb Earth ape, 'member?"

Jopp smirked. "Glad to hear you've accepted your identity. Anyway, they're just movies about an adventuring smuggler."

The approaching vehicle was now less than a mile away, with the dust cloud in hot pursuit. The hum grew into a deep rumble. The two companions stood silently as it closed the gap.

At two hundred yards, Chuck saw that the vehicle resembled a cross between a van and a pickup truck, only much wider across. He covered his ears as the rumble evolved into a roaring cacophony of mechanical clinks and clangs. At one hundred yards, he could see light glinting off the silver finish of the wide front grille. The body of the vehicle sported a checkered green-and-orange pattern.

"Oh, please no," moaned Jopp. Chuck didn't hear this as his hands were still over his ears.

The roaring din ceased as the vehicle screeched to a stop alongside their ship. The trailing dust cloud washed over

Chuck and Jopp. Amid their coughing and wheezing, they heard a hatch slide open. A booming voice cut through the dust. "Woooooooooo! Would ya look at that flapper!"

"Oh—*cough*—god, no," Jopp lamented.

"What—*cough*—what is it?!" shouted Chuck.

The dust dissipated. Chuck rubbed his eyes, coughed a few more times, and looked down. The front half of the garishly colored vehicle's roof slid back. Chuck could make out the silhouette of a figure standing up through the opening. The dust finally subsided completely, and Chuck had to rub his eyes again to make sure he was seeing correctly. The figure in the vehicle was . . .

. . . an alien. But it wasn't just any alien; it was *the* alien. The alien every human thinks about when they think about aliens: bulbous head, ashy gray skin, large black eyes, a tiny mouth and nostrils, denim overalls . . .

Chuck did a double take; the alien was indeed wearing denim overalls.

"It—it's," stuttered Jopp. "It's a . . ."

The alien yelled up at them, "I ain't seen a flapper like that in a humpalope's moon! I bet you can party for days with that baby! How much ya want fer it?!"

Jopp's shoulders slumped forward. "It's a Gorthan."

TEXT UNIT 0010

"A what?" Chuck felt a little lucidity creep back into his consciousness.

"It's a . . . I mean, *he's* a Gorthan," answered Jopp.

Chuck cocked his head. "I've heard that word before." He furrowed his brow and thought for a few moments. His face lit up, and he snapped his fingers. "Oh! That Tahl lady said something to you about a Gorthan. What was it again?"

"Never mind that. We need to get off this planet . . . immediately."

"Why? He doesn't seem so—"

"Hey!" shouted the Gorthan. "You two gon' stand up there yankin' yer dangles all day, or what?"

Jopp sighed and massaged the sides of his head before yelling down, "We're coming!" He turned to Chuck. "All right, let's see if we can't get this guy to give us a lift out of here. Try not to engage him in too much conversation, okay?"

He started heading for the hatch.

Chuck didn't follow. "Why do we want to leave? I thought the company salvage crew was on its way."

Jopp stopped and turned around. His face had that hand-in-the-cookie-jar look. "Yeah, about that . . . I never got a confirmation that they were coming. In fact, I never actually made contact with dispatch. For all I know, Prime Partners has no idea where we are."

He held his hands up apologetically.

Chuck's cheeks flushed, and he huffed, "We were waiting out here for nobody? Why the hell didn't you tell me?!"

Jopp pointed at Chuck. "That right there. That reaction. That's why I didn't tell you. I didn't want you freaking out while I came up with a solution."

The Gorthan's voice drifted up, "This is BOOOORRRRRRRINGGGGG."

Jopp started up again for the hatch, this time at a much-accelerated pace. He called back to Chuck over his shoulder, "Let's go! We need to get down there right now."

Chuck opened his mouth to protest, but Jopp was already down the hatch. Chuck sighed and started to follow. Jopp's voice echoed, "Hurry up! And grab the case!"

Chuck sighed again, made a quick detour to pick up the case, and then headed down the hatch. By the time he made his way down into the central lounge, Jopp was nowhere to be seen. A bright stream of white light poured in through an open door. Chuck stepped through and saw Jopp and the Gorthan standing at the foot of the exit ramp. The Gorthan was doing all the talking, and he looked excited about whatever it was they were discussing. Jopp simply nodded his head at regular intervals. Chuck noted that the Gorthan looked to be just a few inches taller than Jopp. The design on the overalls reminded Chuck of some famous painter. What was his name? The guy who died in a drunk driving accident, whose paintings looked like he just spilled drops randomly across the canvas. Pollop? Bollock? It was something like that. Anyway, the Gorthan's pants reminded Chuck of those paintings. The only other clothing he appeared to be wearing were some bright-green sandals. The whine of the desert winds prevented Chuck from hearing their conversation. He arrived at the foot of the ramp just in time to hear the Gorthan say, ". . . so that's how I almost had a three sex with two Hibas from Klopan 7. . . . Anyway, what the butt were we talkin' 'bout?"

Jopp pointed over his shoulder. "The ship. You wanted to buy it off us."

The Gorthan slapped himself on top of his head. "I forgot that was there! I bet you get some tops partying going on in there."

Chuck raised an eyebrow in disbelief and glanced back up at the looming ship. When he looked forward again, the Gorthan was staring back at him in wide-eyed wonderment.

Chuck gave a little wave. "Hi, I'm Chuck."

The Gorthan looked at Jopp. "What's a chuk?"

Jopp waved Chuck over. "Chuck is his name, and yes, he is from Earth." Then he looked back. "Chuck, this is Dagwam Rocket Beer Washgom. Apparently we're on 'planet WamBam.' Its population is 99.8% Gorthan . . . so hooray for that."

Before Chuck could respond, Dagwam bounded up and slapped him on the shoulder. "Holy face piss! You totally *are* from Earth! That's so tops!"

Chuck nodded hesitantly. "Um, thanks . . . I think?"

Jopp interjected, "Yeah, yeah . . . so about the ship?"

Dagwam spun around. "Oh, snot farts! I keeps forgettin'! So what we got here?"

Jopp plastered a wide smile across his face and gave a dramatic wave toward the ship. "So, what have here is a *slightly* used Class 4 Longstrider: all the latest tech, the exterior is a hypercompressed alloy . . . obviously crash tested."

"Quit dangle stranglin' me," interrupted Dagwam. "What you want fer it?"

"Um . . . twenty thousand Tahlians and a ride to the nearest intersystem shuttle?"

"Tal-yans?"

Jopp sighed and rubbed his temples. "We need to get off this planet. How can we make that happen?"

Dagwam closed his eyes, pinched his face tight, and stood silently for a solid minute. Jopp and Chuck exchanged confused looks. The Gorthan's face lit up, and he threw his arms in the air. "Got it!"

He didn't say anything else, only stared expectantly at the two. A second set of confused looks passed between Jopp and Chuck.

After another awkward thirty seconds, Jopp broke the silence. "Um . . . Dagwam?"

"Rocket Beer."

"Sure, okay . . . Rocket Beer, you said you had an idea?"

"What idea?"

Jopp exhaled in aggravation. "Didn't you just have an idea on how we could get off this planet?"

Dagwam's face scrunched up again in thought. Jopp seriously considered heading back to the ship for another ale. He gave Chuck a brief glance over his shoulder, and then did a double take. Chuck was nonchalantly sipping from a bottle.

"Seriously?" he shot back.

Chuck shrugged. "Slipped it in my pocket on the way out. Don't be mad just 'cause you didn't think of it."

"You could have gotten me one."

"I could have done a lot of things."

"What does that even mean?"

Chuck just shrugged again. Jopp was about to say something when Dagwam exclaimed, "Got it!"

Jopp spun back around. "What's your idea? Don't think, just spit it out."

Dagwam spat a green gob of something on the ground, then said, "You could go to Trash Blast Station. Then you could get a ride to Sauce Port. They got one of them big shuttle things. Lots of weirdo types like y'all come through there."

Chuck whispered to Jopp, "I hope some of that made sense to you."

Jopp ignored him. "So, Dagwam—"

"Rocket Beer."

He sighed. "Okay, Rocket Beer, we need to get to that port, Sauce Port."

Dagwam shrugged. "Well, then y'all should go to Trash Blast Station."

Jopp's cheeks flushed orange, and his left eye began twitching. Dagwam didn't seem to notice. Instead he smiled at Chuck. "Man, I love me some Earth style. It's tops! Y'all know how to party! And that's saying something."

"Um, thanks. . . ."

"We should party. Earth is big shit 'round here. Me and you? Together we could get all kinds of voopah on our yub nubs."

Chuck stammered, "Oh, um, well—"

He was interrupted by Jopp. "Oh, I know, right?! I'm so jealous of him, being from Earth and all." He gave a Chuck a pleading stare.

It took Chuck a second to recognize the "just go with it" face before playing along. "Oh, yeah! I mean, it's supergreat being from Earth. Everything on Earth is so awesome." He glanced at Jopp, whose right hand was hanging at his side, waving him on. Chuck continued, "In fact . . . some of the coolest people I know are actually getting a little bored with Earth and are looking for a new planet to party on."

Dagwam's mouth dropped open. Chuck continued, "You know, I'll bet I could convince them to come here for a party. Your people wouldn't be interested in that, would they?"

Dagwam slapped his hands together. "You pissin' out your mouth?! You serious! That would be the radical!"

Chuck nodded. "Oh, yeah, so radical. I'll tell you what, you give us a lift to that trash station place and enough money to buy a ride to Sauce Port and then off the planet, and not only can you have this ship"—he waved with a flourish at the looming wreckage—"but I'll come back with a bunch of other people like me. We'll throw a massive Earth-style party. What do you think about that?"

Dagwam narrowed his eyes and scratched the top of his head. Suddenly a wide, green tongue flopped out of his mouth. Chuck stared as Dagwam slowly ran his tongue over the palm of his right hand. He then stretched the newly moistened hand out and upward in what looked to be "high five position." Chuck glanced at Jopp, who was nodding furiously. He sighed and then proceeded to give his own right palm a good lick. It tasted like sweat, with just a hint of the ale. He raised his hand in similar fashion, and Dagwam, smiling wide, gave Chuck's hand a solid slap. Chuck winced.

"You got a sale, Earth man!" shouted Dagwam, before he bounded back to his vehicle.

Jopp started after him. He took a few steps and then stopped, looking back at Chuck. "That was good work. You may actually survive this whole ordeal." Chuck responded with his middle finger. Jopp laughed. "Let's go, buddy. We don't want to keep this guy waiting."

Chuck finished what little was left of his ale and casually tossed the bottle aside. He gave the ship a last look, picked up the case, brushed away some blue sand, and hurried after the others.

TEXT UNIT 0011

Haaga Viim stewed in the captain's chair on the bridge of the *Pfraza*. The marauder crew had been lucky in finding a nearby way station. They had been even luckier that the station manager was open to "off-ledger" business transactions, securing them a private hangar. The synthesized voice on the other end of the commline had told him to wait, so he had. The appointed hour came and went with no word, each passing minute giving his quarry a chance to widen the gap. He glanced at his pilot, Vaatu, who was busy looking busy, all while conveniently avoiding eye contact. Haaga's eyes then passed over the Twins, currently engaged in a gridspar match. Finally his gaze fell on his first mate, Shai, arms folded across his chest, thin eyes closed in meditation.

A beeping noise pulsed through the air. Shai opened his eyes and picked up the comm receiver. "Yes." The bridge was silent as the reptilian first mate listened to the voice on the other end. He hung up and looked to Haaga. "Jorwei says there's someone here. He asked that you come down."

Haaga's expression darkened as he pulled his broad orange frame out of the chair. The way station manager had assured them they would not be bothered, and Jorwei would've handled any minor issues on his own. Haaga descended the ship's boarding ramp and saw Jorwei waiting for him on the hangar floor. The Puzuru had a habit of donning shirts only when the situation absolutely required it. This, apparently, was not one of those situations, as his skin's blue-and-white camouflage pattern was on full display. His only articles of clothing were gray boots, gray pants, and the electric pump-shot slung over his shoulder.

Haaga scanned the dimly lit hangar. The ship-sized exit portal and a small doorway were the only things to see in the otherwise featureless room. The two orange-skinned Ochreans sat near the ship portal, and Ghono was leaning his considerable bulk against the door frame. Jorwei motioned toward the latter and explained as they walked over, "It's the station manager."

"Probably trying to squeeze more pecks out of us," grumbled Haaga. He caressed the hilt of the sonic dagger on his belt, wondering if he would have to teach a lesson on the follies of unchecked greed.

"I don't think so," replied Jorwei. "He's got someone with him. Said they instructed him to tell you they'd been sent here by an 'old friend.'"

Haaga grimaced and quickened his pace. Jorwei knew better than to keep the conversation going and clammed up. Haaga spoke to the hulking, crimson Dronla, "Open it, Ghono."

Ghono nodded and wrapped one large hand around the handle and braced himself against the door. Should anything be amiss, he'd be able to slam it closed with the full weight of his massive form. Jorwei positioned himself alongside the door, swinging his weapon around into his hands. Haaga stood back.

They both looked to him, and he nodded. Ghono cracked the door open ever so slightly. Jorwei peered through the opening, and saw two figures waiting expectantly. One was the station manager, a short, obese Yoblon, nervously wringing his hands. The other was taller. That was all Jorwei could discern, as the individual kept himself hidden in a dark cloak, the hood drawn up over his head.

"You can both come in once your friend loses his pretty cape," hissed Jorwei.

The cloaked stranger remained stone still. The portly, yellow-hued Yoblon nervously glanced back and forth. "Uh, um, d—did you tell him that an 'old friend' sent us?"

Jorwei opened his mouth to say something snide, but Haaga cut him off. "It's okay. Let them in."

Jorwei narrowed his eyes skeptically before nodding to Ghono. He then took a step back and leveled his weapon at the doorway. Ghono opened the door just enough for the two individuals to step inside. The cloaked one accepted the invitation, while the station manager hung back. Haaga looked over the stranger's shoulder to the Yoblon and said, "You can go now."

The station manager couldn't leave fast enough. Ghono quickly closed the door and stepped behind the stranger. Jorwei moved next to Haaga, his weapon still pointed at the stranger's chest. "Can we dispense with the needless mystery and get to business?" Haaga said.

The stranger's hands rose deliberately to the cloak's hood. It was pulled it back to reveal sharp, yet distinctly feminine, humanoid features. Her silver skin had the slightest hint of shine, and her bare face and scalp bore a series of magenta tribal markings.

"What's a J'Kari doing associating with the likes of us?" asked Haaga.

The J'Kari's tone was hoarse yet strong. "I'm here to fix what you broke."

Haaga raised a single finger. "Let's get a few things straight. First, the mistake was made by our mutual 'friend' in choosing the staging area." He extended a second finger. "And second, you will check your tone. I don't care how much money is at stake; you disrespect me on my own ship, I'll kill you with my bare hands and flush your corpse into space. Do we have an understanding?"

The J'Kari smirked but nodded in agreement. She removed her cloak and tossed it nonchalantly to the floor. While her presence emanated authority, her attire was your average traveler's garb. Haaga noted it felt almost *too* average, as if she spent far too much effort on trying to look normal. He ignored this for the moment and moved on to pressing matters. "I assume you're here to provide some information on our target's whereabouts."

"You assume correct. They're in the Drecken System. We'll know for sure once we get there, but it seems as if the ship crashed on some Gorthan-infested boondock."

Haaga thought aloud. "So we aren't likely to have a run-in with the ULE. . . . Good. What about Prime Partners? Won't they send a salvage team?"

The J'Kari shook her head. "Don't worry about the company or the Law Cogs. Neither will be an issue."

Before Haaga could ask why, she continued, "Our problem is that it will take a full standard day to reach the system. If they did, in fact, crash, and if they did, in fact, survive, it's unlikely they'll stay with the wreckage; seeing as no salvage team is going to respond to their distress calls."

"And we can't have any witnesses lingering out there, now can we?" added Haaga.

The J'Kari responded with a deadpan "No, we cannot." She stepped toward the *Pfraza*'s boarding ramp. Before she could pass, Haaga held out a thick arm, blocking her way. "I don't recall inviting you aboard my ship."

She glared back. "We don't have time for this."

Haaga returned the glare with his eyes while smiling with his mouth. "There's always time for decorum, and besides, I don't even know your name."

The tattooed, silver-skinned J'Kari responded, making no attempt to hide her annoyance, "Call me Kahpa. Now may we go, *Captain*?"

"All right, follow me." He led Kahpa toward the ship, while Jorwei gave the "round up" signal.

Haaga, Kahpa, and Jorwei made their way to the bridge, while the rest of the crew prepared for departure. They approached Shai's console, and he rose in greeting.

Haaga jerked his head. "This is Kahpa. She can apparently help us find our target."

Kahpa stepped forward and stretched out her hand; a small, white rectangle rested in her palm. "Here are the coordinates of their last location."

Shai took the data tab from her and inserted it into his console.

"Ooooo . . . Jaka!" squeaked a high-pitched voice.

Kahpa turned around to find two oversized cotton balls staring up at her.

"Can I help you?" she asked dismissively.

"Jaka funny!" The Twins laughed.

"Get back to your stations," ordered Haaga. The Twins scurried off. He turned back to Kahpa. "You still haven't told us how you know where they are."

"I don't know *how*. I'm just relaying the information."

"Humpa shit!" spat Jorwei. Haaga waved him off.

Kahpa made a point of looking Haaga in the eye and hissed, "You've spoken with our mutual friend, yes? Does he strike you as someone eager to share information? My job was to bring the coordinates to you and help you acquire the target. How this information was obtained is irrelevant to my job, just as it is irrelevant to yours." She looked back to Shai. "We need to leave immediately. It will take us a standard day to arrive at those coordinates."

"We can't afford a full day," snapped Haaga. "You said the planet was inhabited by Gorthans. By this time tomorrow, that transport will have been completely stripped."

"Well unless this ship is capable of breaking the laws of space and time, we don't have much choice, now, do we?"

Haaga cocked his head toward his pilot. "Vaatu can follow them through the anomaly."

Kahpa scoffed. "Oh, really?" She turned to the pilot. "And just how would you accomplish that?"

Vaatu opened his mouth to reply, but Haaga cut him off. "He owes you no explanation, J'Kari. Your job was to provide us with the target's coordinates. How our ship gets there is irrelevant to your job. Now find a seat and strap in."

Kahpa gave the ship's captain another smirk as she casually chose a chair at an unused navigation terminal.

Haaga stepped over to the pilot's station and quietly said, "You are confident in your calculations?"

"Yes, sir."

Haaga took his position in the captain's chair and commanded, "Light us up."

The ship lurched off the ground. The hangar portal seal peeled back, revealing the spotted midnight of space. Haaga flipped a switch and spoke, his voice echoing through the ship: "The hunt is on in 3 . . . 2 . . . 1."

The young Ochrean pilot gripped his controls and sent them hurtling into the endless night.

TEXT UNIT 0012

The green-and-orange vehicle, or the Rumbler, as Dagwam called it, blazed across the desert, leaving a plume of bluish dust in its wake. It had been roughly half an hour since their departure from the crash site, all of it spent in silence. Well, at least the passengers and driver had been silent. One could attribute the lack of conversation to any number of factors. It could have been the tremendous roar of the Rumbler's engine. It could have been the unrelenting series of vaguely rhythmic bumps and bangs blaring through the vehicle's interior, otherwise known as Gorthan music. Or it could have been the fact that both Chuck and Jopp had fallen asleep in the back.

The Rumbler skidded to a halt, and the backseat sleepers were yanked into consciousness. Dagwam cut the engine and retracted the roof. He stood on his seat and turned around to face the groggy duo. "Wooo! You dudes musta been partyin' hard! I never seen no one pass out like that! Let's go!"

He hopped to the ground. Chuck and Jopp stretched as they took in their surroundings. They looked up at what Chuck thought resembled a house, not too dissimilar from what one might find in an affluent Earth suburb. The glaring difference was that it was seemingly pieced together from three completely different houses. The first floor was unmistakably a log cabin but painted blue. The second floor was divided right down the middle. The upper-right quarter appeared to have been pieced together from thousands of scrap metal bits. Chuck had no idea what the upper-left quarter was made from, but it looked like Swiss cheese. The roof shingles were made of black glass, reminding Chuck of solar panels.

To the left of the house was what could have been a junkyard. It stretched for acres and held at least a dozen large piles of scrap metal. Scattered here and there were the carcasses of small vehicles. Chuck glanced to his right and could see another three or four similar homesteads situated along the horizon. He looked back the way they had come and saw nothing but blue desert. He turned around to see Jopp climbing down after Dagwam, and followed suit. Dagwam loped toward the house, and Jopp jogged after him. Again, Chuck followed.

Jopp called ahead, "Dag—I mean, Rocket Beer! Wait a minute!" Dagwam waited at the front stoop for them to catch up.

"You remember we need to go to Trash Blast Station, right?" asked Jopp.

"Yup."

"So, is this Trash Blast Station?"

"Nope."

Jopp sighed heavily. "Where are we?"

Dagwam peered at Jopp. "We're on planet WamBam. I done said that already. You brain-slow or somethin'?"

Jopp looked at Chuck pleadingly. Chuck pointed at the house. "What is this building?"

Dagwam spread his arms out wide. "Welcome to my estately abode."

Jopp was dumbfounded. Chuck asked, "Why did you bring us here?"

"Man! You fellas really ain't the slickest rud in the gaw, is you? I needs to be getting you your moneys. And y'all can't be traipsin' around wearing them weird clothes. And I sure can't pass up the chance to have a beer with a bona fide Earth man, now can I? Plus, my sisters would kill me if they missed the chance to meet ya!" He turned and went through the door.

Jopp was fuming. Chuck simply shrugged. "Look, this is our only shot to get out of here, right? Plus, I don't know about you, but I would love to get out of this dirty uniform. And he did just offer us a beer. . . ."

Jopp raised an eyebrow, allowing a thin smile to creep across his face. "All right, Earth ape. Grab the case."

They bounded up the front steps and passed through the front door. If someone were to have asked Chuck how he might have described the foyer, he would have responded with . . . *insane*. The foyer was insane. Resting in the center of the room, stretching up to the ceiling, was a pyramid of beer bottles.

A staircase wound up the right-hand wall, its railing coated in brightly colored stones, gems, and crystals. The walls were a collage of posters, not unlike a college dorm room. Amid the pictures of Gorthans in flashy attire and ostentatiously deco-rated Rumblers and what Chuck could only assume were liquor ads, he spotted a few familiar images. One poster displayed a famous Earth rapper, surrounded by a bevy of scantily clad women. Another depicted a neon orange Lamborghini. There was also the classic five-fingered green cannabis leaf. And then he saw a surprisingly tasteful landscape of the Grand Canyon. He opened his mouth to comment but noticed that Jopp had already disappeared through the doorway ahead.

At least Chuck assumed that's where he had gone, as he heard a rhythmic thumping emanating from that direction. He stepped cautiously around the beer-bottle pyramid and headed through the doorway. He turned left, following the music-esque sounds. He passed through another doorway and dropped the black case in surprise.

Jopp was kneeling in the center of the room, an upturned crimson bottle pressed to his lips. Dagwam stood next to him, hands held high, each gripping a dark red bottle. Chuck looked to the right to see three Gorthans seated on a long couch. He noted that they pretty much looked exactly like female versions of Dagwam, except they had hair. Nobody seemed to notice Chuck's entrance. They were too busy goading Jopp on with chants of "Chuz! Chuz! Chuz!" and Jopp eagerly obliged. A bit of the bottle's contents trickled down from the side of his mouth. He finished the drink, wiped his chin, stood up, and let loose a tremendous belch. The four Gorthans erupted in applause. Jopp spotted Chuck in the doorway and pointed. "Chuck! Get in here and have a drink!"

Dagwam spun around. "Oh, gabber gams! I forgot! Nooni! Daymi! Yibbi! Check it out! We got a real live Earth man in our house!"

The three on the couch stared, mouths hanging open. Chuck gave them a little wave, and they squealed in delight. Suddenly Dagwam had thrown an arm around him and was leading Chuck over to the couch. "Earth man Chuck, allow me to introduce my sisters: this one here is Nooni." The one on the left gave Chuck a big smile. Her thin lips and long lashes were neon green. She had a matching shock of green hair that shot straight up in the air for about a foot, and then was folded back behind her.

Dagwam continued, "And here we have Daymi." Her lips and lashes had been tinted fluorescent yellow, and her matching hair had been cut short, forming a mishmash of yellow spikes pointing in every direction. She held both thumbs up and slammed her fists together. Chuck considered returning the gesture, but Dagwam had moved on.

"And finally, we have Yibbi." She had an upturned bottle pressed against her lips. Yibbi's color of choice was electric blue. She had the longest hair of the three, slicked to the side, falling over her left shoulder. She pulled the bottle away and burped out the words "Hey there!" The four Gorthans burst out laughing, and Chuck couldn't help but giggle a bit.

Dagwam composed himself and said, "So anyway, girls, this here is Chuck. Now, me and Chuck and his little yellow butler man—"

Jopp interjected, "Hey!"

Chuck waved him off.

Dagwam continued, "We got us some important Earth-style business to attend to, and I need y'alls' help." They waited expectantly. A few moments passed. Finally, the spiky yellow one named Daymi said, "Dagwam."

"Rocket Beer," he corrected.

She hopped to her feet. "Oh, would ya give that *Rocket Beer* plop glop a rest? You shot *one* beer into space *one* time. That don't make you no hero." Then she turned to Jopp. "Now what did you and the Earth man need help with?"

Dagwam scrunched his face up. Chuck raised his hand. "Um, he's buying our ship in exchange for a ride to that trash station place and some money."

Jopp jumped in. "And I believe he mentioned something about new clothes, too."

Daymi rubbed her chin. "Yeah, that's a good point. Y'all shouldn't be traipsin' around wearing them weird clothes." She turned to the green one. "Nooni, run upstairs and get Dagwam's Earth robe collection." Nooni downed the remainder of her beer, casually tossed the bottle over her shoulder, and moseyed out of the room. Daymi turned back to Dagwam. "Go dig up the money stash we buried a ways back."

Dagwam furrowed his brow. "You ain't runnin' this show, Daymi. I'm the one what found this here Earth man and his metal flapper."

"Bet you a bottle you can't do it in less than five minutes."

"Woooo! You're on, sister!" Dagwam sprinted out of the room.

Daymi turned to the last remaining sibling, the electric blue one. "Yibbi, you got the most important job: get this Earth man and his yellow butler guy—"

"Hey!"

"—some beer." Yibbi wasted no time bolting out of the room.

Jopp wagged a finger at Daymi. "I am absolutely *not* this guy's butler, okay? If anything, he's *my* butler. In fact, if it wasn't for me, he'd probably be dead right now!"

Daymi leaned in. "Ain't you just the cutest. You know, yellow is my favorite color."

Jopp's cheeks flushed purple. "Oh . . . uh . . . oh . . . um . . ."

He was saved by the voice of Dagwam booming down the hallway. "Daymi! Where the phoob is the shovel?!"

Daymi hollered back, "In the kitchen, Butt Milk! Where else do you expect a shovel to be?!"

There was a series of clatters and clangs, followed by a loud "Found it!" then the sound of a door slamming.

A few seconds later, Yibbi returned with a crate of dark red bottles. Without warning she threw one to Chuck, who ducked at the last second. The bottle shattered against the wall, spilling red liquid everywhere. Daymi put her hands on her hips. "Listen, I know it might seem like the best way to drink your chuz is to get it all out the bottle at the same time. But the stupid ground ends up drinking most of it. Trust us, we've experimented."

Chuck started to explain. "I wasn't rea—" He caught the second bottle Yibbi tossed just before it connected with the side of his face. Daymi smiled.

Yibbi threw two more drinks to Jopp and Daymi, then selected one for herself. The three of them stood silently, staring at Chuck.

Chuck's eyes darted back and forth between them. "What?"

Jopp smirked. "They're waiting for you to chug it, man. Good luck. This stuff's a lot stronger than Flanisi."

Chuck took a deep breath, popped the top, and went to work. Whatever this liquid was, it definitely didn't go down as smooth as Flanisi Ale. He closed his eyes to concentrate, and amid the chants of "Chuz! Chuz! Chuz!" he managed to polish off the whole bottle. When he finished, the Gorthan sisters let out a cheer, and Chuck saved himself from a black eye by catching another airborne bottle. He silently prayed he wouldn't be expected to chug this one as well. As if to answer his prayers, Nooni returned with her arms wrapped around a wadded mound of fabrics and unceremoniously dumped it in the middle of the floor.

"Here's every Earth robe we got," she announced just before making a no-look catch on a flying beer.

Chuck set his drink down and began rooting through the pile of clothes. He was surprised to discover that many of the items appeared to actually be from Earth. After sifting through a mélange of seventies-era bowling shirts, ugly Christmas sweaters, an Elvis jumpsuit, and a Shawn Kemp Seattle SuperSonics jersey, Chuck pulled out a nondescript maroon shirt. It was short sleeved and button-down, and looked as if it might have once been the top half of a janitorial uniform. He set it aside and continued sifting through the pile, coming up with a faded pair of jeans and a green trucker hat.

"What ya think of my collection?"

They turned to see Dagwam standing in the doorway. He was coated in a fine layer of blue dirt, a dented box clutched in his right hand and a shovel in his left. His expression held a level of pride one might see from a parent witnessing their child graduate from law school.

"A lot of this is actually from Earth." Chuck was still examining the clothes he'd selected. "How did you get this?"

Daymi spoke up. "Earth style is tops. Them is some valuable robes right there."

"You don't have any normal clothes, do you?" asked Jopp. "Like a basic-fit jumpsuit?"

He was answered with four blank stares from the Gorthans and a shrug from Chuck. Jopp shook his head and settled on a long-sleeved shirt that read "College" across the chest and some gray sweatpants. Daymi ordered Nooni and Dagwam to put away the remaining clothes. She then indicated to Jopp and Chuck that they could get changed in one of the hallway bathrooms, or "plop closets," as she called them.

Four minutes later, Chuck was back in the living room, sipping on a fresh beer. Another four minutes would pass before Jopp rejoined them. It had taken him an extra bit of time to discern that his pants were not secured in place by a firma seal, but rather by two pieces of string.

Dagwam attempted to open the dented box using the time-honored method of banging on it with the shovel. After a half dozen swings, the shovel method proved fruitful, and the lid popped open. Chuck peered over Dagwam's shoulder to see a colorful array of items resembling poker chips and credit cards. Dagwam spent a few seconds sifting through the box before deciding to simply upend it, spilling the contents across the floor. Jopp bent down and picked up one of the credit card–like objects. It was a light shade of tan with pink trim. In one of the corners was a small digital screen, which displayed "32,358." Jopp's eyes bugged out, and he silently waved Chuck over.

"What's up?"

Jopp whispered, "Be quiet." He peered around Chuck's shoulder to see that Dagwam was still engrossed in sorting the colorful items. He then glanced behind him to see that the three sisters had apparently grown bored and had thus left the room. He continued whispering. "This card has over thirty thousand Tahlians."

Chuck whispered back, "I have no idea what that means."

Jopp furrowed his brow. "It means this is worth a good amount of money. You make sure he's not looking when I swipe it."

"I don't want to screw the guy over."

"OH, COME ON!" exclaimed Jopp. Dagwam looked up curiously. Jopp gave him a big grin and a wave. Dagwam returned both gestures and went back to sorting. Jopp resumed whispering to Chuck. "The scrap off our ship is gonna make this guy a fortune in whatever dowfa-shit currency they use here."

"Dowfa?"

Jopp rolled his eyes. "It's a slow fat animal, not unlike an Earth ape. Would you please stay focused? We need money, real money . . . now."

Chuck glared at Jopp. "Not like this." Before Jopp could react, Chuck snatched the card. He turned around and said, "Dag—I mean, Rocket Beer, we'd really like to take this card as payment."

Dagwam looked up, saw the card, and burst out laughing, "Are you serious?! What you want that for?! It ain't worth nothing."

Jopp nudged Chuck in the ribs, but he ignored him. "Actually, it is worth a good amount of money in the place we're headed. We'd appreciate it if you'd let us accept this."

Dagwam's expression morphed into what Chuck had taken to calling his "scrunch mode." They stared silently at each other for an awkwardly long moment.

"Y'all are some tricky negotiators. But you ain't gon' get the best of ol' Rocket Beer! I'll give ya that there card, but you gotta let me give ya this, too!" He was holding out a fist full of green poker chips.

Chuck's mouth fell open in disbelief. Jopp seized the moment and swiped the card back from Chuck. "You steer a tough deal, sir. We accept your terms."

"Tops epic! Let's drink on it!"

TEXT UNIT 0013

Haaga Viim blinked away the white spots that often accompanied an anomaly jump and stared through the *Pfraza*'s main viewscreen. The anomaly had deposited his ship in orbit over a pale blue planet.

Haaga addressed his reptilian first mate. "Shai?"

The lean Soreshi raised his snakelike head. "The coordinates match. This is where they came out."

Haaga heard a sigh of relief escape from the pilot. He turned to his fellow orange-hued Ochrean and nodded.

"You just earned yourself a 5 percent bonus."

Before the pilot could say thanks, a sharp voice cut in. "Let's actually find the target item before you start doling out bonus Tahlians."

The silver-skinned J'Kari calling herself Kahpa leaned over one of the navigation consoles. She read something off her data bracelet and started tapping icons on the screen.

"I don't remember giving you permission to do that," growled Haaga.

Kahpa snarked, "I don't have time for your wobb-waggling power play shit right now."

Haaga stood. "What did you just say?"

Kahpa kept her eyes on the screen and said, "Shhh, let the professional work."

Haaga lunged at her with his left arm outstretched. Kahpa ducked and launched a kick to his midsection. Haaga tucked his right elbow into his side and rolled with the blow, letting his thick arm take the brunt of the strike. He countered with a wide hook, which she sidestepped. She threw a jab at his face, which he blocked with ease. In unison, they yanked their pulse pistols from their respective holsters, leveled the weapons at each other's heads, and froze. They stayed like that, with pistol muzzles hovering inches from their faces, for a full fifteen seconds.

Kahpa broke the silence. "I may have spoken a bit rashly a moment ago. We are under a great deal of pressure, and I am uncomfortable with not being in charge. That being said, this is still your ship. So . . . may I please use the navigation console, Captain?"

Haaga lowered his pistol and nodded. "You may."

Kahpa lowered her weapon as well and turned back to the console. She could have sworn she caught the hint of a smirk in Haaga's expression. She worked at the console for a minute before standing back up to say, "It should take us just a few hours to find the ship. Given the rate of the planet's orbital rotation, they probably came out right where we are now and immediately crashed. The primary thrust cap must have been destroyed."

The cotton ball–shaped gunners known as the Twins shouted, "Thrust cap boom!"

***

Haaga, Kahpa, and Jorwei stared at the ten thousand square feet of nothing that comprised the Prime Partners transport ship's storage unit. More specifically, they stared at the empty space on the wall where a certain black case should have been.

"Un . . . phoobing . . . believable," muttered Kahpa.

Haaga ground his teeth as he said, "I thought you said the storage unit would be secured."

"It was," retorted Kahpa. "The pilot's code wasn't supposed to open the door."

Jorwei ran a patterned blue-and-white hand through his shock of blue hair. "I don't think they used a code." Haaga and Kahpa turned to him. "Did you see the hatch lock? Someone tinkered with it."

"Could have been some Gorthan fungleback," spat Kahpa.

"No," said Haaga. "Gorthans wouldn't care about a black case. They'd be too busy stripping the hull for scrap."

"That makes no sense," hissed Kahpa. "The transporters had no idea what they were carrying. Why would they bother to break the lock? Why would they take the case?!"

Jorwei scratched the back of his head.

"We must be dealing with a couple of real pros."

TEXT UNIT 0014

"Thirteen chuz! Fourteen chuz! Fifteen chuz!"

Jopp stood upside down on his hands, with Chuck and Dagwam holding his legs in place. One of Dagwam's sisters fed Jopp beer via a hose, while the other two counted off the seconds. At twenty-three seconds, the hose slipped from his mouth, and the foamy red libation sprayed him in the face. He sputtered and spat as Chuck and Dagwam helped him back to an upright position amid cheers from the trio of sisters.

"Y'all wanna play Pop Hop?" asked Dagwam.

Before they could answer, Dagwam hollered to his sisters, "C'mon! Let's set up the bottles!"

While the four Gorthans scurried around collecting empty bottles, Chuck took the opportunity to step outside through the back door. He rubbed the alcohol-induced haze from his eyes and stared up at the stars.

What a funny planet, he thought. *It gets dark in the middle of the day.*

He spent a few minutes searching for the Big Dipper, but then chuckled when he remembered where he was.

"What's so funny?"

Jopp had walked up alongside him. Chuck glanced down at his stocky yellow buddy and answered, "Just looking for Earth, I guess."

Jopp raised an eyebrow. "I didn't explain how anomalies work well enough, huh? You see, for all we know, Earth could be—"

"I get it, man. It was just a dumb joke."

They watched the white flare of a comet streak across the sky. Jopp let the last few drops drip from his drink and then flung the bottle into the scrap-laden expanse of Dagwam's backyard.

"So, just what exactly is wrong with you?"

Chuck turned to Jopp with a stunned expression. "What do you mean?"

Jopp looked him in the eye. "This whole situation you've been thrust into, it would be hard to cope with even for someone who'd grown up under the Sentient Coalition. Yet, here you are, taking everything in stride."

Chuck shrugged. "I don't know, man. I grew up on sci-fi. Whether it was movies or books or whatever, if it had aliens and space travel in it, I was all over it."

"What about your people back home? Other than the little chat about our yok-head dads back on the ship's roof, I haven't heard you mention family or friends."

Chuck paused for a moment, then let out a deep sigh and said, "My mom died about a year ago. The funeral was the last time I talked to my dad. He asked me if I was tired of wasting my life and would I like to go back to med school. Unsurprisingly, I had put down a few drinks, so I promptly told him to fuck himself. I have no brothers or sisters. I lost touch with my high school friends when we all went to different colleges. Dropping out of school made it hard to stay close with my college friends, except for my roommates . . . who probably think I'm mixing mai tais in St. Croix right now."

Jopp stared at him blankly.

Chuck shook his head. "Let's just say there's nobody who'll miss me too much."

A loud crash came from inside the house, followed by a howl of laughter.

"And besides," said a smiling Chuck, "this is a hell of a lot more interesting than whatever's going on back on Earth."*

* *Unbeknownst to Chuck, the heroic antics of Noha Sol had just saved the innocently ignorant Earth apes from complete annihilation at the hands of the nefarious Inquisitor Gablax.***

** *This message brought to you by Centauri Films and the upcoming cinematic adventure:* Noha Sol: The Edge of Civilization.

TEXT UNIT 0015

"Are you seriously suggesting we just wait here and hope they show up?"

"I'm not *suggesting* anything," Haaga retorted. "I'm *stating* that that is exactly what we are going to do."

"We should be sweeping the desert," Kahpa snarled. "They can't have gotten too far. They're probably holed up in one of those junkyard shacks."

"And you'd rather knock down the door of each and every one until we find them?"

"At least we'd be *doing* something!"

"Do you have any idea how many of those hovels are out there? Because I sure as shit don't. Here's what I do know: this town, Trash Crash or whatever the hell they call it, is the only town within a thousand kilometers of their ship. So, yes, they may have managed to find shelter in some Gorthan fungleback's lean-to, but they can't stay there forever. They're going to try to get off this planet, which means they'll have to come through here."

Kahpa folded her arms and glared at the orange-hued captain, who leaned back in his chair with a smug expression.

Haaga turned to his first mate. "Shai, send the boys out into the town. Tell them to ask around about a Yoblon and a . . . what was the other one called?"

Shai raised his snakelike head. "It was an Earth ape."

"That's right, a hairless Earth ape." Haaga scratched his chin and continued, "So tell half the crew to ask around about a Yoblon and an Earth ape. Tell the other half to find vantage points on top of the buildings. I want eyes on anyone coming into or leaving town."

While Shai picked up the bridge commline to relay the orders, Haaga turned back to Kahpa. "Feel free to join either team. At least then you'll be *doing* something."

The silver-skinned woman shot him an unamused look, before stomping off the bridge.

***

"This job is a real pile of humpa dung," grumbled Jorwei from atop a three-story building on the edge of the Gorthan town. He put the Amp Lens back up to his face and scanned a barren stretch of blue desert. "Why couldn't we have been hired to steal the first-place jewel from the Miss Venova pageant?"

"I feel confident they don't use authentic diadode gems in that trophy."

Jorwei glanced back at his fellow lookout. "Man, why you gotta nova-burn my fantasy?"

The muscular bulk of Ghono reclined on a chair near the rooftop door. He traced a bloodred finger over one of the many scars covering his right arm and snorted. "You call that garish farce a fantasy? I'd like to drop a fermion bomb on the whole thing."

Jorwei raised his blue eyebrows. "You're just one big umbra pod of fun, aren't you?"

Ghono shot up out of his chair.

Jorwei stepped back from the towering figure. "I was just foolin', man."

Ghono pointed his thick red arm over Jorwei's shoulder. "Look."

Jorwei spun around and saw a cloud of blue dust billowing on the horizon. He used the Amp Lens to zoom in on the vehicle at the center of the cloud.

After a moment, Jorwei turned back to Ghono and said, "Get Haaga on the line."

TEXT UNIT 0016

Chuck hadn't been sure of many things lately. At this moment, however, he was pretty sure he was drunk. He was pretty sure he was hearing a high-pitched noise. He was pretty sure he was in the Rumbler. He was pretty sure he was *driving* the Rumbler. He decided to further assess the situation and opened his eyes.

He glanced to his right to see a passed-out Jopp clutching the black case like a teddy bear. He looked in the back to find the source of the high-pitched sound: Dagwam stood in the back seat, whistling through his fingers. The Gorthan's other hand held a red bottle high in the air. Chuck turned his head forward to see a steering wheel. He also saw two hands wrapped around the steering wheel. A closer examination confirmed that, yes, they were his own hands, and he was, in fact, driving the Rumbler. He looked up from the steering wheel and through the front windshield to see a cluster of low buildings rushing toward them. He hoped the buildings had the wherewithal to steer themselves out of his way. The buildings had gotten very close at this point, and Chuck was annoyed to see

that they had remained steadfast. He looked for some kind of
horn to beep.

Then a gray arm shot forward and slapped a circular, red
button in the center of the vehicle's dashboard. Chuck felt
himself pulled forward as the Rumbler's emergency brakes
did their job. The thick belt strapped across his chest saved
his sternum from meeting the steering column. The vehicle's
wheels ground the dessert gravel into dust, shooting billowing
clouds into the air. Once the Rumbler had completely stopped,
and the dust cloud had completely settled, Chuck could see
a sandy blue brick structure resting mere feet from the front
of the vehicle. He swung his head to the right; Jopp had slept
through the whole thing. Chuck thought it might be a good
idea to wake him up—"Jopp . . . Jopp . . ."—but his yellow
companion remained fast asleep. Chuck leaned in close and
shouted, "Jopp!"

"Don't touch me there!" exclaimed Jopp as his eyes shot
open.

Chuck reared back, bewildered. "The fuck?"

Jopp was rubbing his eyes. "Fuck what?"

"Huh?"

"What?"

"What?"

"Huh?"

"You're confusing me."

"*You* are!"

"What the shit are you talking about?!"

"I don't know!" Jopp then scanned their surroundings with
his half-open eyes. "Where we—Where we are?"

"I don't know!" Chuck threw his hands in the air.

"Where's guy?" slurred Jopp.

"He's right—" Chuck saw that Dagwam was gone.

They were startled by a loud *Wooooooooooooo!* and turned to see Dagwam coming around the corner of the building. He fastened his overalls as he approached the Rumbler. "Ah, man! I had to drain like a humpalope, if ya know what I mean! Welcome to Trash Blast Station!"

Chuck noticed an intense pressure in his bladder.

"I need to pee."

Dagwam smiled and pointed back to where he'd come from. "Just hop 'round that corner to take care o' yer business."

The Gorthan beer was wreaking havoc with Chuck's balance, and it took every ounce of focus and determination not to face-plant as he climbed down from the vehicle. He shuffled toward the back of the building.

He heard Jopp call after him, "Wait!"

Chuck watched as Jopp swung his legs out, missed the first step, and met the ground with his face. For a few long seconds, Jopp laid completely limp. Chuck hoped he hadn't been knocked out. His concerns were assuaged when the stout yellow being let out a muffled groan followed by a loud belch. He pushed himself up off the ground, a fine layer of blue dust decorating his front. Chuck did his best to stifle a giggle; his best wasn't very good. He continued his failing efforts to hold back laughter while reaching out to help dust off his partner. His hand was swatted away by the grumpy Yoblon.

While waiting for Jopp to finish cleaning himself, Chuck took in their surroundings. He couldn't tell if everything looked so hazy because of the beer or because of the dust. His gaze passed slowly across the horizon: a cluster of clay and brick buildings, a herd of giant camels, some wiry trees, a couple of scrap yards, some more buildings. *Wait . . . what?* he thought as his head snapped back. Chuck gawked at a herd of massive beasts. They stood about a hundred yards away and were at least as tall as a house. Their bodies were, in fact, reminiscent of camels. However, their hides were a dark bluish gray with white spots, and their eyes looked like what you might see on a gigantic insect. Jopp stumbled up alongside Chuck and followed his gaze.

"Ugh, fuggin' *humpalopes*," mumbled Jopp.

"Humpa-wha?" asked Chuck, but he saw that Jopp had already continued on toward the back of the building. Chuck hurried to catch up. As they turned the corner, an acidic stench assaulted their senses. Chuck covered his mouth and nose with his hand and looked down to see a large puddle in front of them. It glowed like a white shirt under a black light.

"Ugh, Gorthan piss," grumbled Jopp, as he circumvented the puddle.

"Smells like sulfur and lemon juice," muttered Chuck as he followed after him.

After relieving themselves, the duo returned to the Rumbler to discover that, once again, Dagwam had disappeared.

"Where's guy?" Jopp asked to no one in particular.

Chuck didn't respond but, rather, ambled up to the vehicle. He pulled himself up and almost fell backward. After steadying himself, he gave the interior the once-over. There didn't seem to be any more unopened red bottles rolling around, much to his disappointment. The black case sat on the front passenger seat. Chuck grabbed it and hopped back to the ground to find Jopp staring at him expectantly.

Chuck lamented, "No beer."

Jopp's expression fell. Chuck shielded his eyes from the sun and looked toward the town. They stood at the end of a wide dirt lane. Odd buildings sat tightly together on either side of the road. Dozens of vehicles, not unlike the Rumbler, were parked with no discernible order along the lane. Chuck and Jopp looked at each other, shrugged, and headed into the town. Chuck noted that the buildings, much like Dagwam's house, had been slapped together using a variety of materials. Each structure they passed appeared as if it was trying to outdo its neighbors in its garishness. They paused to stare at one structure that rested some ways back from the street. The path from the street to the building's entrance began with a freestanding stone archway. It was painted gold and seemed to be coated in glitter . . . or whatever the alien equivalent of glitter was. Chuck noted that this archway must have, at some point, not been gaudy enough for the proprietor, because just a few feet behind it, there was another, larger archway. This one looked to be coated in a couple hundred gemstones and crystals. Their gaze continued on to a third archway behind the second. This one actually reached higher than the building itself. It was made of metal and had tubes of neon lights running across its surface.

"Y'all hungry or somethin'?"

This startled the pair, and they jumped back to see Dagwam standing alongside them. He was sipping from a large green bottle.

"Where—*burp*—you . . . go?" slurred Jopp.

Dagwam stared at them quizzically. "Ummmmmm . . ." He went to take a pull from his drink. As the green glass from the bottle entered his field of vision, his eyes lit up. "Ob yab," he garbled through a mouth full of liquid. He spat it out and explained, "I went to get this. C'mon."

"Wait, you said hungry. . . . I'm hungry," said Chuck.

"Well, good! Cuz yer starin' at PcDoylie's Place. They got tops epic humpa stacks!"

"'Humpa stack'?"

"You ain't never had a humpa stack?!" Dagwam tossed the green bottle over his shoulder. "Let's go!" He started heading through the archways.

Jopp protested, "No—*burp*. Nope."

Chuck responded with the fierce determination reserved for the drunk and hungry. "I need food *now!*"

Jopp threw his hands up defensively and nodded. They followed after Dagwam.

Twenty-seven minutes later, the three of them sat at a table, staring at three steaming "Taste Blast" humpa stacks. It had only taken six minutes for them to place an order and have their food prepared. It had taken twenty-one minutes for them to actually get to the counter to order. This was due to the restaurant staff and other patrons insisting that they each got to meet the Earth man individually. Chuck's palm was pretty sore after the sixteenth high five.

Chuck examined his humpa stack. It resembled an exceptionally large hamburger, except the "bun" was orange and the "burger" was gray with glowing white spots. The long, thin strands atop the meat patty could have been vegetables, noodles, or even tentacles for all he could tell. Dagwam wasted no time digging in. Chuck took a bite and rolled it around his mouth. The meat was greasy but not wholly unpleasant. It reminded him of venison but with an almost sweet-and-sour aftertaste. He still wasn't sure what the toppings were, but they had a nice crunch. He glanced over to see Jopp gingerly pick his up and take a small bite. After chewing for a bit and swallowing, Jopp's face relaxed. He saw Chuck looking at him and commented, "'S'okay . . . *burp.*"

The three finished their food in relative quiet, or more accurately, there was no more conversation. The smacking, slurping, and grunting of Dagwam and the other Gorthan diners was anything but quiet.

Shortly after, the trio stood back outside on the street. Chuck patted his now-full stomach and felt sobriety pawing around the edges of his consciousness. Despite his earlier trepidation, Jopp had cleaned his own plate and was picking at something in his teeth while gazing up at the arches. Chuck saw Dagwam's green bottle lying in the dirt. He set down the case, picked the bottle up, and held it out. "You said you went to get this. . . ."

"I did?" He stared at the bottle for a split second before shouting, "Dung dogs! I did! C'mon!" Without another word, he loped down the street.

After a short journey, they stopped in front of the largest building Chuck had seen so far in the town. It stood either four or five stories tall. He couldn't determine the precise number of floors due to the asymmetrical placement of windows and balconies. It reminded Chuck of those cheap apartment buildings you see in college towns, except this building was coated in a splattering of lime-green and neon-yellow paint. Bright lights shaped like bottles hung from the balconies. Painted in bold letters across the building's wide double doors was the word *CHUZ*. Chuck felt reverberations of heavy bass seeping out.

Dagwam flung the doors open and disappeared inside. Chuck started to follow, but Jopp grabbed his arm. Chuck turned back. "What's up?"

"What are we doing here?" asked Jopp. Chuck noted this was Jopp's first fully formed sentence since their arrival in town. He must be sobering up, too.

"We're going to go in here to get a ride off this planet," answered Chuck.

"This is a bar."

"So?"

"So, you think we're going to find a competent pilot with an interplanetary ship, willing to illicitly fly us off-world . . . in a bar, in the middle of the desert, on some insignificant backwater of a planet."

"So?" asked Chuck.

"So, that's kind of . . . ridiculous."

"Well, it worked for Luke!"

"Who the shit is *Lyook*?"

"No one! Listen . . . I know it's ridiculous, but this whole situation is ridiculous! We might as well keep riding that train."

Jopp looked confused. "No, we need a spaceship . . ."

"Not a literal train! It's a figure of—never mind! Let's just go in and check the place out. Worst-case scenario, we grab a drink, right?"

As they reached the doorway, Chuck remembered he'd set the case down when they first arrived at the bar. He jogged back to the street, picked it up, and turned around to see that Jopp hadn't waited. He sighed and shook his head as he opened the double doors. He followed the thump of music across a darkened foyer and through a second set of double doors. Chuck's jaw dropped at the sight laid out before him.

Chuck stood on a small landing. To his left, stairs led down to the main floor. To his right, the stairs ascended along the wall. He looked down and saw dozens of Gorthans dancing erratically in the center of the main floor. He leaned over the railing and looked up; there was no ceiling above the dance floor. He could see clear through to the building's roof. The second, third, and fourth floors wrapped around the structure's walls. Dozens of Gorthans leaned over the railings, and little streams of spilled drinks drizzled down to the bottom floor. Chuck saw that the actual bar ran continuously around the edge of the bottom floor. After a quick scan, he spotted the yellow block that could only be the back of Jopp's head as his yellow friend talked to the bartender. Chuck turned toward the stairs going down. Before he could take a step, he felt two massive hands wrap themselves around his shoulders and yank him back into the darkness.

TEXT UNIT 0017

Jopp leaned on the counter, trying to get the bartender's attention. The female Gorthan was currently focused on a group of four male Gorthans at the other end of the bar. Jopp's impatience got the better of him, and he called out, "Hey!"

The bartender and her favored patrons halted their conversation and turned toward him. After a few seconds of blank stares, one of the male patrons whispered something to his friend. His friend took a long hard look at Jopp before whispering something back. Without another word, the four of them walked away from the bar and into the crowd. Jopp paid this no mind, as he'd achieved his goal in getting the bartender to come over. Before she could ask what he wanted, Jopp barked, "Flanisi Ale!"

She returned the request with another blank stare. Jopp sighed and revised his order. "Just give me something that will get me drunk, please." This time, she smiled and produced a glass from under the bar, held it up to an unmarked tap, and filled it with a foamy red liquid. She slid the glass over to Jopp and said, "Two gorbacks!"

Jopp dug in his pockets and came up with the handful of the poker chips that Dagwam had given them. He separated two from the bunch and tentatively slid them forward, gauging the bartender's reaction. She seemed to approve of the offering and snatched up the yellow discs. The bartender left to take care of some other customers, and Jopp lifted the glass to his mouth. He took a long sip and became aware of some figures standing unnecessarily close to him. He set the glass down and turned around to see the four Gorthan patrons he had interrupted standing shoulder to shoulder, staring at him. Or, at least, he assumed they were staring at him, as they all had their eyes covered with dark lenses. Except for the lenses, the glasses were colored various neon shades. Each of them wore a neon tank top that matched their respective glasses frames. Their shoes reminded Jopp of oversized versions of the ones Chuck had been wearing when they first met. He thought he remembered Chuck referring to them as *sneakers*. After a few seconds of uncomfortable silence, one of the Gorthans spoke. "You the butler, bro?"

"What?" asked Jopp.

"Our boy, Rocket Beer, was in here talkin' all 'bout how he's been partying with a real live Earth man and his yellow butler. So, you the butler, bro?"

"Well, I am traveling with the Earth man, but I'm *not* his—"

Before he could finish, the four Gorthans howled with glee and started head-butting each other. The one who had originally spoken waved at the bartender. She set four more of the red foamy drinks on the bar. They all reached around Jopp and snatched up the mugs. One of them also grabbed Jopp's glass and shoved it in his hand. They started chanting, "Chuz! Chuz! Chuz!" Left with little choice in the matter, Jopp raised his own drink aloft, and the five of them guzzled down the potent beverages. Upon emptying his glass, Jopp unleashed a deep belch, which sent the Gorthans into another frenzy of cheering. The one in the green neon, who had spoken first, dropped himself down on the bar stool next to Jopp. "Bro! How tops is it to party with a real live Earth man?!"

"Oh, uh, it's sooooo tops . . . epic."

"I knew it!" shouted the Gorthan. Then to his entourage he shouted, "Didn't I tell you bros?! Earth mans know how to party for not fake!" Then to Jopp: "Is the Earth man here?!"

Jopp settled in. "Oh, yeah. The Earth man is here, and I can totally introduce you to him, but I need another drink first."

"Most definitely!" concurred the Gorthan, and then to his compatriot in neon orange: "Bro! Get our new bro here another cold crusher!"

"On it!" he replied and disappeared into the crowd.

Jopp turned to his new friend with a perplexed look. "Where's he going? The bartender's right behind us."

The Gorthan glanced over his shoulder to see the bartender standing there, smiling blankly. He looked at Jopp. "Good point, my yellow bro! I'm sure he'll figure it out. He's the smart one." Then he turned back again to the bartender. "More chuz!"

TEXT UNIT 0018

The strong hands let go, and Chuck sprang into action. He spun around to face his ambusher, the black case held high in a defensive position, and found himself staring at a broad, muscular chest. His eyes crept upward until they found the being's head, which was brickred and somewhat small compared to its body. The being smiled and said, "Chuck! What are you doing here?"

Chuck's mouth fell open. He dropped the case and stammered, "Bhan-Bhana—"

The being thrust his right hand forward, seizing Chuck's, and gave it three vigorous shakes. "Bhanakhana Bhen Bhindo! Yes! From the Prime Partners dispatch hangar yesterday!"

"Yesterday?"

"Yes! Do you not remember us meeting?"

"Yeah, I do, but . . . wasn't that just, like, earlier today?"

Bhanakhana looked concerned. "I am afraid not. It was most assuredly yesterday when our first meeting occurred. I have been traveling since then, and only just arrived here within the hour."

Damn, how long were we drinking at Dagwam's? "Why are you here?"

Bhanakhana looked amused. "Funny that you are asking me such a thing. I am a sentologist. I am here to write a dissertation on Gorthan culture and why they seem to be obsessed with Earth."

I'd read that, thought Chuck.

Bhanakhana continued, "Seeing as this establishment currently holds 83 percent of the town's population, I felt it was the most appropriate venue in which to begin my studies. As I approached from the south end of the lane, I was shocked to see you walking in. Perhaps the more pressing question is, why are *you* here?"

Chuck relayed the whole story: the pirates, the explosions, the anomaly, the crash, the black case, Dagwam, the Rumbler. Everything. As Chuck spoke, Bhanakhana's expression was a rolling wave of excitement and worry.

Bhanakhana folded his gigantic arms across his chest and studied Chuck for a few moments. "You and your comrade have certainly gotten yourselves into quite the predicament. I would strongly suggest you get in touch with Universal Law Enforcement as soon as possible. Do you know what that is?"

"They're sort of like the police, right?"

Bhanakhana nodded.

"Correct. The Universal Law Enforcement Agency should be able to assist you. They do not have much of a presence on this planet. However, I do believe they have a station in a nearby system. Do you have the means to get yourself there?"

Chuck shook his head. "Nope. That's why we're here, to find a ride off this planet."

"You came to a bar, in the middle of the desert, on an underdeveloped planet, in order to secure off-world passage? I am sorry, my friend, but your premise is quite ridiculous."

Chuck rolled his eyes. "So I'm told."

Bhanakhana clapped his hands together. "Nevertheless! If there is any way in which I may help you in the securing of interstellar travel, please let me know."

"That would be great! Thank you."

"We should exit this establishment and go to the hangar port. There, you should be able to secure passage to this planet's shuttle station."

Chuck nodded. "We need to get Jopp, first."

"Ah, yes, your stout yellow companion! Where might he be?"

"I saw him at the bar." Chuck jerked a thumb over his shoulder.

"Splendid! Let us retrieve him posthaste."

"Uh, yeah."

They exited the recessed alcove and stepped back onto the landing that overlooked the main floor. Chuck scanned the room; it wasn't difficult to spot Jopp. It was helpful that he was the only Yoblon in the building. It was more helpful that he was currently standing on a bar stool, holding court for a handful of neon-draped Gorthans.

Chuck sighed and pointed.

"Oh, hell. There he is. Let's go grab him."

He received no response from his new crimson companion. Chuck thought Bhanakhana might not have heard him, and turned back to repeat himself. What he saw caused the color to drain from his face. Bhanakhana stood like a statue, and his face bore a worrisome expression. Standing behind him and slightly to the right was an individual Chuck had never seen before. The individual's features were humanoid and sharply female. Her skin was silver, and her bald head and face were covered in magenta markings. Standing to her right was an individual Chuck had definitely seen before. He recognized the same angry face that had been displayed on the viewscreen of their transport ship. It was the marauder captain. He held an object that Chuck felt very comfortable assuming was a gun. Chuck waved to the orange-skinned pirate, and his voice cracked sharply as he said, "Hiiiiiiiiiii . . ."

The pirate's expression grew grimmer, if that was even possible, and he tilted his head. "Up the stairs. And put your phoobing hand down before I cut it off!"

Chuck looked down, and the shock of the current circumstances had apparently caused a bit of numbness, as he had been unaware that his right hand was still waving. Chuck took his left hand and pushed his right back down to his side.

The pirate huffed, "Now pick up the case, and get up the stairs!"

TEXT UNIT 0019

"So then I says to him, 'Hey buddy, get your own globnob!'"

The Gorthans burst into a fit of raucous laughter. Jopp leaned his head back and drained his drink. He pulled the empty mug away from his mouth and unleashed a thunderous belch, which sent the Gorthans howling yet again. *Maybe this place isn't so bad, after all,* he thought as he surveyed the crowd from atop his bar stool perch. He tapped the green-clad Gorthan on the shoulder. "Chooch, I feel deep space calling. Where's the personal waste room?"

Chooch stretched a gangly arm, covered in glowing green bracelets, toward the back of the bar and said, "Plop closet's back that way, bro."

Jopp hopped down from the stool and announced, "I'll be right back. Get us another round, and I'll tell you all about the time I jumped the Mishinyo Rift with the grand chancellor's daughter." Another cheer rose as he began making his way through the crowd.

Jopp exited the restroom while fumbling with the drawstring of his sweatpants.

"Stupid Earth leggings," he muttered to himself. "Can't wait to get ahold of some *real* . . ." He would've continued his grumblings, had he not walked face-first into a wall. At least he assumed it was a wall, as it was hard, solid, and unmoving. Jopp cursed and rubbed his wide, flat nose, which was feeling just a bit flatter at the moment. He dropped his hand and looked up at what he'd walked into . . . and immediately wished it had been a wall. An Ochrean loomed in front of him. The orange-skinned being was thick and broad and wore what Jopp considered to be an excessively menacing expression. Jopp glanced to his right to see a blue-and-white jigsaw pattern covering the skin of a wiry Puzuru. Jorwei's expression was more amused than menacing, but Jopp wasn't paying attention to that. He was more focused on the electric pump-shot pointed at his face.

Jopp didn't know how to react. He settled on giving Jorwei a tiny wave. "Hiiiiiii . . ."

Jorwei cocked his head toward the front of the bar. "Let's go."

"To get some drinks?" squeaked Jopp.

The Puzuru smirked and replied, "Oh, *we'll* most definitely be getting drinks later. *You*, unfortunately, won't be joining us."

"That's rude."

The smirk was gone, and Jorwei barked, "Now let's *go*. Get up the stairs."

"Look, fellas . . . I think there's been a mista—"

Before Jopp could finish, the Ochrean punched him in the stomach. Jopp fell to his knees, coughing up a bit of purple blood. Jorwei leaned down. "Don't make this harder than it has to be."

Jopp glared up at him and snarled, "Your mother was a sloober."

Jorwei raised the butt of his weapon, as if to strike Jopp with it. Before he could deliver the blow, a gray finger tapped his shoulder. He turned around to see a Gorthan, dressed completely in neon green. "Bro! What are you doing to our butler bro?"

"I'm not a butler!" said Jopp and coughed.

No one paid attention.

"This doesn't concern you," hissed Jorwei. He started to turn back, but the Gorthan grabbed his shoulder. He wheeled around and shoved the Gorthan back. "Fuck off, you little fungleback."

Shattering glass burst around them, and the Ochrean collapsed to the ground. Standing behind him was another neon-clad Gorthan, the handle of what used to be a glass mug in his hand. He pointed at Jorwei and shouted, "You wanna tussle, bro? You got one!"

Jorwei attempted to raise his weapon, but the two gangly arms wrapping themselves around him prevented that from happening. He dropped the gun and tried to pry off the tight embrace. The Gorthan shouted in his ear, "You shouldn't push Chooch, bro!"

The Puzuru leaned his head forward.

"Who the fuck is Chooch?" he shouted as he slammed the back of his skull into the Gorthan's face. The Gorthan let go of him and staggered backward. Pink blood trickled down from his left nostril. Jorwei wheeled around to face him.

The Gorthan wiped the blood from his face with the back of his hand and hollered, "I'm Chooch!" And he dove into the Puzuru, sending them both rolling across the floor.

Jopp looked around at the erupting chaos. Some of the partying Gorthans had stopped to watch the scuffle. Some took it upon themselves to start new brawls among each other. His gaze drifted upward until it froze on the stairway between the second and third floors. More specifically, his gaze froze on four individuals marching up the stairs. While he recognized neither the large Dronla nor the silver-skinned J'Kari, he was pretty sure the gun-toting Ochrean was the marauder captain from earlier, and he damn sure recognized Chuck. He tripped over something and almost fell. Jopp looked down to see Jorwei's electric pump-shot. He picked it up and, despite his natural inclinations, resolved to save the dumb Earth ape.

Jopp took a step toward the stairs but stopped when two figures appeared on the landing leading from the main entrance. They blocked the only path to the stairs. One was a reptilian Soreshi, and the other was one of the biggest Dronlas Jopp had ever seen. He had scars running up his red right arm to his neck. The two individuals wielded rifles and were scanning the crowd. Jopp's stare was met by the narrow eyes of the Soreshi, who nudged his partner and pointed at Jopp. They started heading toward him, shoving Gorthans out of the way.

"Shit!"

Jopp spun around, looking for another way out. Besides the bathrooms, he saw only one other door. He sprinted for it, dodging an airborne glass and a flying bar stool along the way. The door shrieked as he wrenched it open, spilling Jopp into the harsh sunlight. He got up and closed the door, looking for some way to lock it. He figured he had about thirty seconds before they burst through after him. Jopp scanned his surroundings: he was in an alley, and a heap of scrap metal leaned against the side of the building. It was all small bits and pieces, save for one item. He saw one long, thick slab of metal. It looked like it could have, at one point, been the wing on a PON-y Class express mail transporter. Jopp dropped his new weapon and ran to the metal scrap. He gave it a push; it stayed put. He leaned into it; it didn't budge. He saw the door begin to open and howled as he heaved with every ounce of strength left in his body. The metal slab gave way and fell over with an echoing thud, slamming the door closed. Immediately, something began hammering the door from the inside, but the scrap metal held fast. Jopp exhaled in relief, sweat dripping from his forehead. It wouldn't be long before they decided to come around from the front. He grabbed the electric pump-shot and followed the alley around to the back of the building.

Rising up before him was perhaps the most rickety metal staircase Jopp had ever seen. It zigzagged all the way up to the roof, and Jopp noted at least a fifth of the steps were missing.

"Fuck that," muttered Jopp, as he scanned the different avenues of the alley. To his dismay, he saw that each of the paths dead-ended at the walls of other buildings. *Of course Gorthans would build alleys that lead nowhere.* He looked back up at the staircase.

"Fuck me," he grumbled as he began to climb.

TEXT UNIT 0020

Chuck and Bhanakhana stood on a rooftop populated entirely by empty beer bottles and purple stains that smelled faintly of sulfur and lemon juice. The tattooed silver-skinned female was standing behind Chuck, one hand holding a gun to the back of his head, the other holding the case. The pirate captain stood behind Bhanakhana. He spoke into his data bracelet. "We're in position."

Chuck cowered as a massive black ship descended from the clouds overhead to the rooftop. The scene reminded Chuck of a large mural he once saw as a child at a museum. It depicted a pterodactyl swooping down upon unsuspecting prey. At the time, he thought it was the coolest thing ever and had spent the next few weeks pretending to be the extinct predator, much to the chagrin of his parents, teachers, classmates, and small pets. The scene didn't feel so cool now that he was playing the part of the prey.

The ship lowered until it hovered just a few feet above the rooftop. A ramp extended down, and an alien that looked very similar to the captain, although shorter and broader, exited the ship. He carried a weapon that resembled the grenade launchers Chuck had been so fond of in his video games back on Earth. The silver-skinned alien must have noted this as well, as Chuck heard her say, "Isn't Shuuja's weapon a little much, Haaga?"

He heard the captain, presumably Haaga, reply, "Shuuja likes his weapons. Better to have it and not need it, right?"

"Let's just get going." Chuck heard the eyeroll in her tone.

"Fair enough. Get him on the ship."

The silver-skinned alien nudged Chuck with her weapon and snarled, "Get on the ship, Earth ape."

Chuck plodded forward.

Bhanakhana turned his head to the side and addressed his captor. "Are we not following?"

"No, *we* are not," replied the captain, "*I* will be joining them shortly. *You* will be staying here . . . permanently."

Bhanakhana took a deep breath and replied, "I see."

Chuck and his captor had reached the base of the ship's ramp when he heard a sound like a raw steak smacking a brick wall. They spun around to see the orange body of the pirate captain crumpled on the ground. Bhanakhana stood over him, massaging his massive left fist with his equally massive right hand. The silver-skinned alien and the other pirate raised their weapons, and Bhanakhana made a move for the captain's gun. Chuck knew he wouldn't be fast enough, and he opened his mouth to call out.

There were a crackling noise and a flash of blue light; no sound escaped Chuck's lips. He felt every single muscle in his body contract simultaneously. The pain was unlike anything he'd ever experienced. He couldn't speak, couldn't move, couldn't think; he could only stare as the rooftop rushed up to meet him.

TEXT UNIT 0021

Chuck lay facedown on the rooftop. People were shouting, though he couldn't discern who it was or what they were saying. A pins-and-needles sensation flooded through his body. He began flexing his fingers. In perhaps what was the single most difficult task he'd ever performed, he managed to push himself up onto his knees and looked around. He quickly learned who was doing the shouting; Jopp stood in front of him, screaming in his face. It took another second before Chuck could comprehend the actual words being shouted, and even then it was little more than a jumble of *Get up*, *Let's go*, and *Fuck*.

There was a crash, and Chuck swung his head to see a motley blue-and-white skinned alien burst through the door out onto the rooftop. Chuck heard Jopp yell, "Shit!" and turned in time to see him raise a weapon at the newcomer. With a thunderous crack, a flash of jagged blue streaks shot out from the weapon at the blue-and-white alien. Jopp's target dove behind a broken table, as his weapon continued to spew lightning. Still on his knees, Chuck saw the silver-skinned alien get to her feet. She wobbled a bit and then began staggering toward the

ship's ramp, black case in hand. The orange-skinned pirate—
Chuck thought he'd been called Shuuja—had also risen. As
he reached for his grenade-launcher thingy, a blur of red flew
across Chuck's field of vision. Bhanakhana and Shuuja began
trading haymakers. Chuck's legs felt like rubber as he climbed
to his feet. He saw the silver-skinned woman reach the base of
the ship's ramp and raced after her.

She was halfway up the ramp when Chuck caught her. His
motor skills were still shaky, and he clumsily barreled into her
back, sending them both tumbling off the ramp. They slammed
back down on the rooftop mere inches from the edge. Chuck
felt all the air rush out of his lungs. He gasped for breath as he
sat up. The silver-skinned alien was also wheezing and clutching her chest. The case lay between them. They both saw it and
made a grab for it at the same time. She got there first and slid
it away. Chuck lunged forward and caught the corners. She had
a much better grip, however, and she gave a ferocious tug. The
case immediately slid out of Chuck's hands. The momentum of
her pull caused her to roll backward. Chuck gasped as she, and
the case, slipped off the edge of the roof.

Chuck sat there, blinking and staring at the empty space
where the silver alien had just been. A strong hand gripped his
arm and yanked him to a standing position. He looked up to
see the stern face of Bhanakhana staring back at him. White
blood trickled from a cut across his chest, and he held the
pirate's "grenade launcher" in his other hand.

"We must go."

Chuck nodded and looked past him. Jopp was still firing
wildly toward the rooftop door, and Haaga was starting to
regain consciousness. Chuck called out, "Jopp!"

Jopp didn't turn around but simply pointed with one hand
to the back of the building, "Staircase! Over there! Hurry!"

Chuck and Bhanakhana sprinted to the two rusted railings sticking up from the back wall of the building. They looked down at the rickety metal structure.

"This is perhaps the most dilapidated stair structure I have ever laid eyes on."

"Eh, I've seen worse," replied Chuck. Bhanakhana looked at him skeptically. Chuck shrugged.

"College town student housing."

Bhanakhana opened his mouth to comment, but Chuck was already over the edge. The staircase creaked and groaned as they cautiously made their way downward. They were half-way down when they heard a loud bang and looked up to see Jopp come flying over the roof's edge. He skipped the first flight of stairs entirely and planted hard on the fourth-floor landing. The metal structure let out a shrill whine, and one of the bolts holding the upper railing in place popped out of the wall. It clinked and clanked its way down past Bhanakhana and past Chuck and landed in the dirt below with a tiny puff of dust.

Jopp cursed under his breath. "Shiiiiiiiiiiiiiiit . . ." And then he called down, "You better move! Now!"

The creaks and groans turned into rending shrieks as a half dozen more bolts popped out of the wall and sailed down after their comrade. Jopp flew down the stairs, taking three and four steps at a time. The fifth-floor section of the stairs ripped completely from the wall and curled out over the alley. The bolts continued to pop as more and more of the structure tore loose. Chuck and Bhanakhana reached the ground and quickly got out of the way of the falling debris. Jopp was still a full flight up when the metal structure gave a giant cry and tore completely free from the building. Jopp cried out, "Goddamn Gorthans!" and he hurled himself away from the structure. He hit the ground, rolled away, and came up limping. The structure let out one final scream as it collapsed upon itself. They looked up to see two orange heads and a blue one peering over the roof's edge.

Jopp held up his middle finger and yelled, "Eat my yub nubs!"

The trio sprinted around the corner of the building and froze. Lying in the dirt was the body of the silver-skinned alien. A pool of dark blood slowly seeped out from under her lifeless form. The black case lay a few feet away. Jopp took two steps forward before his injured leg buckled. Chuck moved to help him, but Bhanakhana beat him to it and hoisted Jopp up as if he was an infant. "Please allow me to assist you."

Jopp grumbled something unintelligible, before relenting and allowing himself to be carried. Chuck snatched up the case, and they ran down the alley toward the main street. As they approached the alley's end, two figures jumped in front of them with weapons drawn. One of them was the other orange-skinned Ochrean, whom Jopp had run into near the bar's bathroom. The other looked like Bhanakhana, except for the series of crescent-shaped scars that marked his right side. The orange-skin said, "Drop the case."

Bhanakhana's eyes narrowed as he studied his fellow Dronla.

"I know of you from somewhere. . . ."

The scarred Dronla returned the look, adding a cruel smile as he said, "I'd expect so."

"You're—"

He was cut off by the roar of an engine as a green-and-orange vehicle suddenly crashed into the two assailants. The Ochrean was instantly crushed under the tires, while the crimson Dronla jumped up at the last second. He slammed into the hood and rolled over the top, coming to an unconscious rest in the dirt. Bhanakhana, Jopp, and Chuck gawked as the roof of the vehicle slid back, and Dagwam hopped out. He didn't acknowledge the three individuals standing in front of him but rather opted to address the one underneath his vehicle. "Hey, buddy! You all right? You shouldn't be jumpin' out in front of the Rumbler like that! Hey! I'm talking at you, man! Ain't you ever been told it's rude not to answer people when they talkin' at you?"

Chuck piped up, "D—Dagwam?"

The Gorthan spun around, and his expression lit up.

"Well I'll be shat out a humpalope! I thought y'all had done disappeared! Missed a hell of a tussle, that's for sure!" He then gave Bhanakhana, who was still cradling Jopp, the once-over. "Now how 'bout that! I never seen a butler have his own butler for carryin' him around 'n whatnot!"

Jopp started, "I'M NOT A—"

Chuck interrupted, "Never mind that! Dag—I mean, Rocket Beer, we need to get out of here as fast as possible!"

A wide grin spread across Dagwam's face.

"Let's ride!"

TEXT UNIT 0022

Haaga Viim shouted from the bridge of the *Pfraza*, "Fire!"

The main viewscreen displayed two red projectiles tearing into the ground below, barely missing a swerving orange-and-green vehicle. He turned his swollen and bruised face to his first mate, grumbling through gritted teeth, "Shai, what the phoob are the Twins doing?"

"I believe they are attempting to disable the target without damaging the cargo."

Haaga bellowed toward the front of the bridge, "Quit playing around and annihilate the vehicle!"

He turned back to the viewscreen to see the target turn down an alleyway, narrowly avoiding the next blast. The ship corrected course to stay above the vehicle; however, the various outcroppings and awnings spanning the alley obscured their sight lines.

"Level every building if you have to!" he commanded.

The Twins glanced back at their captain, then at each other. They shrugged, turned back to their sight finders, and unleashed a barrage of cannon fire on the ground below. Their shots demolished a makeshift bridge, sending rubble careening down. Another blast tore the whole side off a building yet still failed to slow the vehicle. Haaga looked up and saw the hangar port come into view. He noted that the cluster of buildings hemming in the alley was about to end, and there would be about a half mile of open ground before they reached the hangar.

"Vaatu! Get us out ahead of them! We'll hit them as they exit the alley!"

The ship jerked and shot forward. They flew a few hundred yards across the open ground before spinning around to face the row of buildings. The front cannons trained on the mouth of the alley, ready for their target to emerge. They waited. . . .

TEXT UNIT 0023

"What'd ya say?!"

"I said stop!" Chuck felt the humpa stack in his stomach attempt a comeback tour as Dagwam slammed on the brakes. As the Rumbler came to a screeching halt, something crashed into the back of Chuck's seat with a thud.

"What the shit?!" the something said.

"You okay, Jopp?" Chuck called back.

"Fuck you," Jopp-the-something replied.

"Why have we ceased moving?" Bhanakhana was wedged in behind the driver's seat, Shuuja's large weapon propped up next to him.

The Rumbler rested in the cover of the alleyway, less than a quarter mile from its end. Chuck pointed to the open expanse between them and the hangar. "I think I saw the ship shoot past us. They might be waiting out there."

"Y'all want to go back to the party?"

"No!" the three answered in unison. Dagwam was visibly disappointed.

"Well, we obviously cannot stay put."

"No shit, Big Red."

Bhanakhana turned to Jopp with a perturbed expression. "Do you have anything useful to contribute, or is cursing your only method of communication?"

Jopp smirked, reached out, and patted the pirate's large weapon. "I think I might have an idea. . . . Oh, and fuck you."

Chuck and Dagwam responded simultaneously, albeit with opposite levels of enthusiasm, "Oh, shit."

TEXT UNIT 0024

"Captain?"

Haaga ignored Shai and called out to the gunners, "Ready the decimator shells." The Twins gave a surprised glance back before eagerly turning to their controls.

"Captain?"

Haaga continued to ignore his first mate. "On my mark, raze every building until they have nowhere to hide."

"Captain?"

Haaga finally acknowledged him. "What is it, Shai?"

"I'm reading a peculiar heat signature. . . ." Shai trailed off, a confused expression glued to his face.

"And? What about it?"

"It's . . . I mean . . . there are no other active interplanetary ships in our vicinity, yet I'm getting readings akin to that of a fusion reactor firing off. . . ."

"Where is it coming from?"

"There." Shai raised a scaly finger, and Haaga's gaze followed it to the mouth of the covered alley. Just then they heard a pop and a thunderous roar, and the orange-and-green vehicle shot out from concealment. It was making no attempt to maneuver but rather seemed to be coming right at them. The viewscreen zoomed in to reveal that the vehicle's top had been retracted. Haaga was about to order his gunners to fire but stalled when he saw the stout yellow Yoblon stand up on the back seat of the vehicle. The Dronla held him in place as he hefted Shuuja's concussion cannon. Haaga could have sworn he caught a smirk on the yellow one's face as he pulled the trigger.

TEXT UNIT 0025

Tires squealed as the Rumbler propelled from the shadows into the open expanse. The wind stung Jopp's eyes and would have knocked him back had Bhanakhana not been there to hold him steady. As he zeroed his sights on the hovering black mass, he mumbled to himself, "You hijack my rig? This is what you get, winklinkers." He pulled the trigger, the weapon went *thunk*, and a rocket fired out.

At the last moment, the ship swerved to avoid a direct hit. The rocket glanced off the ship's side and detonated, tearing off a chunk of the armor plating. Jopp screamed, "Hit it!"

Dagwam hollered with glee and slapped a button on his dashboard. The engine let out a furious bellow, and the Rumbler stalled for half a second before blasting forward. It took everything Bhanakhana had to keep Jopp from flying out of the vehicle. When he was sure Bhanakhana's grip was steady, Jopp wheeled himself around to stare behind them. The Rumbler's exhaust port was trailing a tail of green fire. Jopp saw that the marauder's ship had spun around and was gaining on them. He thought he should do something about that and hoisted his weapon back into a firing position. He took aim and let off another rocket. His shot was a tad high, and he watched it merely graze the ship, which then promptly answered back with a pair of crimson cannon blasts.

Up in the front seat, Chuck looked ahead to the approaching hangar. On any other planet, he guessed the building wouldn't be very remarkable. On this planet, however, it *was* remarkable in that it was the only building built with some sense of practical architecture. It was at least twice as large as any other building in the town, and wide-paned windows punctuated the gray metal walls. Chuck glanced behind them, saw how close the ship had gotten, and began frantically scanning the hangar for an opening. He suspected they wouldn't have the luxury of circling the structure until they found a proper door. As if to drive the point home, a red beam blasted into the ground nearby, causing his teeth to rattle. Chuck looked to his right to see that the concussion from the blast had created a spider-web crack in his side window. He stared at it for half a second, before calling back to Bhanakhana, "I have an idea!"

Everything after that was a blur. . . .

Jopp got off his third and final shot just before Bhanakhana pulled him down inside the vehicle.

The Rumbler's roof slid closed as the marauder's ship unleashed another barrage.

Jopp's rocket connected with the ship's left wing. Black smoke poured from the gaping wound, and the ship began to spin out of control.

The ship's volley connected with the ground just behind the Rumbler. The force of the explosion propelled the vehicle into an airborne end-over-end roll, sending it crashing through a hangar window. It skidded across the hangar floor, leaving glass shards, metal bits, and green scorch marks in its wake.

When the smoldering husk finally came to rest, Bhanakhana wasted no time in kicking out the back door. After extricating himself, he reached back in to pull out an unconscious Jopp. Dagwam and Chuck had already gotten themselves out, and the former was currently helping the latter free the black case. It had gotten wedged under the crumbled dashboard, and they fell backward when it finally came loose. Chuck dusted himself off and then pointed to Jopp's limp form in Bhanakhana's arms. "Is he okay?"

"He is breathing." Bhanakhana nodded toward the wreckage. "What was *your* idea?"

Chuck shrugged. "Um, drive through the window. . . ." He looked back to see Dagwam staring at the hunk of metal formally known as the Rumbler. "Ah, man, I'm sorry about your car."

Dagwam turned around with—to Chuck's surprise—a big smile. "Y'all see how we smashed that window?! Wooooooooooooo! We was tumblin' like a wiverbush weed on a windy day! That was so tops! And the way Yellow Man there was givin' that big black flapper what for? They ain't know what hit it!"

"Um, okay," was all Chuck could muster.

"We must go. My vessel is this way." Bhanakhana headed off across the hangar, Jopp in tow.

Chuck waved to Dagwam. "You can come with us. It might not be safe here."

Dagwam shook his head. "Nuh-uh, man! No way! I'd have to have dung for brains to leave now."

"Huh?"

He laughed. "You pretty tops, Earth man! But sometimes I wonder iffin you don't think so good. I just spent the last day partying with a real live Earth man, whose butler caused the biggest tussle we've had this year, and half the town is all tore up, due to us racing that space flapper! Dontcha get it?"

Chuck didn't get it.

Dagwam clapped his hands. "I'm 'bout to be famous! You know how much voopah I'm gonna get?! The ladyfolk are gonna be all over me!"

Chuck's mouth dropped open. "Uh, have fun, I guess . . ."

Bhanakhana's voice boomed across the hangar floor, "Chuck, we must leave immediately."

Chuck looked back. "Anyway . . . thanks for everything."

But Dagwam couldn't hear him; he was too busy chatting up some female Gorthans. Chuck shook his head, smiled to himself, and hustled across the hangar.

Bhanakhana stood next to his ship, or at least, what Chuck could only assume was his ship. Less than forty-eight hours ago, he would have seriously questioned the flight capabilities of the object before him. However, at this point, skepticism was essentially expunged from Chuck's thought process. The object Bhanakhana stood next to was two stories tall and equally as wide; its surface shone like polished chrome. It was a perfect cube, with grooves forming five-by-five grids on each side. Chuck asked, "Where's Jopp?"

"He is resting in the med bay. He is still unconscious but will likely survive." Bhanakhana turned to lead him into the cube.

Chuck followed. "Cool ship."

Bhanakhana glanced over his shoulder. "I can adjust the temperature if it is not to your liking."

TEXT UNIT 0026

Bhanakhana's cube ship hurtled through space with a black, six-winged pterodactyl in hot pursuit. They had been traveling for three hours and were just half the distance to the nearest mapped anomaly when the marauders caught up. The assailants fired shot after shot, each one missing the mark by a wide margin. The cube ship darted back and forth, seemingly giving minimal deference to the laws of physics. Chuck gripped his armrests so tightly that he felt his hands go numb. The Longstrider crash landing was a theme park kiddie ride compared to this. Chuck watched on the panoramic viewscreen as another fiery barrage sailed past them. He called out, "I assume we can't keep this up forever!"

Bhanakhana called back, "No! We cannot!"

"Doesn't this ship have any defensive weapons?!"

"I am a professor of sentology! I study passive indigenous cultures! Firefights are not exactly commonplace in my work!"

Chuck's mind wandered to thoughts of how Jopp was doing back in the medical bay. At the time of their departure, he had still been out cold, so they had strapped him to the cushioned examination table. At first Chuck felt a little guilty; there was no way Jopp had stayed unconscious through the ship's erratic maneuvering. He imagined waking up to the sound of explosions and finding oneself inexplicably tied down to a medical table would leave one feeling quite agitated. He visualized Jopp's face, twisted up in anger, hurling curse-laden insults to an empty room. The faintest hint of a chuckle crept its way up Chuck's throat. The brief moment of internal levity was immediately squelched by the violent vibrations of a narrowly missed shot.

"They seem to be closing in!" shouted Bhanakhana.

"What can we do?!" replied Chuck.

"If you believe in some form of deity, I would suggest making peace with it!"

Chuck contemplated that statement. While he'd been brought up in a household that prescribed to some generic iteration of Christianity, it had never really taken root. In college he'd taken World Religions as a means to spend some time with a girl he liked. The course touched on everything from Islam to Shinto, and none of it had really hit home for Chuck. It was at this point in his thought process when Chuck realized the ship was no longer moving. He looked to Bhanakhana. "Um, why did we stop?"

"Our assailants have broken off their pursuit."

"Well, that's good, I guess. Right?"

Bhanakhana didn't respond. Chuck drummed his fingers on his leg.

"Why do you think they gave up?"

Bhanakhana extended his arm, pointing to the viewscreen. "I would assume that is why."

Chuck looked up and saw a towering vessel looming before them. It looked like someone had taken a skyscraper-sized aircraft carrier and rotated it ninety degrees to a vertical position.

Violet lights ran up and down the length of its charcoal-gray surface.

Chuck swallowed nervously. "Wha—What is that?"

"That is a Universal Law Enforcement frigate."

"So, they're like police?"

"That is correct."

"Well, that's great, right?"

"Possibly."

"Possibly? What's not great about this?! They just saved us."

Bhanakhana slowly turned his head to look at Chuck directly. "They gave no chase to our assailants. They seem to be fixated on us. Do I need to explain why that may be concerning?"

A pulsing beep interrupted Chuck's reply. Bhanakhana turned back to his console and pressed a button. A gruff voice came through the line. "*Galactic citizen, this is Unit Chief Gadwey of the ULE frigate* Strike Down. *We request that you submit to a vessel audit. Will you comply?*"

Bhanakhana responded, "Affirmative, *Strike Down.*"

"*Good. Prepare for docking.*" A pale lavender light shot out from the frigate. It enveloped them and began to pull the cube ship closer.

Bhanakhana spun around to face Chuck. "It is absolutely critical that you are completely honest with me, Chuck."

Chuck nodded.

"The events that transpired between our first meeting and now—they occurred exactly as you described them to me? You have neither altered nor omitted any detail?"

Chuck nodded again. "Everything happened just like I said."

"And you vow that you bear no ulterior motives in this ordeal?"

Chuck shook his head. "I'm just trying not to die, man."

Bhanakhana ruminated on this for a brief moment, before standing up. "Very well." He walked over to where the black case had been strapped down and unfastened the restraints. He then carried it to the back corner of the room and knelt down where the floor met the wall. He reached a hand out, pressed lightly on an unseen button, and the floor panel slid back, revealing an empty space.

"What are you doing?" Chuck had crept close to peer over Bhanakhana's shoulder.

"I assume you would prefer it if this particular item was not confiscated, yes?"

"Oh . . . um . . . yeah, I guess so."

"They will not find it here. These compartments were designed to remain hidden to virtually all scanning technology."

Chuck smirked. "So you're such an upstanding citizen that you don't have any weapons on board, but you've got secret smuggling compartments?"

Bhanakhana replaced the floor panel and stood. "I said that I do not enter into firefights. I never claimed that I do not have the occasional need for discretion in my studies."

Chuck smiled. "I'm just joking with you."

Bhanakhana peered at him. "Ah, yes. I remember reading an article about how your species quite often mischaracterizes humor."

Before Chuck could offer a retort, they felt the ship lurch to a halt. The viewscreen showed they had been pulled into some sort of hangar. Identical rows of ships lined the walls. Chuck was pretty sure he could spot a fighter jet when he saw one. Everything from the ships to the hangar itself was colored with some combination of gray, black, and varying shades of purple.

A rectangular patch of light materialized on the far wall, and in strode half a dozen darkly clad figures. Their matte black armor bore no seems. Their helmets were smooth and completely featureless: no eyes, no mouths, nothing but black. The only difference between the figures and the shadows they cast was the glowing violet light on the left breasts of the figures' armor. As they moved closer, Chuck could see that the light was in the shape of a ring, with four glowing dots situated at each of the cardinal directions.

The dark menagerie came to an abrupt halt some feet from the ship, and an amplified voice sounded. *"Galactic citizen, thank you for your cooperation. Please open the vessel's primary entrance."*

Bhanakhana pressed a button, and the cube ship's front port slid open. The black-clad figures disappeared from the viewscreen as they entered the doorway. A few seconds passed with Chuck and Bhanakhana staring silently at the now-blank screen. They then looked at each other and, in unison, blurted out, "Jopp!"

They turned and rushed out of the control room. After a short sprint down a twisting hallway, they burst into the ship's lounge and were met by the gun barrels of half a dozen armored agents.

"Don't move," commanded the one in front. Bhanakhana stood as still as a statue. Chuck's hands shot straight up in the air. Despite the lack of facial features, the black figures were visibly taken aback. Chuck glanced at Bhanakhana, who was staring at him in dumbfounded awe.

"What are you doing?!" he whispered hoarsely.

"I'm surrendering," Chuck whispered back.

The commander stepped forward. "Why is this individual presenting the Sallinthir mating stance?"

"The what?!" yelped Chuck.

The commander spoke in an almost patronizing tone. "Please lower your appendages, citizen. We do not desire to copulate with you."

Chuck lowered his arms, cheeks burning red with embarrassment.

The commander turned his head toward Bhanakhana. "Are there any other sentient beings on board this vessel?"

Bhanakhana answered in a measured tone, "Yes."

"How many are there, and where are they located?"

"There is one additional being. His current location is the medical bay."

The commander gestured with his weapon. "Show me."

***

Jopp stared out across the crystal-clear expanse of the ocean and smiled. He felt the waves lapping at his bare toes and dug them into the soft pink sands of the Dandune beach. In his right hand was a tall frosty glass, filled to the brim with a glowing orange liquid. He raised the glass to his lips and took a long pull. He swallowed and let out a deeply contented sigh. "Nothing like the first sip from your fourth Nebula Punch of the morning."

A soft, feminine voice answered his musings. "You can say that again, lover."

Jopp glanced to his left, where his arm was draped around the shoulders of the most gorgeous Yoblon woman he'd ever seen. She looked up at him and smiled. He returned the smile and then shifted his gaze back to the horizon. *This is true bliss,* he thought. *No more slavery under some corporate tyrant, no more psychotic pirates trying to kill me, no more Gorthans . . .* Jopp couldn't remember the last time he'd been this happy. He heard his lovely companion whisper his name. He looked to see that she was no longer under his arm.

"Jopp."

He spun around to see that she was now halfway up the beach.

"Jopp."

He tried to move toward her but found that his feet were stuck.

"Jopp."

He tried to call out but found that he had no voice.

"Jopp."

He felt the ground start to shake. The vibrations reverberated through his whole body. He looked up to see that his lady friend was no longer in sight.

"Jopp."

A jagged crack appeared in the ground between Jopp's feet. He gawked as it shot forward, splitting the ground in front of him. It continued until it hit the horizon. Jopp watched in horror as the crack appeared to shoot up into the sky.

"Jopp."

The crack widened, as if the sky was being pulled apart. Jopp's mouth fell open as something moved into the black space that the crack had formed. It was a round, pinkish mass. Features began to form; an awkward nose grew from the center of the mass, two oval eyes appeared, and the thin line of a mouth spread open.

"JOPP!"

Jopp shot up suddenly, narrowly avoiding butting his head into the pinkish face mass. He massaged his antennae in an attempt to quell the pounding in his head. He rubbed his eyes and took in his surroundings. He was sitting in a stark white room, one he was pretty sure he'd never seen before. He became aware of something right next to him and looked up to see Chuck, the pinkish face mass, staring back at him. Behind Chuck was the hulking crimson form of Bhanakhana. The two of them stepped aside, revealing a half dozen armored shadows with weapons drawn. Ten whole seconds passed in silence as Jopp looked from the black figures, to Bhanakhana, to Chuck, and then back to the black figures. He then fixed his gaze on the well-armed cadre standing out in front and said, "I didn't do it."

TEXT UNIT 0027

Haaga Viim leaned back in his chair, an upturned glass resting on his lips. When the glass was emptied, he wasted no time in refilling it with more of the cloudy liquor. He swirled it around casually, letting his gaze pass over the three individuals currently seated in his quarters. A slightly bandaged Jorwei and a heavily bandaged Ghono reclined on the couch, each nursing glasses of the same liquor. Shai sat in a chair across from Haaga. He also held a glass of the liquor, despite the fact that he never drank.

"So, what was a Class 12 ULE frigate doing out in the middle of nowhere?"

Haaga's question was answered with silence.

"And why did they let us go?"

More silence.

Haaga glowered and grumbled, "Don't all speak at once."

Jorwei cleared his throat. "What about that other Dronla? Where did he come from? Damn bloodskin." He shot a nervous glance at the scarred Dronla, Ghono. "Eh, no offense, G-Man."

Ghono waved him off. "I feel the same. There are far too many weak-willed bleeding hearts sullying my race's gene pool."

Haaga gestured to Ghono. "I don't suppose you know who he is?"

"No, but he seemed to know me."

Haaga turned to Shai. "You're awfully quiet."

Shai breathed deeply and spoke in a calm, collected manner. "At this juncture, I think it is safe to assume that there is more going on here than we know."

"No shit."

Haaga and Shai shot death glares at Jorwei, who drew his fingers across his lips in an exaggerated *I'm zipping it* motion. Shai continued, "Given the losses we've sustained and this newfound intervention by the ULE, a serious argument could be made for abandoning the contract."

Jorwei clapped his hands. "Hell yeah! Screw this job! We want to get ourselves killed or, worse, locked up over some little case and a damn Earth ape?!" He snapped his fingers. "You know, I think I already got an idea for a new score! We aren't far from the Yuro System, where they got that new Equa Train running. It'd be no problem to—"

"Humpa dung!" Ghono spat. "I don't walk away from contracts, and besides"—he grimaced and pawed at the bandages around his torso—"I owe them some pain."

Haaga sat back in thought. As if on cue, his commline started buzzing. He flipped the switch. "What is it, Vaatu?"

"*Captain, you have a call from—*"

"An old friend?" Haaga finished.

"*Um, yes.*"

Haaga looked to his crewmen. "Give me a minute."

When his three guests had exited, Haaga flipped a second switch. "Hello."

The synthesized voice once again echoed through Haaga's quarters. *"Congratulations! I didn't think it was possible for this situation to get any more phoobed up! I obviously underestimated you."*

"Are you—wait, you already know?"

"That you leveled half a city? And that our target is now in the custody of the phoobing Universal Law Enforcement Agency? Yes, I know that."

"How do you know all that?"

"Well, Haaga, when a high-ranking ULE officer is murdered, it tends to draw a bit of attention."

"Who—" Haaga felt his stomach turn as a wave of realization washed over him. He leapt to his feet and slammed his hands down on the desk, "The J'Kari! Kahpa! You put a ULE officer on my ship without telling me?!"

"Listen—"

"No! You listen! We are done! You hear me?! I'm keeping what's left of the first payment, taking my crew, and laying low until this blows over. And *you* should pray our paths never cross again, because I promise you I will tear out your tongue just so I can shove it back down your throat."

A full minute passed before the synthesized voice responded. *"How colorful. Open the final payment account."*

"What?"

"Open the final payment account."

Haaga growled and punched in the series of commands that would access his various bank accounts. He pulled up the account in question and his one good, nonswollen eye widened with shock.

"Well?"

"Is this a joke?"

"No. You'll know when I'm joking. My jokes are hilarious, but that's beside the point. Back to the account."

"You seem to have added an extra zero."

"*That's right. Ten million Tahlians. You just got a 1,000 per-cent raise. The money is actually sitting in your account at this very moment. All you have to do is enter the confirmation pass-word, which I'll give to you once I get that case. If the password isn't entered within the next seventy-two hours, the funds will be rescinded.*"

"Oh, that's all? Why didn't you say so? I'll just head back over to the Class 12 frigate. You know, the one that's probably hunting me down as we speak? I'll simply ask if I can borrow a piece of evidence linked to the murder of an agency officer. I'm sure they'll have no issues with that."

"*Sarcasm doesn't suit you. Stick to the tough guy act. Now turn on GMM.*"

"Why?"

"*Just turn on your news feed.*"

"I grow tired of your cryptic nonsense," grumbled Haaga has he pulled up Galactic Mass Media. He scrolled through the trending stories:

. . . trade negotiations breaking down between the Vashnii and Yoblon governments . . .

. . . infamous Dazlinian heiress arrested for her third piloting-under-the-influence offense . . .

. . . the mysterious murder of a ULE agent . . .

Haaga highlighted the last one, and a video began to play. The screen displayed the exterior of the Gorthan bar as a green-skinned reptilian woman spoke into the camera.

"*I'm standing outside a local liquor dispensary on the Gorthan-inhabited planet of Drecken Minor, where Cherrine Kahpanova, a vice director in the Universal Law Enforcement Agency, was found murdered.*"

The video cut to a still of the deceased. The person in the picture had shoulder-length black hair and was dressed in a

ULE uniform, but Haaga still recognized her as the same J'Kari woman who had boarded his ship yesterday.

"Details are vague, but it is believed that a wild Earth ape and a rogue Yoblon transporter are the culprits."

The video cut again to a piece of security footage.

"This recording shows the two suspects entering the establishment. Mere minutes after this footage, a massive riot broke out among the bar's patrons. It is believed that the two suspects instigated this riot as a means of distraction. Our sources tell us they lured the victim to the roof, where they proceeded to throw her over the edge. The real question here is not who or how but, rather, why?"

The video then cut to a studio where three individuals sat around one side of a circular table. The middle one, a salmon-hued female Tahl, looked into the camera.

"Thank you for that report from the field. I'd like to hear some opinion from our guests. Any theories, Patriarch Haks?"

She was gesturing to the insectoid on her right, who slammed two of his four clawed hands down on the table.

"It is time we stopped coddling the hairless Earth apes and started seeing them for what they really are: an inevitably dangerous threat to sentient life throughout the universe! The Sentient Coalition needs to authorize a total assimilation of planet Earth!"

The other guest, a muscle-bound female Dronla, chose this moment to interject.

"Let me guess. It should be your Vashnii Armada that carries out this 'assimilation,' correct? You warmongers are simply looking for an excuse to invade yet another underdeveloped planet—"

Haaga cut off the broadcast. The synthesized voice spoke again. *"Ah, why'd you turn it off? It was just getting good! At one point, they had to restrain the Vashnii patriarch from climbing across the table! Anyway, you notice anything in that story? Better yet, you notice anything* not *in that story?"*

"There was no mention of us."

"*And you're welcome for that. You and the J'Kari female were featured quite prominently in the original security footage."*

"How?"

"*Don't worry about that. Worry about how you're going to get that case out of ULE custody."*

TEXT UNIT 0028

Chuck sat in a stark white box of a room. Besides himself, the only other objects were the chair he was sitting on, the white table in front of him, and a second chair on the other side of the table. A panel slid open on the far wall, and a black-clad agent entered. Chuck stared quietly as the moving shadow crossed the room and sat down in the empty chair. Neither spoke for the next minute. Chuck almost broke the silence but caught himself. He thought back to all those interrogation scenes he'd watched on TV. *My lips are sealed,* he thought.

The agent reached both hands up and pressed two fingers to each side of the helmet. There was a faint hiss, and the agent pulled off the featureless mask. Chuck's lips were immediately unsealed as his jaw fell open. The face behind the mask was utterly stunning. She was definitely of the same race as the silver-skinned alien from earlier. This one, however, had jet-black hair that fell past her shoulders. A purple tattoo shaped like a backward seven adorned her right cheek. Her almond-shaped eyes were a pale shade of lavender. She narrowed those piercing eyes at Chuck, who at that moment would've done anything to gain the favor of the woman behind them.

"So, tell me, Earth man. . . ." Her voice was calm and inviting. Chuck was readying himself to tell her that yes, he would run away with her.

"Why did you kill Vice Director Kahpanova?"

***

"I do not know that individual."

Bhanakhana had just been asked the same question as Chuck. Similar to Chuck's room, the agent conducting the interrogation was a silver-skinned, tattooed J'Kari. Dissimilar to Chuck's room, the agent was a male, and the perpetual sneer he wore was far from attractive.

"So you just happened to be fleeing the scene with the prime suspects, and you're telling me you don't know anything about the murder?"

"I was not fleeing from the scene of a murder. I was fleeing from the criminal assailants who were attempting to kill us. From the vantage point of this frigate, I would have thought that an obvious observation."

"Insubordination and disrespect won't get you very far."

"I intend no offense. I merely find it curious that my vessel has been impounded, yet no action was taken to pursue a vessel so obviously engaged in illegal activities."

"That vessel wasn't linked to the murder of a ULE officer!" The agent slammed his hand down on the table.

"As I mentioned a moment ago, I do not know the individual of whom you speak."

The agent slid a mobile viewscreen across the table. Bhanakhana looked down, and recollection rolled over his face. She had hair and was wearing a uniform, but he was definitely looking at the J'Kari from the rooftop struggle.

The agent saw the realization on Bhanakhana's face and smirked. "Now, shall we start our discussion over?"

***

"So, what's the ULE's policy on fornication? Are you guys like the Orpulus monks, or do they let you Law Cogs enjoy a little lunar lovin'?"

"Mr. Wenslode—"

"A little of the nebula nasty?"

"Mr. Wenslode—"

"A little constellation consummation?"

"MR. WENSLODE!"

"Call me Jopp."

The Yoblon ULE agent sitting across from Jopp ground his teeth; a purple vein pulsed on his forehead. "Mr. Wenslode, I would advise you to take this seriously."

Jopp leaned back in his chair and propped his feet up on the table. "I am taking this very seriously! We Yoblons weren't meant to be celibate, you know. It's been known to cause serious emotional issues."

The agent glared at Jopp, who smiled back. After a few deep breaths, the agent said, "Moving on to the charges. . . ."

***

"I didn't even want to be here! A few days ago, I didn't know aliens even existed! Next thing I know, I'm getting forced into working for that company!"

The female ULE agent rolled her eyes "Uh-huh, right. Prime Partners Intergalactic Consortium hired you, an Earth man, to work for them."

"Yes! It was one of those purple 'tall' guys...Quo-something."

She smirked. "Oh, sure, the head of the largest corporation in the known universe personally hired you, an Earth man. That makes perfect sense. On an unrelated note, do your people have a concept of sarcasm?"

Chuck sighed and slumped back in his chair. The female agent drummed her fingers on the table. Chuck then sat up straight. "Okay. You don't believe me? Fine. What's your theory? Tell me a more plausible explanation for how I, an 'Earth man,' wound up here."

She stopped drumming her fingers and stared at him. He folded his arms across his chest and leaned back. Her smirk disappeared. She opened and then closed her mouth. Her brow furrowed in frustration.

Chuck leaned forward. "Well, when you think of something, let me know. In the meantime, I would be happy to tell you the rest of my story."

This time it was she who leaned back, arms folded. She gave him the go-ahead with a silent nod.

***

"I first met the Earth man called Chuck on the main commerce hangar of Prime One. I was conducting research for an upcoming thesis and had docked at Prime One in order to procure supplies before beginning the next phase of my project. While awaiting the delivery of my order, I noticed the Earth man."

"What a convenient coincidence," snarked the agent.

"It was no accident that we became acquainted. The humans of Earth are not even aware that our society exists, yet here was one milling about on the flagship of the wealthiest organization in the known universe! Academic curiosity demanded I make his acquaintance."

"Oh, yeah, sure. I always try to make friends with the animals whenever I take my younglings to the zoo."

"I find your parental tactics questionable. Back to my point: a portion of my thesis brings into question the official status of Earth humans' sentience. I hypothesize that they may, in fact, qualify for a higher classification."

"Why not? And while you're at it, let's give humpalopes the right to vote!"

Bhanakhana gave the agent a perplexed look. "I find your snide comments to be unprofessional as well as a hindrance toward your goal of revealing the truth behind the death of your associate. I would very much like to continue without the interruptions."

The agent scowled at Bhanakhana for a few moments before grumbling, "Go on."

Bhanakhana looked quite pleased with himself. "Thank you. Now, I feel I would be remiss if I did not inform you that humpalopes lack the necessary development in the cerebral cortex to comprehend a governmental voting system. . . ."

***

"What about the Kapua? Are they allowed to be ULE agents?"

"Mr. Wenslode—"

"They don't even have physical bodies. How would you even fit a sentient, shimmering cloud into one of those snazzy black uniforms? Oh! I know! You could build some kind of floating orb for them. You know, paint it black—"

"Mr. Wenslode—"

"There's not a criminal in the galaxy who would know what to do against a platoon of black floating orbs! It could be your secret weapon!"

"Mr. Wenslode!"

"Call me Jopp."

The purple vein on the agent's forehead had gained a twin. The agent fumed in his chair, and his voice cracked a bit when he spoke. "Mr. Wenslode, you are facing the most severe of punishments should you be found guilty! Your lack of coop-eration will only make your predicament worse for you! Now please answer my questions!"

Jopp gave the agent an apologetic expression and nodded in agreement.

"What exactly were you doing on that planet?"

Jopp tapped his chin in thought. A wave of sad realization slid over his face. "Oh, wait. We have a problem. How would the black floating Kapua orbs use weapons?"

***

"So out of nowhere these space pirates—"

"We just call them pirates."

"Huh? Oh, what?"

"Never mind. Please continue." The smirk had returned to the agent's face. Chuck noticed it seemed more amused than derisive this time around.

"So, uh, yeah. The pirates attacked us . . . and we're about to die . . . and then Jopp finds this anomaly." Chuck paused, waiting for some cynical comment. It never came. The agent simply stared at him expectantly. "We come out the other end of the anomaly, and immediately the ship starts busting up."

"Forcing you to crash-land on Drecken Minor," she added.

"Yes!"

"What happened to the ship's cargo?"

"Oh, well there wasn't—I mean, we left it with the ship when a local Gorthan offered us a ride."

"Ah, yes. Enter the Gorthans." She shook her head slightly.

"I know, right? They are something else! Seriously, how are they part of your big multiworld society, but Earth isn't?"

The agent sat up straight; her face had become stern and stoic. She looked Chuck dead in the eye. "The Gorthans were the first race to successfully navigate an anomaly. They have no idea how to map one or how to duplicate a trajectory, but their bravery to at least try laid a critical piece of the foundation for the society we have today. What has your planet done for the universe?"

***

"It was quite stunning, to say the least. Once again, I found myself staring at a real live Earth man. How could an Earth man be on Drecken Minor? He appeared quite similar to Chuck. However, it can be difficult to discern one Earth human from another."

"Let me guess, 'academic curiosity' demanded you go see if it was the same guy."

"Most certainly! As I am sure you have surmised, it was, in fact, the same individual." Bhanakhana beamed before recounting Chuck's story of everything that had happened since their first meeting.

The agent held up a hand. "Wait a minute. So the Earth man claims he was hired by Prime Partners and attacked by marauders before escaping through an uncharted anomaly, which just happened to spill out in orbit above the very same planet you were arriving on? And you believed him? I thought you were supposed to be smart."

"What you perceive as a coincidence is, in fact, an astounding revelation. For the past fifty standard annuals, Gorthan popular culture has exhibited an explosion of Earth-based influence. My theory is that the Gorthans have known about the uncharted anomaly for quite some time."

"Gorthans don't have the wherewithal to fully map an anomaly."

Bhanakhana shook his head. "I never claimed that they did. I hypothesize that they are aware of the anomaly's existence, and that it will occasionally take them to Earth. That's all the information a Gorthan would need to attempt a jump. They are fascinating beings."

The agent waved him off. "Don't try to derail me with your philosophical musings. Even if all of that is true, which it probably isn't, it gets you no closer to clearing your name. Stop stalling and tell me what happened to Vice Director Kahpanova!"

***

"Don't get me wrong: I dig the uniforms."

The agent sitting across from Jopp was holding his head in his hands, staring down at the table.

"You got that whole mysterious shadowy vibe. It's very intimidating."

The agent slammed his hands down on the table and glared at Jopp through bloodshot eyes. "Mr. Wenslode, please stop wasting my time."

"Wasting your time? How could you say that? I shared my first sexual experience, gave you my recipe for scrambled fujo, and told you about that time I dosed Quib and hallucinated that my bed was trying to eat me."

The agent stood up. "None of that relates to the murder of Vice Director Kahpanova. I'm done with you."

"Actually it does. You'll see; it'll all be clear once I finish. That is, unless you want to be on record as ending an interrogation before the suspect completes his statement."

The agent slumped back down in his seat.

Jopp scratched his head. "Where was I? Oh, yeah. I guess my real issue with the uniforms is that insignia. Whose idea was that? Didn't anybody notice it kind of looks like a dowfa's anus?"

***

"I swear I'm not lying!"

The agent was on her feet, leaning forward. One hand was bracing her upper body against the surface of the table. The other held Chuck by the collar. Their faces were inches apart, the agent's eyes burning with rage. She shoved Chuck back into his chair and picked up her helmet.

"I will not sit here and listen to you spin lies about the vice director!" she spat.

Chuck was fidgeting nervously. "Look, I don't know what else to say. That's how it happened."

"You expect me to believe that a vice director in the Universal Law Enforcement Agency was actively assisting a lowly band of criminals in the apprehension of an inconsequential Earth ape and a burned-out Yoblon?! And that she died by accidently falling off a roof during a firefight?!"

"I don't expect you to believe anything! I don't know anything about the Universal Law thing or pirates or criminals or Yoblons or anything! I'm just telling you what happened!"

The agent turned and stomped out of the room.

***

"The damage to the town was a result of our assailants firing upon us as we made our way to the hangar."

The agent rolled his eyes. "Sure, the 'pirates' and the 'mysterious black ship.'"

"I never referred to them as pirates, and I never classified their vessel as mysterious. After reaching the hangar, we fled in my Estal Cube. The assailants gave chase until we came into contact with your frigate, which brings us to the present."

Bhanakhana spread his hands wide, palms up, as if to say *that's all there is.*

The agent glanced at his notes, then back at Bhanakhana. "You still haven't explained why they were chasing you."

"Why they were chasing Chuck and Jopp is unknown to me. I was simply attempting to assist an individual in need."

***

"So then I says to him, 'Hey buddy, get your own globnob!'"

TEXT UNIT 0029

Two black-clad agents flanked Chuck as he walked down the white corridor. The Earth man wore white pants and a white shirt. They reminded him of the medical scrubs he'd seen on one of those TV shows where the doctors spend all their time sleeping with each other instead of curing illness. Chuck hadn't lasted long enough in med school to ever actually wear a pair himself. Much like the Prime Partners medical bay, the prisoner intake department employed a thorough disinfectant process, which accounted for the extra hitch in Chuck's step.

They turned a corner and entered a long hallway, bordered on both sides by glass. Chuck glanced left and right, seeing that the glass panes acted as the front walls of jail cells. Every inmate gawked as Chuck passed. He recognized many of the species, but there were plenty of new ones as well. There was one inmate that resembled a beetle standing on two legs. Another looked like someone had placed the head of a parrot on the body of a gorilla. The next being that caught his eye looked like a five-foot pineapple with arms and legs. The cell after that housed a giant wad of blue goo, who was currently stuck to the cell's back upper corner. A series of blue streaks on the front wall of the blue goo wad's cell spelled out "Phoob the Law Cogs." Chuck stared openly at one cell housing a yellowish-green cloud. It sparkled as Chuck passed, sending shivers up his back.

He was too busy staring back over his left shoulder to notice that his escort had stopped. He felt a firm hand grasp his shoulder and pull him back. He turned to see two familiar faces. They were dressed in the same white scrubs as Chuck and standing behind the glass of their own cells. Bhanakhana sat up straight on his cot. Jopp was lying down, his hands resting behind his head, gazing up at the ceiling. The empty cell between the two of them was missing the front glass pane. One of the guards gave Chuck a little push, and he plodded into the empty cell. He crossed the threshold, and there was a hissing noise as the front glass pane slid into place.

Chuck saw that the cots all ran along the back wall of the cells, essentially forming one long bench. He plopped himself down and reclined against the wall. No sooner had the guards turned the far corner than Chuck heard someone say, "Man, you look like shit. White is not a good color for you, Earth ape."

Chuck glanced right to see Jopp leaning against the glass wall that separated their two cells. The Earth man chuckled. "Yeah, well, you look like a hardboiled egg, Lemonhead."

Jopp responded with a middle finger.

A deep voice sounded from Chuck's left. "Either my TellAll is malfunctioning, or I need to learn more about the nuances of Earth linguistics. Did you refer to his cranial region as a sour fruit?"

Bhanakhana sat on the end of his cot, as close to the glass divider as possible. Chuck's eyes filled with guilt as he looked up at the muscle-bound Dronla. "I'm so sorry we got you mixed up in this mess."

Bhanakhana shook his head. "I have spent the past hour ruminating on this matter. I do not regret my decision to offer aid."

"But you wouldn't be here. . . ."

"This is true. However, I would rather be sitting in this cell, knowing I made the ethical decision, as opposed to walking away from an individual in need."

"You're a better man than I am, Big Red," called Jopp.

Bhanakhana nodded. "This is something we can agree on."

Chuck stifled a laugh. Jopp shot him a glare. Chuck fidgeted with his pants. "Man, I thought the Prime Partners medical exam was rough. These people really clean you out."

Jopp snorted. "Oh, yeah. The ULE gets real thorough. . . . Buncha despotic dick bags."

"Your profanity notwithstanding, I concur that our hosts are less than gracious. When this matter is resolved, I fully intend to file a formal complaint. The agent who conducted my interrogation was quite rude."

Jopp laughed. "Ha, I almost made my guy cry!"

They looked at Chuck expectantly. "Oh, uh . . . yeah. My agent was. . . . They were all right, I guess."

Bhanakhana and Jopp exchanged glances. Chuck attempted to change the subject. "So, uh, how much trouble are we really in here, guys?"

Jopp shrugged.

"I have sent word to my legal advocate," Bhanakhana replied. "We will know more tomorrow."

Chuck sighed and stretched out on his cot. He didn't even remember falling asleep.

TEXT UNIT 0030

Haaga Viim lay on the floor of his ship's bridge. His upper half rested against the back of a chair. The cut over his swollen right eye had reopened, allowing tiny drops of blood to trickle down his face.

Shai was unconscious and draped across a control console. Haaga's pilot lay facedown in the middle of the room. The twin gunners were nowhere to be seen.

Black scorch marks peppered the various surfaces of the room. Haaga felt the ship pitch slightly. He heard a low tone resonate through the air, indicating that another vessel had docked with them.

Then Haaga heard it: the rapping of boots on metal. He looked toward the open door. He watched as three black-clad ULE agents strode onto the bridge, weapons at the ready.

"Thank the gods!" Haaga cried out. "I thought I was going to die! Please help me!"

They slung their weapons over their shoulders and rushed up to him. The lead agent knelt down. "We caught your distress signal."

"Please . . . see to my crewmen first. . . . I think they might be dead."

The lead agent waved his hand, and his two comrades each went to check on one of the bodies. The lead agent turned his head back to Haaga. "What happened here?"

Haaga's words came in raspy spurts. "We were . . . transporting medical supplies . . . for destitute children on Drecken Major. . . . We were attacked by . . . marauders. . . ."

He began coughing.

The lead agent patted his shoulder. "It's going to be okay. The ULE will handle this."

"Um, sir?"

The lead agent looked to the secondary agent next to Shai. "What is it?"

The secondary agent was tinkering with a small oblong tool. "This individual is not dead. In fact, my scanner readings indicate he is in perfect health."

"Wha—" Before he could finish, the lead agent felt something press up under his chin. He slowly turned his head to see that Haaga's expression of terror had morphed into a sinister grin.

In an instant, Shai and the pilot hopped up, weapons trained on the other two agents.

Haaga pressed the pulse pistol a little firmer against the lead agent's jaw. "It looks like my crew is going to be okay. Isn't that just miraculous?"

***

Haaga sat across from the lead agent on the bridge of a ULE orbital cruiser. The agent's helmet sat next to him on the control console, so Haaga could see the agent was a J'Kari male.

His black hair was cropped closely to his silver scalp. Violet tattoos covered the left half of his face and neck.

Haaga caught his own reflection in a blank viewscreen and did a double take. The face staring back at him was not his own, but rather bore the sharp features of an older J'Kari. His new steely skin looked very dark. His head was bald, and a thick strip of white hair ran along his jawline. The bridge door opened, and in walked three ULE agents, helmets in hand. The first two were also J'Kari, one with slicked-back black hair and the other sporting a shaved head. The third had an owl's head attached to a massive frame of a body.

Haaga gestured to the large, feathered one. "Ghono, get on the navigation console."

The beak opened and said in a high-pitched squawk, "How did you know it was me?"

Haaga rolled his eyes.

"Why are you doing this?" asked the real J'Kari agent.

Haaga turned to him. He pointed a finger back at himself. "Holoskins are capable of some amazing things. Just like that"—he snapped his fingers—"and I'm no longer an Ochrean. . . ." He glanced at the badge on the table. "I'm Key Major Ferru. Hmmm, he sounds important." Haaga continued, "But there is one thing these great gadgets can't materialize." He held up a black card with fluorescent markings. "ULE credentials. We still need the real thing. Only way to get those is off a real agent."

He tossed the card onto the desk. "Here is the situation: you are going to take us to the frigate currently in orbit over Drecken Minor. All we need is one little case, which is most likely sitting in the confiscation vaults. No one will miss it. While we do that, your fellow agents will remain on my ship as insurance. If we aren't back in twelve hours, they die. If everything goes well, we return your associates, and we all go our separate ways. No one needs to get hurt."

The agent peered back at him. "I'm supposed to believe you won't just kill us once you're done?"

Haaga leaned forward. "I would love to, but dusting a crew of ULE agents would bring a lot of attention. I'd prefer to avoid attention, if possible. And before you ask, no, I am not worried about you hunting us down. I'm willing to bet you don't want a service record that contains an incident where you allowed your ship and crew to be captured by criminals."

The agent scowled at Haaga for a few moments before turning to his controls. "You said they were near Drecken Minor?"

TEXT UNIT 0031

Chuck awoke to the hiss of his cell door opening. He sat up and saw an agent stepping through the doorway. The agent pressed a small remote, and the front glass panel slid closed. The agent reached up and removed the featureless black helmet, revealing herself to be the same agent from Chuck's interrogation.

"May I speak with you?" she asked.

A voice from Chuck's right boomed, "Oh, ho *ho*! Your interrogator was 'all right,' huh? You were holding out on us, Earth man!"

Chuck turned to see Jopp leaning against the glass with a devilish grin. He gave the agent a wink. "How you doin', sweets?"

The agent gave Jopp a patronizing smile as she pressed another button on the remote. The three glass walls of Chuck's cell instantly clouded over. Jopp's comments became barely audible muffles. Chuck could just see a shadow against the new opacity of the glass.

The agent dragged the cell's sole chair over to a spot a few feet in front of Chuck's cot. She set her helmet on the ground, placed the cell remote on her belt, and removed a pistol from her holster. She then sat down across from him, the pistol resting casually on her thigh.

"You try anything and I turn your head to ash, understand?"

Chuck nodded.

"My behavior was inappropriate during the interview. I should have never put my hands on you. I understand if you wish to file a complaint with my superiors."

Chuck glanced from the pistol on her thigh to her face. "Uh, don't worry about it?"

Then, surprising even himself, he chuckled. "Honestly, that might have been the friendliest conversation I've had in the past two days."

She arched an eyebrow. "So you do understand sarcasm."

Chuck shook his head. "No, I'm serious. This whole intergalactic society thing you have is utterly insane."

"I appreciate you accepting my apology, but I still shouldn't have lost my composure. It's just that the vice director . . . she . . ."

The agent trailed off.

"She was somebody to you."

The agent stared at the ground. "The ULE Academy is hell. There's an 88 percent dropout rate. She was my mentor. I wouldn't have made it through without her."

Chuck offered an awkward "I'm sorry."

She either didn't hear him or chose to ignore it. She seemed to be talking more to herself than to Chuck at this point. "She was a good agent. She spearheaded the task force that ended the Uhton genocide. Who knows how many lives that saved? I can't believe she would go bent."

Chuck had no response, but he was pretty sure she wasn't expecting one. She looked up at him. "I haven't slept. I spent the night scouring files, data logs, security records . . . anything

I could get my hands on that might prove she wasn't bent. And, do you know what I found?"

Chuck didn't know, but he was pretty sure she was about to tell him.

"I found a perfectly detailed record of everywhere she'd been, and why she'd been there," she said with a grimace.

"Um . . . isn't that a good thing?" Chuck asked.

"I said her records were perfect. I didn't say they were accurate."

Her expression darkened, if that was even possible. "One entry in particular stood out: about one and a half standard annuals ago, my unit was stationed in the Warsan System. We received an unexpected visit from the vice director. She told us she'd received intel on a group of marauders holed up in the marshes of Warsan Prime. Our orders were to take them down—arrest if possible, terminate if necessary. We followed the coordinates she provided and came across this sleek three-story metal structure, just sitting in the middle of a damn swamp. We breached the door and immediately got hit by gunfire. We returned in kind, dropping two of them before beginning our sweep of the building. When it was over, we'd dusted twenty-one and captured two, losing three of our own in the fray. We led the prisoners back outside to find the vice director waiting with her security detail. She thanked us for our service and then said she'd be personally taking the two prisoners in for processing. Mission accomplished."

Chuck fidgeted under her stare, which threatened to burn his eyes out. "So . . . um . . . wha—what's . . ."

"What's the problem?" she finished for him.

All he could muster was a slight nod.

"The official report shows twenty-three hostiles killed in action. Do you remember how many I told you we terminated?"

Chuck swallowed some spit. "Tw—Twenty . . . one."

She leaned forward, her eyes burned like two violet flames.

"I've borne witness to the deaths of sixty-two sentient beings. Some were good people; some were monsters. The face of each and every one is carved into my brain. Twenty-one hostiles and three agents died that day in the swamp . . . no more, no less."

"Could she have made a mistake?" blurted Chuck.

She stared back at him with an almost pitying expression, as if he was a puppy who'd just bitten his own tail. The stare became a smile, and she began chuckling to herself. It was then Chuck's turn to stare, as her chuckle evolved into a hysterical fit of laughter. She rocked back in her chair, clutching her side. Chuck turned his head left and right, not knowing what he was hoping to see. Her guffawing subsided, and she wiped a tear from her eye.

She looked Chuck up and down and let out a sigh.

"Whew! You are a strange breed, Earth man! You are facing life in prison, and I happen to stumble upon a discrepancy that gives the slightest of indications something illicit might have been going on with the vice director. I give you the absolute tiniest modicum of a chance at giving your insane story some credibility . . . and what do you do? You completely dismiss it! And to accomplish what? Make me feel better?"

She stood up and holstered her pistol.

"No, Earth man, there was no mistake. Our files are retina-checked. Vice Director Kahpanova's own eyes read every line of that report three times before signing off on it. She purposely entered a false number. Now I don't know what actually happened in that little Gorthan borough you smashed up, but I'm going to find out."

She turned and headed for the front wall panel. When she reached it, she looked back at Chuck and added, "Thanks for the laugh. I needed it."

"Uh, you're welcome, I guess."

She opened the front panel, and Chuck called out, "Hey, what's your name?"

She looked back over her shoulder. "It's Rohi . . . Rohi Kahpanova. The vice director was my mother's sister."

Her gaze lingered on Chuck a moment longer before she turned to head down the hall. The front panel hissed as it closed behind her. Chuck's head swam as he tried to make sense of what just happened. A beep shook Chuck out of his thoughts. The cloudy cell walls turned transparent again, revealing Jopp still standing up next to the glass . . . only now he was shirtless . . . and flexing. The yellow Yoblon's expression fell when he saw that Chuck was alone.

"Ah, man! I was gonna show her the goods!"

TEXT UNIT 0032

The Class 12 ULE frigate *Strike Down* had a newly appointed chief arms guard, and he stood at attention as the visiting officers descended from their ship. He had received notice of this visit barely an hour ago. His unit scurried about, making sure everything was in order here in the frigate's confiscation vaults. As they approached, he studied the five visitors. One was a hulking Aviape. He felt relief to see the remaining four officers bore the same silver skin and various tattoos as he did. It's not that he disliked other races; some of his best friends were Yoblons and Venovans. It's just that he felt more comfortable dealing with fellow J'Kari. He didn't think it was speciesist at all. . . .

The chief arms guard snapped out of his reverie just in time to offer a salute. A J'Kari bearing the rank of unit leader was the only one to reciprocate. The other four were busy looking around the hangar in a curious fashion. The unit leader saw the chief notice this and barked, "Chief!"

The chief arms guard's eyes snapped forward. The unit leader gestured to the rather large J'Kari officer on his left. "Key

Major Ferru is here on a very important matter. We understand you recently apprehended individuals suspected of murdering a vice director."

The chief nodded. "That is correct."

The unit leader continued, "Key Major Ferru's task force has been tracking these vile criminals for quite a while. This incident is only the latest in a slew of heinous crimes. We suspect they were in possession of vital evidence at the time of arrest."

The chief kept nodding. "Oh, we found lots of strange stuff on their ship. Would your team like to examine the evidence?"

Before the unit leader could answer, the large key major put his hand on the chief's shoulder and smiled. "That would be most helpful. I'll be sure to make a note of your assistance in this vital investigation."

The chief beamed. "Right this way!"

***

"It's not here."

Haaga, currently known as Key Major Ferru, stood in the center of evidence vault 042. The unit leader, also known as Haaga's hostage, and Jorwei, also known as Jorwei, were standing on either side of him. The three of them had sifted through every item in the vault: the collected evidence consisted of plants, preserved animal skeletons, and countless trinkets indigenous to the various planets from Bhanakhana's travels. What was painfully missing, they noted, was a black case.

"Well, that's a shame for you, but we need to go," the unit leader said. "The chief out there has been too busy polishing your official yub nubs to remember standard procedure. As soon as he logs your visit into the database, it's going raise some flags."

Haaga/Ferru stepped forward, putting his face inches from the unit leader's. "I will kill every living creature on this frigate before I leave without that case."

"They probably stashed it on their ship."

Haaga/Ferru and the unit leader turned to Jorwei. He explained, "His ship's an Estal Cube. It's probably got some supersecure lockbox on it; something that wouldn't show up on a basic scan."

"Looks like we're off to the impound hangar," grumbled Haaga/Ferru.

"Well . . ." Jorwei trailed off.

"Well what?"

"Well, for one, we'll never find it. Not unless we completely take apart the ship."

"Then we fly it out of here and strip it later."

"Unless it's got a bio-lock."

"What exactly are you trying to say to me, Jorwei?"

Jorwei gave him that *don't shoot the messenger* look. "We need *them*."

The holoskin-coated face of Haaga/Ferru twitched and flickered. He turned back to the unit leader. "Take us to the holding cells."

TEXT UNIT 0033

". . . and that was the second time my girlfriend tried to kill me."

Jopp, Chuck, and Bhanakhana sat at a white cafeteria table. Seated across from them were three other inmates. One looked like a ball of black fur, with facial features pushed closely together. Another looked like a slug with arms. The third was a big pile of teal slime. That was all Chuck knew about them, as every second of the last ten minutes had been filled with the sound of Jopp's voice. Chuck swirled his spoon around the bowl of brown slop sitting in front of him.

"What is this?" he wondered aloud.

The ball of black fur emitted a series of high-pitched whistles, clicks, and pops. Chuck glanced at Bhanakhana and Jopp, who simply shrugged.

The slug with arms spoke. "It's . . . a . . . protein . . . puree . . . specially . . . formulated . . . for . . . the . . . U . . . L . . . E . . . detainment . . . division."

Chuck scooped out a spoonful of the slop and sniffed at it before taking a bite. It reminded him of rice pudding. He was going for a second bite when Jopp gave him a playful punch in the arm. "So, what's the deal with that little solar flare of an agent?"

Chuck mumbled through a mouthful of protein puree, "Huh?"

Jopp nudged Bhanakhana in the side. "Our Earth buddy here got a special visit earlier."

"It wasn't a big deal," protested Chuck.

Jopp gave Bhanakhana another nudge. "A visit from a very attractive female agent."

"She just had a few extra questions."

"And she blanked the walls so I couldn't hear you two." Jopp went for another nudge, but a giant red palm caught his elbow.

Bhanakhana looked down. "That is a most unpleasant feeling." He then looked to Chuck. "I am not an expert in the matter, but that course of action does not sound like Universal Law Enforcement standard protocol."

Jopp rolled his eyes. "Oh, wow, there's actually something you're *not* an expert on?!"

Bhanakhana looked confused. "Why, yes. In fact, there are a great many subjects on which I would not consider myself to be an expert."

Jopp waved him off. "And sadly, the standard practices of super-jettie ULE agents is part of that list. Now, back to the matter at hand."

"Guys, Rohi was just there to talk about the investigation!" blurted Chuck.

Bhanakhana arched an eyebrow. Jopp spun back around, a wide grin plastered across his face. "Oh, really? *Rohi* just wanted to talk, huh?" He looked back at Bhanakhana. "You hear that, Big Red? *Rohi* just wanted to talk." He looked to Chuck. "So tell me, buddy, what did *Rohi* want to talk about?"

Chuck opened his mouth to respond but froze when his eyes caught something. Jopp and Bhanakhana followed his gaze to see a group of inmates approaching. The three beings seated across the table must also have noticed the approaching group, as they were hastily attempting to vacate their seats. The inmates walked up to the end of the table, closest to Bhanakhana. There were four of them, all Soreshi. The green scales on their arms looked stretched over the thick cords of muscle. The biggest one stepped forward. His python-like head looked from Bhanakhana to Jopp to Chuck. He opened his jaw and said in a scratchy rasp, "I'm called Jash. I run this house block. You don't eat, sleep, or breathe unless I give you my permission." He placed his hand around a bowl of the protein puree. "And I didn't give you three my permission." He slid the bowl off the table. It clattered on the floor, spilling brown slop all over.

Bhanakhana stood and turned to face Jash. "That was rude."

The other three reptilians spread out. Jash stretched his arms wide. "You feel like dying today, bloodskin? Make a move."

Jopp jumped up on the table. "All right! That's enough!"

Everyone turned to look at him. He stomped to the end of the table and pointed a finger at Jash. "Listen up, *Trash*!" His pointing finger swung back to Chuck. "You see that guy, right there? He's an Earth ape . . . and he's with *us*!"

Jash peered around Jopp at Chuck, gave the Earth man the once-over, and then looked back at Jopp. "Yeah, so what?"

"So, everyone knows you don't mess with Earth apes! They can melt your brain with their eyes!" Jopp pointed two fingers back at his own eyes.

Jash looked from Chuck to Bhanakhana, then back to Jopp. "Humpa shit. I don't believe you."

Jopp put his hands on his hips. "Oh, yeah? Ask *him*." He tilted his yellow head toward Bhanakhana. "He's a sentologist. He knows all about Earth."

Jash looked expectantly at Bhanakhana, who was staring at Jopp in utter confusion. Jopp gave him a wide-eyed *just go with it* look. Bhanakhana furrowed his brow. He opened his mouth, closed it, then opened it again. "The humans of Earth have shown themselves to be quite unpredictable, as well as occasionally being capable of"—he paused to shoot a quick glare at Jopp—"spontaneous feats of violence."

Jopp's face fell. Jash looked around at his crew. "Let's learn these crazy yoks a lesson."

The three other reptilians advanced. Bhanakhana wasted no time diving forward, splitting the difference between two of the assailants, driving his boulder-like shoulders into their respective guts.

The third reptilian lackey made for Jopp, who opted to implement the "food fight" defense. A bowl of brown slop flew through the air, narrowly missing the attacker's head. The next two bowls connected with his chest and legs but did little to slow him down. Once he saw his cache of protein-laced ammunition had been exhausted, Jopp gritted his teeth and took a running start to the edge of the table. He leapt into the air and cried out, "Oh, shiiiiiiiiiiiiiiiiiiiiiiiiit!"

His heel connected with the face of the slop-covered Soreshi, and the two of them tumbled across the floor. It was at that moment that Chuck felt clawed fingers dig into his arms. He was hoisted into the air and tossed across the table—he bounced off the opposite bench on his way to colliding with the floor. He groaned and gasped for breath. He heard approaching footsteps and tried to pull himself across the sleek white tiles. A raspy voice cackled, "Earth apes! Deadliest of beings!"

Chuck continued to scramble for cover. The grating tones continued to taunt him. "What are you waiting for, Earth man? Aren't you going to melt my brain with your eyes?"

Chuck felt the clawed fingers dig into his shoulders and yank him up from the floor. He was spun around, coming face-to-face with a sneering Jash. "You know, I can't remember the last time I ate something alive. I think it's time I treated myself."

He opened his mouth, revealing row upon row of hooked teeth. Chuck saw a thick red finger appear and start tapping Jash's shoulder. The reptilian let go of Chuck and turned around just in time to catch a glimpse of a huge red fist. There was a sound like a baseball bat hitting a watermelon as the fist made contact with Jash's face. His body crumpled to the floor as Bhanakhana's hefty frame loomed over him. Chuck's eyes moved up from the unconscious reptilian mass to meet the concerned gaze of his large red companion.

"Are you all right?" Bhanakhana asked.

Before Chuck could answer, a familiar voice called out, "Real smooth, Big Red!"

Bhanakhana and Chuck looked across the room. Jopp was on the floor, leaning up against a table. Propped up next to him was one of the reptilians. The thug was unconscious and wearing an upturned bowl on his head. Bits of protein puree dripped to the ground. Jopp pressed a piece of torn cloth to a cut on his forehead and huffed, "Spontaneous feats of violence? That's the best you could come up with?!"

An alarm blared, causing all the inmates to hit the deck. They placed their various hands, tentacles, and other appendages behind their heads. A dozen black-clad ULE agents rushed in carrying clear oblong shields. Bhanakhana and Chuck joined their neighboring inmates on the floor.

Jopp started slow clapping. "Good jobs, guys! Real efficient response time!"

TEXT UNIT 0034

Rohi Kahpanova took a moment to massage her temples before digging into yet another witness report. There had been almost two hundred Gorthans in that saloon, and each and every one had been more than happy to give their own version of the events. The statements were incredibly detailed and quite . . . colorful.

"The tussle got started by three o' them Squidlings from Tentaclon. . . ."

"There was ten of 'em, and they was all gold-skinned Vixenettes . . . and they definitely wanted a piece o' my man business."

"Then I drank, like, twenty chuz!"

"If I hadn't a' been there . . . everyone woulda been turnt into humpalope dung."

"Then he says, *Get your own globnob!*"

She sighed, put down the info log, and pinched the bridge of her nose. She reached down to open her bottom drawer, revealing a gold bottle. She pulled the top off and held it up to her nose, inhaling deeply. Her fingers flexed as she stared at the empty glass on her desk. She stretched out to grab it. Her graceful fingers wrapped around the glass, and she paused. She sat like that for a few moments. Her gaze passed from the bottle to the empty glass to the pile of work on her desk. She exhaled in annoyance and let go of the glass. She capped the bottle and returned it to its home in the drawer. She was just about to get back to reading when she noticed a blinking light on her console, indicating she had a new notification. She opened the message and was on the commline before she'd even finished reading. After a series of clicks, a tired voice answered, *"Confiscation vaults."*

"This is Division Officer Rohi Kahpanova. I have a notification here telling me that someone has been in the vault pertaining to incident 0000102214. Who was in that vault?"

"No problem, D.O. What is your clearance code?"

"Clearance code KRG0201."

"Checking. . . . Code confirmed. Okay, D.O. Let's see. It looks like a key major named Ferru was cleared to examine the evidence."

"Key Major Ferru . . . I don't know any Key Major Ferru . . ."

"Um . . . no offense, D.O., but aren't there, like, over a thousand active key majors?"

"One thousand and thirteen," she mumbled under her breath. Into the comm she said, "Send me the video logs of the key major's visit."

"Affirmative, D.O."

A new notification popped up, and she terminated the call. A screen opened on her console, showing an overhead shot of six figures making their way down the hallway leading to the confiscation vaults. Rohi recognized the chief arms guard heading up the pack. The other five were new to her. They walked the length of the hall and entered the vault. A casual eye wouldn't have noticed anything out of the ordinary. Rohi ran it back and watched again. And then again. It was on the third viewing that she saw it, right as the group was making their way past the camera.

It was the tattoo on the key major's left jawline; it was obviously meant to be a traditional J'Kari symbol for strength . . . but it wasn't quite right. The pointed ends curved in the wrong direction. She quickly waved through a holographic settings menu until she came to an icon labeled "Distortion Detector." In an instant a blue filter tinted her screen. Rohi glared at four of the six agents. Where their heads should have been, the screen was lit up with four orange lights.

"Holoskin," she murmured to herself as she picked the commline back up.

Another series of clicks and a different voice answered, *"Oversight and Administration."*

"This is Division Officer Rohi Kahpanova. I have an important message for Key Major Ferru. Is he still aboard the frigate?"

"One moment, D.O. . . . Okay, it looks like the key major is still on board."

"Where is he?"

"It looks like he just passed clearance in the inmate holding unit."

"The holding unit . . ." Rohi's eyes flared. She slammed the commline down and sprinted from her office.

TEXT UNIT 0035

"Well, that was fun." Jopp scratched at the fresh bandage on his forehead.

"No, that was fucked up." Chuck pawed at one of the nicks in his arm, courtesy of Jash's claws.

Jopp leaned against the glass separating their two cells. "Wabbah in one hand, Glajax in the other."

"What?"

Jopp smirked. "Never mind." He nodded. "What's up with him?"

Chuck glanced back to see Bhanakhana sitting on his bunk. His legs were crossed, his hands were resting on his knees, and his eyes were closed. Chuck turned back to Jopp. "He said something about rebalancing . . . or recentering himself."

Jopp arched an eyebrow. "He's kinda weird, huh?"

Chuck shrugged. "Weird has pretty much lost all meaning at this point."

Jopp rubbed his chin. "I'll tell you one thing, though. He's not a bad guy to have on your side when the plop glop hits the acceleran. You see the way he handled those Soreshi punks?"

Chuck sighed. "No, I was too busy getting tossed around like a rag doll."

"What's a—"

"Never mind. So, you seemed to hold your own. How'd you manage that?"

Jopp folded his arms. "You're damn right I held my own. I've taken on tougher guys than that scaly scumbag. It was a piece of jubla."

Chuck gave him a knowing look. Jopp rolled his eyes and threw his hands up. "All right! You got me. That guy was kicking my ass."

"So how'd he wind up unconscious?"

"He slipped on a puddle of that protein stuff and hit his head. Boom—out cold."

"Wait, how'd the bowl get on his head?"

Jopp grinned. "I thought it'd be funny."

"I found it quite amusing."

Chuck spun around to see Bhanakhana standing up. He gave them a warm smile. "How are you both feeling?"

Before either Chuck could answer earnestly or Jopp could answer sarcastically, a harsh buzz began to echo through the holding unit. They looked around to see the other inmates pressing their faces against the glass, trying to see down the hall. The buzzing ceased and was replaced by the clicking of boots. Jopp had joined the other inmates in straining to get a look. Chuck glanced sidelong at Bhanakhana. "Why do I have a bad feeling about this?"

Bhanakhana seemed to think for a moment before responding. "Perhaps you are evolving some form of extrasensory perception. Is that typical of human maturation? If so, I will need to make some adjustments to my thesis."

"Um . . ." was all Chuck could muster, noticing that the boot clicking had grown louder. He and Bhanakhana looked just in time to see eight uniformed ULE agents enter the hallway. Three wore the featureless black helmets. One had the head of an owl and was at least as large as Bhanakhana. Three were of the same silver-skinned, tattooed race as Rohi. The remaining agent was also one of the silverskins, except he was noticeably taller and wider than the other two. Chuck's eyes followed the black menagerie as they clicked and clacked their way down the hall.

He felt a knot forming in his gut. They got closer, and the knot tightened. A little closer, even tighter. They were just about to pass Chuck's cell. He closed his eyes tighter than the knot in his stomach and whispered to himself, "Please don't stop. Please don't stop."

The boot clicking stopped. Chuck opened his eyes to see the eight figures facing him. The larger silverskin glared as he pointed at Jopp, then Chuck, then Bhanakhana.

One of the helmeted agents clicked a remote, and Jopp's front wall slid open. Another agent trained a rifle on him, while one of them approached with green glowing restraints.

Jopp held his hands up defensively. "Whoa, whoa. C'mon guys! It was just a little cafeteria tussle . . . and they started it anyway!"

The agent with the rifle stepped forward, pressing the barrel to Jopp's forehead. His tone was ice cold. "Stay silent or you will be gagged. Comply with inmate transfer protocol or you will be terminated."

Jopp's eyes were crossed, staring up at the weapon resting against his forehead. "You got it."

The rifle was removed from his head, and the restraints were clamped to his thick yellow wrists. They led him out into the hallway, and then repeated the process with Chuck and Bhanakhana.

The group of eight agents and three inmates walked down the hallway. The larger silverskin, who was apparently the leader, and the remote-wielding helmeted agent headed up the column. Behind them followed Chuck, Jopp, and Bhanakhana, each flanked by a pair of agents. They came to a door that led into the main cell block. The helmeted agent in front pressed a button on his remote, and the door slid open. The shorter agent in front stepped into the hall, while the large officer in charge halted abruptly in the doorway. Chuck tilted his head to the side, peering around the considerable bulk of the head officer, and his mouth fell open in shock.

Standing at the other end of the hall were three other agents. They leveled their rifles at the approaching column. The two flanking agents wore the faceless black helmets, while the one in the middle did not. It was Rohi, and she was wearing a familiar expression. Chuck had seen that expression before, back in the interrogation room. He decided murderous pirates and reptilian convicts had nothing on that expression.

The helmeted agent out front stepped forward. "Division Officer Kahpanova, what do you think you are doing?!"

Her voice thundered down the hall: "Drop your weapons and step away from the prisoners!"

The helmeted agent looked back to the larger officer in front of Chuck. "I am dreadfully sorry, sir." Then to Rohi he shouted, "Key Major Ferru has clearance to transfer these inmates. Stand down, Division Officer."

Rohi shook her head. "That is not Key Major Ferru."

Before the agent could react, "Key Major Ferru" tore the remote from his hand and shoved him to the floor. The "key major" then stepped backward through the door.

"I'm afraid she's right." He pressed a button, causing the door between them and the main hall to slide closed. The door's lock light turned from green to red. The agent pounded his fist against the glass as Rohi's team rushed forward. "Key Major Ferru" grinned and pressed a second button, causing every single cell door in the main hall to slide open.

Chaos ensued as the inmates spilled into the hall. Echoes of shouting, punctuated with rifle fire, resonated through the door.

Chuck turned around in time to see one of the other helmeted agents ram the butt of his weapon into the chest of the giant owl-faced agent. While the blow cracked Owl Face's chest plate, it seemed to have no effect on him. He responded by slapping the gun away as if it were an insect. His left hand shot out and gripped the helmeted agent by the neck. With relative ease, he hoisted the agent aloft and tossed him into the wall. Upon seeing this, the second helmeted agent dropped his weapon and put his hands behind his head in surrender. The crack in Owl Face's armor sparked a few times, and then Chuck, Jopp, and Bhanakhana gawked as his face started flickering. After a few seconds of static, they were no longer seeing Owl Face. They now saw a bloodred face with crescent-shaped scars along the right cheek.

"Dammit, Ghono!" cursed the imposter key major.

The red-skinned Ghono held his arms out to the side. "It's not my fault!"

"Fuck it!" The "key major" tapped a button on his belt, and his face began to dissolve. An unpleasantly familiar orange-toned visage now glared back at the prisoners.

"Oh, shit," muttered Chuck and Jopp in unison.

Haaga ignored them and rushed to one of the helmeted agents who had been escorting them a moment earlier. He pulled a pistol from his belt and held it to the agent's temple. "How do we get out of here?"

"There's no other way. You might as well give up now."

Without a word, Haaga lowered the pistol and fired a round into the agent's foot. He screamed as he collapsed to ground, clutching at his wound. Haaga turned the weapon on the last helmeted agent. Before he could ask again the agent exclaimed, "You can go back past the cell block we got these prisoners from! Cut through the cafeteria cabin's kitchen and circle around the main hall!"

"Ghono! Toss these two in a cell!" Haaga called. The towering, scarred alien scooped up the two helmeted agents as if they were children and hurried back down the hall.

The muffled sounds of a riot reverberated against the still-locked door. Haaga turned to the remainder of the group. "Might as well ditch the holoskins."

Chuck followed his gaze to see that of the three originally unmasked agents, only one still bore the features of a tattooed, silver-skinned J'Kari. One of them had changed to the same rough orange hue as the leader, and the other's face bore a blue-and-white jigsaw pattern. The latter ran a hand through his thick blue hair. "What about them?" he asked while cocking his head to their prisoners.

Haaga stepped forward. "You do exactly what I tell you to. If any of you resist in the slightest, I will shoot out both your knees and have Ghono carry you." Then to his blue-haired associate: "Jorwei, you and Shuuja watch our back. We need to move, now!" As if to accentuate the point, an alarm began to blare.

They took off at a brisk pace, heading back the way they'd come. They turned down the hall where Chuck, Jopp, and Bhanakhana had been housed, and saw that every cell was empty. Well, almost every cell. Chuck's old cell now held two ULE agents. Ghono was waiting for them. He folded in alongside Haaga, and they continued on.

"I thought I only opened the cells on the main hall. Where are the inmates from this block?" whispered Haaga.

"No fucking clue," grumbled Ghono.

Chuck glanced back over his shoulder, catching grim looks from his friends. The group rounded another corner and made for the double doors that led to the cafeteria cabin. Without hesitation, Haaga and Ghono burst into the room.

"I think we found the other inmates," Ghono muttered.

The cabin was currently undergoing a thorough ransacking at the hands of the prisoners, who all froze when they saw the armed group. As if on cue, the doors at the opposite end of the cabin flew open, and a whirlwind of agents and more rioting inmates tumbled into the cafeteria. This prompted the food looters to go from a state of shock into utter chaos. Some tried to hide, some tried to run, and the rest decided to join the fray.

Haaga screamed, "Get to the kitchen!" and they began shooting their way toward the back of the galley. Inmates dropped left and right in their wake. Chuck saw the glowing yellow cloud envelop two other inmates. They immediately fell to the floor and began grasping at their necks. He heard a cry and looked back to see three of the reptilian Soreshi descend on the one agent who had not been wearing a holoskin. This was apparently of little concern to the others, as the other Ochrean and Jorwei made no attempt to save him, opting instead to prod Jopp and Bhanakhana forward. The door that led to the kitchen and escape from this madness was approaching fast. Chuck heard a cross between a growl and a squawk, and he looked to see the parrot-headed gorilla beast leaping through the air. Jorwei and the other Ochrean turned their weapons on him, but Chuck never saw what happened.

At that same instant, he was shoved to the ground with such force that it caused him to skid across the floor, coming to rest halfway underneath a table. The skid tore skin from his forearm, and he sucked in air as he saw the beading blood drop-lets. Chuck thought he must be going crazy, because he could have sworn it was Bhanakhana who pushed him. He pulled himself fully under the table and surveyed the carnage. In that sea of white scrubs, black uniforms, and blood, his friends were nowhere to be found. He saw a hulking creature—which may or may not have been made of millions of green leafy vines braided together—slam a ULE agent to the floor. This agent wasn't wearing a helmet, and her jet-black hair was splayed wildly about. Chuck saw her face, and his stomach dropped. It was Rohi, no question. She lay stunned on the floor as the vine beast reached for her rifle. Before Chuck knew what he was doing, he was on his feet, sprinting. The vine beast picked up the rifle. Chuck leapt clear over a table. The vine beast aimed the rifle down at Rohi. Chuck let out a guttural howl and dove through the air. His shoulder made contact with the midsection of the vine beast, and they went tumbling down together. When he'd come to a stop, Chuck rolled onto his back. He opened his eyes, and the last thing he remembered was a green leafy fist rushing toward him.

TEXT UNIT 0036

Chuck's eyes fluttered open. He looked up at a ceiling, white paneled with thin, bright lights arranged in rows. At least he thought that's what he was looking at. His mind felt quite foggy. Being on his back made sense; however, he found it odd that he lay in a bed rather than on the cold floor of a prison. His head rested on a pillow, and he glanced down to see a thin sheet draped across his lower half.

Chuck sat up too quickly and winced as a throbbing pain shot through his head. He tried to massage his temple, but his right hand only moved a few inches. He peered down to see that it was cuffed to the railing of the bed. A fresh bandage rested under his right eye, where the scary plant person had hit him.

He noticed a figure sitting nearby. He blinked a few more times, and the figure's features came into focus: jet-black hair that fell past the shoulders, smooth silver skin, and almond-shaped eyes glowing with an almost iridescent hue of lavender.

"Hello," said Rohi Kahpanova. She leaned forward in her chair. "How are you feeling?"

Chuck tried to raise his right hand, was reminded of the wrist restraint, then used his left hand to rub the back of his neck. "My head feels like Bhanakhana used it as a punching bag. Other than that, I think I'm okay."

He noticed a small bandage above her left eye. "So, uh, how are *you* feeling?"

She allowed the faintest hint of a smile. "Physically? I'll be just fine. Professionally? Mentally? Those are different stories."

"Where are we?"

"We're in the holding unit's med bay. You've been out for a while."

Chuck fought through the haze, trying to remember. "What happened? What about Jopp and Bhanakhana?"

Rohi's expression was grim. "They're gone."

"What?!"

"They escaped in your friend's ship during the riot."

"How?"

She sighed. "You saw it for yourself. That prick unlocked every single cell in the holding unit, unleashing three hundred and fourteen irate inmates. Every agent in the vicinity was too focused on quelling the chaos to give an apparent key major and his attaché much scrutiny."

Chuck wrestled with this information. "I just . . . I just don't see how they could've gotten away. I mean, you figured them out."

She shook her head. "All I figured out was some imposter in a holoskin was snooping around the confiscation vaults. I'm more confused than ever right now. They had real credentials. You can't fake those." She narrowed her eyes. "You know who they are, don't you?"

Chuck held his hands—well, just his left hand—up defensively. "I don't know anything about them, except they've been trying to kill us since Day One."

"They were the ones who attacked you in that town?"

Chuck nodded enthusiastically. "Yes!"

"And they were the ones Vice Director Kahpanova was helping?"

Chuck nodded, albeit much less enthusiastically. "Yes."

Rohi leaned back in her chair, crossing her arms. "Another thing that's bothering me about all this: one of the real agents killed in the riot wasn't even stationed here."

"Let me guess," Chuck injected. "It was the one killed in the cafeteria by those snake guys, the Sora-sheeny or something like that. He was like . . . like you."

She arched an eyebrow. "Like me?"

"I mean . . . you know . . ."

"Our kind is called J'Kari. And yes, the agent I'm referring to was killed by the *Soreshi* in the cafeteria cabin."

". . . with the candlestick," Chuck muttered to himself.

"What?"

His cheeks flushed. "Uh, never mind. Yeah, I, uh, think he was working with them."

She pursed her lips. "Yes, we realize that. What we can't discern is *why*. This guy was running a patrol detail two systems over. We have his ship in our hangar, and we have no idea as to the whereabouts of his squad."

They sat in silence for a few moments before Rohi leaned forward with a stern expression. "So, how about you tell me your story again. Only this time, you tell me the *full* version."

"Uh . . . um . . . I mean . . ."

Her expression was unwavering.

He sighed deeply and then recounted the series of events that had led up to now; except this time, he told her about the black case. By the time he had finished, she was glaring at him. Her eyes looked like a pair of purple bonfires.

"You should have told me about the case immediately," she huffed.

"I'm sorry," offered Chuck. "Bhanakhana said we shouldn't tell anyone until we knew more about what was going on."

"We aren't just *anyone*. We are the Bjor-damn Universal Law Enforcement. You should have said something!"

"Wait a second!" Chuck snapped back, his forceful timbre surprising not only Rohi but himself as well. "You said the imposters were in the evidence vault before coming to the holding cells!"

"So?"

"So, if I had told you about the case, you would have confiscated it. It would have been in the vault. They would have taken it and disappeared, leaving me and my friends stuck in jail; charged with murder. At least now you know we're telling the truth."

"Oh, sure, your friends are so much better off now," she shot back.

Chuck furrowed his brow and tried to cross his arms. Only his left arm was successful. His right stayed cuffed to the railing. He felt silly with just one arm draped across his chest and heaved a disgruntled sigh as he let it fall to his side.

Rohi's expression softened. "Look, I'm sorry. We've got over a hundred units dispatched. They so much as come near a civilized system, and we'll get them. An incident like this doesn't blow over easily with High Command. They're nothing if not a prideful lot."

Chuck nodded in assent.

"Is there anything else?" she asked. "Any little detail you can think of that might point us in the right direction? Anything out of the ordinary?"

"*Anything out of the ordinary*? My whole existence for the past three days has been *out of the ordinary*. I don't know what you expect me to . . ." Chuck paused and scratched his head. Rohi watched a flood of realization light his eyes up. He snapped his fingers and exclaimed, "Poe!"

"Huh?"

Chuck waved his hand in a circular motion, as if he was trying to remember something. "You know . . . Po or Yo or Zo or something like that! He, uh, runs the company . . . that we were working for . . . Prime Partners . . ."

Rohi raised her eyebrows and asked, "Do you mean Quo? As in Quo Agban Delanius Zarvinston XXIX, executive regent for Prime Partners Intergalactic Consortium? Is that who you mean?"

"Um, I guess so. . . ."

She stared at him incredulously. "Okay, Chuck from Earth, tell me how the wealthiest being in the known 'verse is involved in all this."

Chuck took a breath. "Well, I met him when they first picked us up on Earth, and I got the impression he wasn't too fond of Jopp."

"I can't imagine why," she said with a snort.

"He was there when we left, too. He had been on our ship. He came out, walked up to Jopp, and said something about 'personally' making sure everything was 'in order.'"

Rohi sat up straight in her chair. "That's like the most ominous statement I've ever heard. It just occurred to you now that he might have been involved?!"

Chuck shrugged as if to say *What do I know?*

Rohi sat back. "What in the hell have you gotten yourself into, Earth man?"

Chuck sighed. "So, what now?"

She stood up. "You just piled on a whole heap of dowfa shit. I need to go and discreetly sift through it."

"Ew."

Rohi chuckled. She took a step closer to the bed, and her fingers looked like they might graze Chuck's hand. At the last moment, she pulled back. If Chuck didn't know any better, he'd have thought she was blushing. She looked him the eye. "Thank you . . . for earlier. In the cafeteria cabin."

"Oh"—Chuck shrugged—"it was nothing."

She shook her head. "Launching yourself into a raging Herbling to save me was not nothing. Thank you."

She was halfway to the door before Chuck could say, "You're welcome."

TEXT UNIT 0037

Haaga Viim peered out the cube ship's viewscreen as the planet Roqua came into focus. To the overwhelming majority of the universe, Roqua was the literal definition of an outer-rim back-water. Ninety-nine percent of the planet was submerged under one gigantic ocean. Underwater mountain ranges with peaks that dared break the surface were all that passed for land on this planet. Haaga Viim ordered Bhanakhana to fly to one of these peaks. Bhanakhana complied without hesitation, as he had to all of Haaga's commands during this trip. The gun barrel held to the back of his head by Jorwei had seen to that.

The rocky peak they were approaching was so large it could have been a mountain in its own right. From the north, the rock face curved around in typical conical fashion. Bhanakhana couldn't make out any conceivable destination for the ship.

"Make your way around to the south side," commanded Haaga.

Bhanakhana swung the ship left to follow along the cliff face. Violent waves hammered at the bare brown stone. The ship continued around to the east side, and the mass of rock maintained its featureless theme. When the ship crested the southeastern curve, the rock face suddenly fell away. Bhanakhana nearly lost control of the ship when he saw what was looming in front of him. The southern side of the peak curved inward, forming a gigantic cove. It wasn't the cove itself that stunned Bhanakhana but rather what was sitting at the center of it.

Built into the cliff face, stretching maybe five miles wide and two miles high was a makeshift city. The word *makeshift* came to mind because there was apparently very little rhyme or reason to its layout. Some sections hugged the cliff tightly, while others branched far out above the churning waters below. Some structures were built from high-grade pressed metals, some were poured concrete, and some were even made of wood. At the city's summit, Bhanakhana saw a long rectangular tower, built from gleaming black obsidian. Most of the city was tightly packed together, the buildings forming an almost zipper-like pattern along the rock wall. He saw a massive dome, its pure white surface shaped like interlocking hexagons. It was offset from the rest of the city, connected by a narrow bridge that clung to the smooth stone wall. The city was very much alive, as there was an almost constant stream of ships flying in and out.

"Pa Tahae," uttered Jorwei in an almost affectionate tone.

Bhanakhana couldn't help himself. "Thief City? It actually exists?"

"You're lookin' at it," answered Jorwei. "But, uh, just shut up and keep flying," he added after catching a look from Haaga.

"Simply marvelous," Bhanakhana said to himself.

Haaga pointed him toward the center of the city. They flew over a line of snugly built shacks and found themselves hovering over an open-air platform. It was teeming with activity, a sea of people flowing underneath. Bhanakhana noticed rows of blue carts and wondered if this might be some sort of market or bazaar. He made a mental note that, were he so fortunate to survive this ordeal, he would definitely be back to study this "civilization."

Haaga indicated a gap between two large buildings. "Down there."

They flew the ship into the gap, which was actually an alley. The alley curved around the back of one of the buildings, and then curved again directly into the cliff face. When the ship turned, Bhanakhana could see that a small hidden cave had been carved into the rock. The cave was empty, except for the sharp angular silhouette of the *Pfraza*. Bhanakhana felt his stomach drop with dreadful recognition, as the cube ship's light glinted off the vessel's black armor. A flash of sparks drew his attention to one of the wings, where a pair of round white creatures were working on the damage done by one of Jopp's rockets.

"Set it down," ordered Haaga, and Bhanakhana obliged. As soon as all thrust engines had been powered down, Bhanakhana felt a prick in his neck. Then everything went dark.

TEXT UNIT 0038

A hand clasped tightly over Chuck's mouth, waking him from a very pleasant dream involving a hot tub and a certain silver-tinted woman. He opened his eyes and wondered if he was still dreaming because the very same woman was staring back at him.

"Rmhm?" he mumbled.

"Shhhhh!" she hissed. "Don't you know what this means?" She squeezed his mouth tighter.

"Smmrry."

She rolled her eyes and removed her hand. "Just be quiet, okay?"

Chuck nodded silently and watched as she unlocked his wrist from the bed railing. He sat up slowly and looked around the darkened med bay. He and Rohi were the only conscious people in the room. She held a finger to her lips with one hand and motioned for Chuck to follow with the other. They tiptoed their way past the sleeping and/or sedated inmates, through the door, and out into a dimly lit hallway.

Once she'd sealed the door, she spoke in a low, deliberate tone. "At the end of this hall is a supply closet. Inside is a ULE uniform. Put it on. I'll keep watch out here."

"What are you doing?" whispered Chuck.

"I'm breaking you out. I thought that was pretty clear," she rasped back.

"Why?"

"Because you have nice eyes. Are you seriously asking me this right now?"

"I just thou—"

"Get your ass in that closet and change."

Fifteen seconds later Chuck was in the storage closet staring at the featureless black uniform of a ULE agent. Forty-five seconds after that he was still staring at the uniform when a knock came at the door. He cracked it to see a frustrated glare.

"Are you done yet?"

"I have no idea where to even start," Chuck replied.

"Lava Pox! Move over." She pushed him back and slid inside the closet.

"Well, you can start by taking off your clothes," she ordered.

Chuck flushed pink. "Um, couldn't you, like, give me directions through the door?"

She responded through gritted teeth, "Take. Your. Clothes. Off."

Chuck sighed and removed his prison scrubs. This experience was quite different from how he'd imagined the first time being undressed with Rohi would be. He thought he caught her eyeing him discreetly, but it could have been in his head. She picked up the pelvic unit of armor, and handed it to him. "Just step into it. It'll adjust to you."

Chuck stepped into the armor unit as if he was putting on a pair of underwear, hot from the dryer. As soon as the black armored briefs reached his hips, they constricted to a snug yet comfortable size. Chuck wiggled his hips a little. "Hmmm, supportive."

Rohi rolled her eyes again. "Let's go."

Chuck slid on the other pieces of ULE armor: the thigh guards, the boots, the chest piece, the sleeves. Each one formed perfectly to its target body part. More surprising than the fit, as far as Chuck could tell, was that the suit seemed to be regulating his body temperature. He'd found the holding unit and med bay to be a tad on the cold side. Inside the suit, it was a comfortable seventy degrees. He nodded in approval. "Nice duds."

"Duds?" asked Rohi. She shook her head. "Never mind. I don't want to know." She shoved the smooth black helmet into Chuck's hands. "Put this on, and don't take it off unless I tell you to."

Chuck nodded.

"You are Second Lieutenant Kr'shur. Remember that."

Chuck snickered. "Lieutenant Kr'shur? Can my first name be W'sley?"

"What? No, it's Poff." She held up an ID card. "What's so funny?"

Chuck shook his head. "Nothing." He then slid on the helmet. He was surprised at how light it felt. The air in the hallway had tasted stale; inside the helmet it was fresh and smelled like . . . *Is that linen?* Chuck thought. A small display in the upper-left corner told him the temperature, the breathability of the air, and how many other ULE agents were in the immediate vicinity.

"This is a lot more comfortable than I thought it'd be."

"Oh, I'm so glad you like it," she snarked. "Now let's *go*."

They stepped out into the still-deserted hallway, and Chuck followed Rohi to the end. She paused at the door. "You ready?"

Chuck saluted. "Second Lieutenant Kr'shur at your service."

"What are you doing?" She was looking at his hand.

"Uh, saluting?"

"That's not how you salute."

Rohi reached out and closed Chuck's hand into a fist. Then she pushed his bent elbow into the side so Chuck's forearm was angled vertically. Finally she rotated his fist to make the palm face forward.

"That's how you salute."

Chuck looked at his fist, hovering a few inches from his cheek and then back at Rohi with an arched eyebrow.

"Fight the power?"

"What? You know what, never mind. Put your hand down. Don't salute. Don't do anything."

Chuck gave an exaggerated snap to attention. Rohi sighed. "I must be fucking insane."

She opened the door, revealing a circular vestibule. There was a desk along the right wall. The guard seated behind it looked like Jopp, albeit much pudgier. His head leaned against the wall, and his mouth hung open. Chuck knew sleeping on the job when he saw it. Rohi strolled right up and rapped forcefully on the desktop.

The guard snorted and woke with a start. "Oh! D.O. Kahpanova! I'm—I'm so sorry. . . . I . . ."

Rohi put on a smile so warm it could've melted a glacier. "Don't worry about it, Vrek. I know things have been stressful at home. The new baby is what, your sixth?"

"Seventh." He sighed. "And she simply will not sleep through the night."

Rohi patted his hand. "It's okay. I took the liberty of signing myself and the second lieutenant in already. We got a break in my case and needed to verify the intel with one of our more cooperative inmates. We didn't want to leave with you still asleep, in case anyone less understanding than us happened to drop by."

The guard wiped his forehead. "That's mighty tops of you, D.O. Thank you!" Then to Chuck: "Thanks to you as well, Lieutenant . . . Kr'shur, was it?"

Chuck gave a stiff nod. Rohi jumped in. "Well, okay then. We have a long night ahead of us following up on this lead. Have a good one, Vrek! Try drinking a cup of wahu. That helps me get through the all-nighters."

He smiled. "Will do, D.O. Have a good night."

Rohi and Chuck walked out of the room into another hallway.

"What if he hadn't been asleep?" asked Chuck once he was sure they were alone.

"Vrek always falls asleep."

"But, I mean, what if he hadn't? That's a pretty flimsy plan. . . ."

She shot him a look. "If you don't like my methods, I can always take you back. I'm sure you won't have a problem patching things up with your buddy, Jash."

Chuck might have strained his neck with how fast he shook his head. They passed through another series of hallways without any further conversation, nodding hello to the occasional passerby. The last door they went through led into a hangar.

Dozens of ships rested in three perfect rows. Chuck guessed the ships in the first row were fighters. They had compact, single-seater cockpits. Their wings were at least twice as wide as the ship was long and were replete with weaponesque adornment. The ships in the second row looked like tank-sized minivans. The ships in the third row looked like the ships in the first two rows had reproduced. All of them were the same dark charcoal with electric violet trim.

Chuck followed Rohi up to the two agents stationed behind a booth. Both were J'Kari, like Rohi. One was a male with a tattooed face, and he looked busy typing something into his console. The other was a female with matching symbols inked under each eye and black hair tied up in a tight bun. Chuck made a mental note to ask Rohi later what the deal was with her species' tattoos. He made another mental note to use more tactful phrasing when asking the actual question.

Rohi addressed the female, "How's your evening going, Xeli?"

She leaned heavily on her elbows. "Holy humpalope dung, Rohi. It's finally settling down. Every inspector squad looking to make a name for themselves has been through here demanding priority flight status. They all want to be the hero who catches the impostor agents, not to mention the escapees."

Rohi nodded casually. "Not surprising. This whole thing looks pretty bad for the agency. Whoever nails these yoks is going to look real good to High Command."

The agent rested her chin on her fist. "Come to think of it, I expected you to be the first one here. I mean, given your connection . . ."

Rohi donned a sly grin. "It's called investigating, Xeli. All those other thrust-heads aren't going to do anything but eat star dust. Why chase after them when I can figure out where they're going and get there first?"

Xeli beamed. "Always a step ahead, Rohi. That's why you'll be magistrate some day."

Rohi gave her a playful wave. "Oh, I doubt that, Xeli. But anyway, my officer here and I need to follow up on this lead. We need to sign out one of the orbital cruiser units."

Xeli leaned back and began typing, still grinning. "No problem. I've got a brand-new one that's all yours." After a couple more keystrokes she said, "You're all set in dock C117."

"Thanks, Xeli." Rohi turned to leave but stopped when she felt a hand placed on hers.

"Go get 'em," Xeli whispered with a wink. In that moment Chuck was eternally grateful that his face was hidden behind the helmet.

A noticeably flushed Rohi turned back to Chuck. "Let's go."

They hurried down the third row of ships until they reached dock C117 and found themselves looking up at one of the transport/fighter hybrid ships. A door opened on the side, and Chuck followed Rohi through a small antechamber and into the three-seater cockpit. Rohi took her place in the pilot's chair, while Chuck sat to her right. She placed her hands on the console, bringing the ship to life. They lifted off and made for the hangar exit. They stopped just before the transparent electro-mag barrier, which separated the pressurized hangar from the vacuum of space.

Rohi spoke into her commline. "Patrol unit requesting final clearance, authority of Division Officer Kahpanova. Flight Clearance Code 548125."

A synthesized voice responded, *"Clearance accepted. Proceed."*

Chuck felt himself pulled against the back of his chair as Rohi rocketed them forward.

After ten minutes of silent flying, Rohi said, "You can take the helmet off now, you know."

"I like it in here," mused Chuck. He saw the unamused expression on Rohi's face and added, "I actually don't know how to take it off."

"There's sort of an indentation behind each of your ears. Press your fingers into them at the same time."

Chuck felt around until he found the grooves and pushed his index fingers to them simultaneously. There was a hiss, and the helmet expanded. It slid easily over Chuck's head, and he placed it on the floor next to his chair. Rohi was giving him an odd look, and he was just about to ask why when he caught his reflection in the mirrored surface of the dormant console screens. The helmet had left his hair in considerable disarray: the right half was completely matted down, while the left was sticking out in all directions. Chuck ran a hand through the tangled mess. "So why did you do that?"

"Do what?" Rohi asked.

"Break me out."

She pressed a button and swiveled her chair to face him. "My job is to solve major crimes. For instance"—she gestured at Chuck—"the murder of a vice director is a pretty fucking major crime. Now, a lot of division officers only care about the numbers: their closing ratios. It would be so easy for me to sit back, let you get convicted, and tally another close. But here's my problem: I believe your crazy story."

"Thank you," offered Chuck.

"Don't thank me yet. Here's *your* problem: there's no solid evidence to support your story."

Chuck sat up. "That insanity back in the holding cells wasn't evidence enough?!"

Rohi shrugged. "An argument could easily be made they were your accomplices attempting to help you escape. Think about it."

"What? That's . . . but . . ." Chuck thought about it.

"See? We need to get real proof there's something else going on. And if we're lucky, save your friends in the process."

Chuck wasn't sure how he felt about the hierarchy of those goals. "So why do you care?"

"For one thing," Rohi responded, "it's not enough for me to just close cases. I do what I do because I like to stop assholes from carrying on with their assholery."

Well put, thought Chuck.

Her face darkened. "And I also want to take down the real people responsible for the vice director's death. I'm not saying I believe she was innocent. I don't know what caused her to get mixed up with the scum. What I do know is she did a hell of a lot of good for a lot of people. And I don't believe one or two bad mistakes erase all the good someone's done. She deserves justice, too."

Also well put.

After a quiet two minutes, Chuck cleared his throat. "So . . . uh . . . you and Zelly, huh?"

Rohi's face pinched. "Xeli and I had one 'encounter' some years ago. Let's just leave it at that."

"Hey, that's cool. I just didn't know you were . . ." He trailed off.

Rohi was calm but direct. "You didn't know I was what?"

"You know . . ."

"No, I don't know." She cocked her head to the side.

"That you're a . . . a . . . ," Chuck stammered.

"Spit it out, already."

"You're gay."

Rohi burst out laughing. Chuck felt every ounce of blood in his body sprint to his cheeks. She settled herself and wiped a tear from her eye. "Wow, Earth man, I knew your kind was behind the times, but c'mon! You mean to tell me your people still put sexuality in basic boxes like homo- and heterosexual?"

Chuck was at a loss for words. She gave him a look like one would give a puppy who didn't realize what they'd done wrong. "It's all just chemical reactions, you know? Just because I was attracted to a female J'Kari yesterday doesn't mean I won't be attracted to a male Puzuru today. You get it?"

Chuck nodded. They sat for another minute or so in quiet, before a wry smile spread across Chuck's face. "So does that mean you really do think I have nice eyes?"

She glared at him and grumbled, "I should've made you keep the helmet on."

TEXT UNIT 0039

Haaga Viim stared down at Jopp and Bhanakhana. They sat with their wrists bound, and a taut cord tethered the restraints to the chairs, forcing their hands to rest in their laps.

"Where is the case?" he asked.

When his question was met with silence, he looked to the men at his side and nodded. Without a word Ghono stepped forward and drove his bulky crimson fist into the center of Bhanakhana's abdomen. He let out a pained grunt, and his head bobbed.

"Hey," Jopp began to protest, but was interrupted by Jorwei saying hello by way of his knuckles. Jopp's head snapped to the right, a slim gash opening under his left eye.

"Fuuuuuck!" gasped a wincing Jopp. "Why do you have to be such a dick?"

Jorwei shut him up with a backhand slap.

"Where is the case?" Haaga asked a second time. Bhanakhana remained silent save for some heavy breathing.

"We sold it for a case of Froth and an evening with two lovely Venovan escorts," quipped Jopp. This earned him and

Bhanakhana a quick succession of punches to their heads and stomachs. Haaga waved a hand, and wheezing and coughing replaced the sound of flesh striking flesh.

Jopp spat out a gob of purple blood. "All right, all right! You got us! We buried the case in the desert back on that Gorthan dustbowl. Take us back, and I'll show you where it is."

Haaga looked Jopp straight in the eye. "Where is the case?"

Jopp glared up at him. "I left it at your mother's house, after she made me breakfast."

Haaga looked to his side and nodded. Ghono stepped forward and yanked up on Jopp's left antenna, eliciting a sharp yelp. A humming white blade with a bright blue edge appeared in his other hand. It disappeared from Jopp's view, and a moment later he let out an agonizing howl. Ghono stepped back again; in one hand he held the blade, now stained purple, and in the other he held the top half of Jopp's left antenna. His eyes met Jopp's, and he smirked as he dropped the two inches of yellow flesh to the floor, squishing it under his boot. Jopp's breath was coming in short, painful gasps. His skin paled.

"I now remember your identity."

Four sets of eyes turned to Bhanakhana, who sat up straight. He fixed a hard gaze on Ghono. "You are Ghongorus Non Ghoy, Scourge of Shworzen, Shame of the Dronla."

Ghono gave a dramatic flourish with his knife-wielding hand and bowed. "You are correct. Although I never cared for that last moniker. In my opinion, it is weak-minded saps like you who are the true shame of our kind."

"You butchered dozens of innocents."

"More like hundreds, and they weren't that innocent."

"Enough!" boomed Haaga. Ghono nodded and stepped back, a faint grin still visible at the corners of his mouth. Haaga leaned close to Bhanakhana. "Either you tell me where the case

is this instant, or I have him"—he tilted his head at Ghono—
"continue to remove pieces of your little friend here."

Bhanakhana glanced at Jopp, who was staring at him with
pleading bloodshot eyes. He turned back to Haaga. "You will
need to release me from this chair. The location is bio-locked."

Haaga stepped back and drew his pistol, leveling it casually at Bhanakhana's chest. He glanced at Jorwei and nodded
in Bhanakhana's direction. Jorwei approached and untethered
Bhanakhana's restraints from the chair. He stood up to his
full height. Haaga had to look up to meet his eyes. "If you try
anything . . ."

"You will kill me," Bhanakhana finished. "Yes, I believe you
have made that concept quite clear." Haaga's pistol followed
Bhanakhana as he walked across the room. When he had just
about made it to the far corner, he paused and turned back
around.

"I will need him as well," he said, indicating Jopp with his
bound hands. "Both our bio-signatures are required to open
the compartment."

Haaga's expression was grim. "Oh, you just remembered
that now?"

Bhanakhana's expression was unflinching. "I must have
suffered a momentary lapse in memory, due to the duress of
our current situation. Please forgive me."

Ghono said, "No problem. Which finger do you need? I'll
toss it over."

Bhanakhana was unfazed. "I employ Vita Tech bio-locks.
Necrotic flesh will not activate them."

Haaga shot Ghono a look that said *shut up* in a thousand
languages. To Jorwei, he nodded in Jopp's direction. After
unlocking Jopp's restraints, Jorewei pulled him to his feet and
pushed him in Bhanakhana's general direction. Jopp staggered
his way across the room, wincing in pain. Bhanakhana knelt

down in the corner, facing away from the rest of the room. Jopp joined him and whispered hoarsely, "What the fuck are you doing?"

Bhanakhana rasped back, "Press you finger to the panel. Be ready to close your eyes, cover your ears, and run."

"How the hell are we supposed to cover our ears?" He rattled his wrist restraints.

"Is there a problem?" sounded Haaga's voice from behind them.

"Not at all," called Bhanakhana as he pressed on the floor panel, causing it to slide open. Sitting inside the compartment was the case. Jopp watched as Bhanakhana reached in and palmed a small metal cylinder in one hand before grabbing the case handle in the other. He gave Jopp a meaningful look, stood up, and turned around. Jopp followed suit. Their captors' eyes lit up when they saw the case clutched in Bhanakhana's fist. Bhanakhana and Jopp began to walk toward them. They were about halfway when Jopp heard Bhanakhana calmly say, "Now."

Jopp had barely a second to close his eyes before the room exploded in a flash of brilliant light. His vision was a blur, and his hearing was filled with a painful ringing, but he remembered to run. He made out the vague features of a massive red figure wearing white clothes in front of him, and he followed it like a compazz star. They twisted and turned through the hallways of the cube ship, and just when Jopp felt his vision clearing, he was momentarily blinded by the sun as they burst outside. He no longer felt the reverberating clang of his boots on metal but rather the dull slapping of his boots on cement. The ringing in his ears started to fade and was quickly replaced by angry curses and shouts. They sprinted around a corner and found themselves in a bustling market square. Bhanakhana seemed to be on hiatus from his strict sense of manners as he bowled through the crowd, though Jopp thought he heard a few *Pardon me*s and *So sorry*s.

The crack of a mecha rifle tore through the air, causing the market patrons to panic and flee. Jopp risked a look over his shoulder and saw Haaga, Jorwei, Ghono, and the other orange-skinned alien shoving their way through the crowd. Even though they were a good fifty yards behind, Jopp could easily make out the rage on their faces. He faced forward in time to see Bhanakhana turn down another alleyway, and he followed. This alley was long, narrow, and completely deserted. The over-hanging roofs of the bordering buildings blocked out the sun, accentuating the rectangle of light at the end of the alley. They were almost to the end when the crack of another rifle shot echoed off the walls. Jopp saw the case fly from Bhanakhana's hand and clatter onto the concrete. He looked back to meet the fiery stares of their pursuers, now only thirty-some yards away. He must have been looking back a lot longer than he thought because he tripped over the fallen case, causing him to tumble into a now-stationary Bhanakhana.

More specifically, Jopp collided with the back of Bhanakhana's knees, causing them to buckle, spilling them both over the ledge at the end of the alley. After a short fall, they slammed into one of the many sloped awnings and out-croppings that zigzagged across Pa Tahae's face. This one was comprised of a smooth and flimsy metal, offering no purchase. The pair promptly slid off the edge and fell a few feet before hitting the next one. This process—the thud of the landing, the scrambling and scratching for a grip, the cursing from Jopp as they fell again—repeated itself another half dozen times. They finally landed with a thump on a wooden, cloth-latticed roof. Other than the duo's groans and grunts, everything was silent.

"What the fuuuuuuck . . . ," moaned Jopp as he sat up.

"What the fuck indeed," muttered Bhanakhana from his prone position.

Jopp raised an eyebrow. "Did you just curse, Big Red? You must be spending too much time with me."

"Much to my dismay, I must concur."

"Ah, you know you love me," teased Jopp. Before Bhanakhana could retort, the roof began to creak and shudder.

"Oh, you've got to be shi—" was all Jopp could utter before the roof gave way with a tremendous snap.

They landed in a pile of splintered wood, torn cloth, and dust. When everything was calm, they sat up to look around. The room was dark and dusty, and the scent of burning metal lingered in the air. Bits and pieces of various electronic devices littered the surface of a workbench to Jopp's right. He saw Bhanakhana staring intently ahead. Jopp's eyes followed the stare, and he was startled when he saw a face leering back at them.

Reclining on a vibrating lounge couch barely ten feet away from them was a rather portly Bogtek. His sickly green skin flowed in flabby rolls down his bare arms. His globe of a gut strained against the fabric of his tank top. Resting on his chest was the first of his four chins. The corners of his arch-shaped mouth were turned up in a smirk, forming something of a mis-shapen W. His tiny nose was turned almost perfectly upward, giving Jopp an excellent view of his nasal passage. Two large, circular eyes rested below a heavy brow. The top of his head boasted only a few wispy hairs. Small pointed ears poked out from behind his chubby cheeks. He looked from Jopp to Bhanakhana then back to Jopp, seemingly eyeing their wrist restraints and white prison scrubs. He smacked his lips a few times and said in a deep, spittle-filled voice, "Dis outta be good."

TEXT UNIT 0040

Chuck had been to New York once as a kid. His father had some big conference there, and his mother had somehow convinced the esteemed Dr. Higgins to let the wife and child tag along. Chuck's mom had taken him to all the standard tourist locales: the Statue of Liberty, Times Square, Central Park . . . but the one image that really stuck with young Chuck was the city skyline. He remembered the sheer awe at beholding such a towering mass of concrete and steel. He thought about that now as he stared at the megalopolis known as Pa Nui.

New York was a one-horse town compared to the chromatic conglomeration that rose up before them. Pa Nui was a city without a planet. Technically, it was a space station—a space station the size of a small planet, or a large moon, depending on who you asked. The city looked like an enormous sphere had been sliced through the middle. Where the top half of the sphere should have been stood about a thousand tightly packed skyscrapers, each one draped in elaborate neon light.

"Holy shit," gasped Chuck.

Rohi grinned. "Yeah, Pa Nui can have that effect the first time you see it. Two hundred million sentient residents. Another fifty million passing through on any given day. Drink it in, Earth man."

As they approached, Chuck noticed dozens of rigid tentacles branching out from the city's midsection. When they got closer, he saw that the "tentacles" were actually lines of ships queued up to enter the city.

Rohi noticed Chuck's gaze and chuckled. "Rush hour."

She flipped a switch, and the lights outside their patrol cruiser started flashing.

"One of the perks of this job," she quipped as they sped past the waiting ships.

If the spaceship gridlock was any indication, they had entered a main thoroughfare. Chuck looked up toward the tops of the nearby skyscrapers. His view was hindered by a honeycomb of tubes that ran between the buildings. Animated billboards coated the walls along the thoroughfare. He saw ads for Flanisi Ale and that bacon-flavored food, Rzackio. He recognized the Prime Partners logo above a smiling alien family with the slogan "Bettering the Future, One System at a Time!" His eye lingered a bit on the image of a scantily clad woman with long yellow hair and powder-blue skin. The ad read "Venova's Finest."

"See something you like?" commented Rohi.

Chuck felt embarrassed for half a second, but then steeled himself and responded with a nonchalant "Maybe."

Rohi raised her eyebrows but had no audible response. She turned onto a side passage.

"So you think this is where they took them?" asked Chuck.

Rohi shook her head. "I doubt we're that lucky. Your friend's Estal Cube is on the top of the ULE watch list. It won't get anywhere near the city perimeter without an alert going out. They need to dump the cube as soon as possible."

"So why did we come here?"

"We've got a lead with that Prime Partners executive scrogbag and his ominous comments. What's good about it is someone as high profile as him won't be hard to find. What's bad about it is someone as high profile as him is essentially untouchable without indisputable evidence, which we don't have. We need to catch him in the act."

Chuck nodded.

Rohi inhaled deeply. "The other problem we have is that if Quo really is behind all this, the hired help will likely tie up all loose ends prior to our meeting him."

"And by *loose ends* you mean Jopp and Bhanakhana," added Chuck.

Rohi's silence answered his question. She turned them onto another wide pathway. Chuck decided he wasn't done with the conversation. "Why exactly are we here?"

Rohi paused for a minute, then took a breath and replied, "You remember what I said about assholes?"

"Prevent the assholery," answered Chuck.

"Right. So, you see, sometimes I'm forced to let an asshole continue his assholery in order to stop a bigger asshole from carrying on with bigger assholery."

"We're meeting an informant?"

Rohi shrugged. "Something like that, but don't use that word in front of him."

She turned them into the airlock of a bright-green high-rise. Once the bay door sealed behind them, she landed the ship and powered down. Then she got up. "Just follow my lead and, as usual, say as little as possible."

Chuck stood up to follow, reaching for his helmet.

"Leave it," she ordered. "He doesn't like covered faces."

"Who is *he*?" Chuck asked, but Rohi was already on her way out the door. He hurried after her. They exited the ship and found themselves looking up at two rather large individuals. Both stood at least six and a half feet tall and were damn near as wide across. One was a hulking Aviape, his gorilla-like body topped with a head that reminded Chuck of the bird from that one cereal—the one with the loops that taste like fruit. What was it called?

Chuck flinched out of his daydream when his eyes fell on the other individual. The leaf-and-vine coated visage of a Herbling peered back at him. Chuck instinctively scratched at the cut under his eye. They were wearing what Chuck could only assume was this society's version of a suit. Except for a little extra shine, the pants weren't too different from a nice pair of slacks. Their suit jackets didn't button down the middle, but rather the right flap extended across their chests and fastened in a seam that ran down the left breast and abdomen. The Aviape's suit was dark gray with silver pinstripes that ran diagonally. The Herbling's suit was black with a lime-green pinstripe that ran in a more traditional vertical pattern.

Rohi threw on that scorching smile. "Hi, boys!"

"Whadda ya want, Law Cog?" squawked the Aviape.

"Oh, c'mon, Nudd. You know he's expecting me," she responded playfully.

Nudd nodded at Chuck. "Who's dis guy?"

Rohi gave a casual wave in Chuck's general direction. "Oh, him? He's just my new trainee. Don't worry; he's in the orbit."

Nudd looked at the Herbling, who pulled out a mobile commline and turned around. He took a few steps away from them; Chuck couldn't hear anything but a few unintelligible mumbles. The Herbling put the commline back in his pocket and turned back. He nodded to Nudd, who in turn nodded to Rohi. "Okay, he'll see ya."

They led Chuck and Rohi out of the airlock and up a wide, sloping hallway. They passed through an archway, and for the umpteenth time in the past few days, Chuck found himself dumbstruck with what he was seeing. The ceiling was at least three stories high and supported by rows of thick gold columns. In between them and the far side of the room, which Chuck couldn't even see, frothed a sea of activity. Hundreds of small crowds clustered around flashing tables. He recognized a gridspar match in full swing. Somewhere a siren sounded, followed by a raucous cheer. He saw stacks of colorful cards being pushed around the tables.

"It's a casino," Chuck mused aloud.

Nudd chortled. "Ya gots a real inspectah on ya hands here, Law Cog."

Rohi gave Chuck the *shut up* look he was becoming all too familiar with. They followed their hosts along the wall, circumventing the controlled chaos of the gaming tables. Eventually, they came to a bank of gold-plated elevators. There were six doors on each side and one at the end, which was guarded by another large, besuited Herbling. He pressed the call button as they approached. The gold doors slid open, and Chuck, Rohi, Nudd, and the first Herbling stepped onto a circular platform. They began to ascend.

After rising five or six stories, the gold-and-beige elevator walls disappeared, revealing the bright pulsing cityscape. It was all Chuck could do to hold back a gasp as the neighboring buildings fell below them. Higher and higher they climbed, their glass tube illuminated by the surrounding lights.

When they finally came to a stop, Chuck could see the rooftop of every skyscraper in their immediate vicinity. The elevator doors opened, and they stepped into an extravagantly decorated foyer. Crystal-clear water poured from the cup of a beautiful stone-carved, two-headed humanoid woman into the pool at her feet. Two elegant couches flanked the fountain, their spiraling gold frames seeming to defy the laws of physics. Plants unlike anything Chuck had ever seen lined the walls. A tall pair of doors occupied the wall space directly across from them. They looked to have been hewn from a dark and rich type of wood. Concentric circles had been carved into the surface, like unending ripples on water. Nudd and his comrade led them up to the doors and gave them two firm knocks.

An unseen voice ordered, "Pwoceed within."

Nudd pushed one of the doors open and indicated that Rohi and Chuck should enter. They passed the threshold and entered a room that made the antechamber look dull by comparison. Green marbled stone covered the walls. Two thin sheets of water fell along the stone into narrow troughs. The troughs formed something of a river that not only ringed the whole room but also zigzagged its way across the floor. This series of narrow rivers divided the room into a handful of white marble islands. Tiny bridges connected the "islands" over the trickling water. Half of the island landings housed large detailed sculptures. The running theme looked to be barely dressed women from a variety of alien races. An unnecessarily wide stone desk with a figure seated behind it took up space on the far side of the room. Chuck followed Rohi over the small bridges toward the desk. As they moved forward, Chuck's eye was drawn to the view behind the desk. The entire back wall was a single pane of glass. He could see the glow of the city stretch for miles.

They got closer, and some movement pulled Chuck's focus to the desk itself. Green, blue, and white shapes swirled against a dark backdrop, seemingly moving within the physical material of the desk. He'd seen this before, in the conference room on the Prime Partners cruiser. Chuck and Rohi came to a stop next to a pair of green marble chairs sitting in front of the desk.

Chuck tore his gaze away from the desk and was startled when he saw the figure seated behind it. For a split second, Chuck thought he was looking at a human. Upon closer inspection, he saw that the individual was definitely not human. He had narrow shoulders, and even under his gold-and-green-checkered bathrobe, Chuck could tell he had bony arms. His leathery skin was a deep mahogany with an oily shine. His nose was round, and he sported a droopy pair of jowls. A curly brown mustache blanketed his upper lip. He had a bulbous head with two tufts of brown hair along the sides. Where his ears should have been protruded two short nodes. His eyes were hidden behind circular, orange-tinted glasses that sat below bushy brown eyebrows. Chuck's parents once had a time-share in the Bahamas, and he thought about all the retirees who'd seemingly been obsessed with turning themselves into burned raisins. This guy would fit in nicely with that crowd.

"Hello, Mr. Brondo," cooed Rohi.

More like Mr. Bronze-o, thought a quite pleased-with-himself Chuck.

"Division Officer Kahpanova. It is a pweasure to see you. Won't you and your fwend have a seat?" Mr. Brondo gestured to the white chairs. Rohi sat, and Chuck followed suit.

Mr. Brondo looked Chuck up and down. "You are fwom Earth, are you not?"

Rohi jumped in. "Well, yes, you see it's part of—"

Mr. Brondo cut her off by raising his hand. "Division Officer Kahpanova, I bewieve I was speaking to your fwend." He clasped his hands together and made a show of facing himself directly toward Chuck.

Chuck looked to Rohi, who could only shrug and give an encouraging nod. He looked back to Mr. Brondo. "That is correct. I am from Earth."

"I was unaware that Earth had been invited to join the Sentient Coawition. I must wepwace my powitical contacts with more wewiable sources."

Rohi opened her mouth, but Mr. Brondo's outstretched palm silenced her. He stared at Chuck expectantly. Chuck felt a bead of sweat form on his brow. He cleared his throat. "Well, uh, you see, Earth is not officially part of the Coalition. I'm part of an experimental . . . task force. The, uh, Coalition reached out to a select group of the most highly intelligent Earth apes—I mean, *people*—and recruited us."

Mr. Brondo leaned forward. "To what end?"

"Well . . . no criminal in the universe would suspect an Earth ape to be investigating for the ULE. They'd never see it coming." Chuck glanced at Rohi. Her expression was blank.

Mr. Brondo stroked his chin. "So tell me, Agent Earth Man, why have I seen your face pwastered all over the news of wate?"

Chuck had nothing to say to that. Rohi attempted to join in. "I can offer clarity on that, if you are agreeable to it."

Mr. Brondo turned to her. "I am always agweeable."

Rohi smiled warmly. "Of course you are. What you have been witnessing play out in the news is this new campaign in action. Our new agent here was able to ingratiate himself with the criminals suspected of murdering a ULE vice director."

Mr. Brondo raised his eyebrows. "I would never expect an Earth man capable of such things."

"That's exactly why the program will work. That is, as long as you can prevent yourself from sharing that informational tidbit with your network of friends," she added.

"Pewish the thought," exclaimed Mr. Brondo before quickly changing the subject. "So, Agent Earth Man! I noticed you wooking at my desk pweviouswy. Authentic storm stone is vewy ware and expensive, but I bewieve a specimen as beautiful as this is worth the pwice. Wouldn't you agwee?"

Rohi decided it was time to take the reins. "Mr. Brondo, as much as I'm sure my associate and I would enjoy discussing the latest trends in office decor, I'm afraid I must insist we keep to business."

Mr. Brondo looked disappointed for a moment before offering a bright smile. "But of course! How may I be of assistance?"

"Well, as we just mentioned, my associate and I are trying to solve the murder of a ULE vice director. As you might expect, it is important we make an example of the perpetrators."

"Certainwy," agreed Mr. Brondo, "wetting twansgwessions go unpunished is no way to maintain one's power . . . or so I've been told."

Rohi nodded. "Our sentiments exactly. But the thing is, we've hit a little snag."

Mr. Brondo leaned back and twirled his mustache. Rohi continued, "There was an inmate riot in my frigate's holding unit yesterday. It resulted in the deaths of three agents, and our suspects escaped in the process."

"How embawassing for you."

Rohi shrugged off the comment. "Yes, it was. They escaped in a late-model Estal Cube. By now they've assuredly gone into hiding."

Mr. Brondo placed a palm to his chest. "And you think I know where they might be?"

Rohi gave him a hard stare. "I think if you don't know already, you know someone who does. I also think you owe me one after the Shankil incident."

Mr. Brondo pressed his fingertips together pensively and furrowed his brow. "You weawize if I do this for you, it will bawance the scales. You wish to use your one favor to aid your Earth man?"

Rohi looked at Chuck, then back to Mr. Brondo. "Yes."

He slapped his palms on the desk. "Vewy well! Pwease enjoy a compwimentawy dwink in the Moon Bar. I will have your information in a few short hours."

TEXT UNIT 0041

Chuck put the frigid bottle of Flanisi Ale to his lips and drank deeply. He set the bottle down and let out a satisfying *ahhh*.

Rohi's disapproving stare was quite clear, despite the Moon Bar's dim lighting.

"What?"

"How can you drink at a time like this?"

"Why wouldn't I?"

She spread her hands. "I don't know. Maybe because you're an escaped fugitive impersonating an agent and suspected for the murder of a high-ranking ULE commander. Or maybe because in three days, when my activity logs are audited, they're going to figure out it was me who broke you out. Or maybe because our one and only shot at saving your friends hinges on an eccentric psychopath."

Chuck picked his beer back up. "From where I'm sitting, you pretty much just summed up every reason why we *should* be drinking."

As if on cue, their waitress, a short buxom Yoblon with lilac hair spiking out from her yellow scalp, stopped by. "Can I get youse two anythin' else?"

Chuck shook his bottle. "I'll take another one of these." He smiled at Rohi. "Anything for you?"

She rolled her eyes. "Fine. I'll have the . . . meteortini."

The waitress beamed. "Shor thing, sweets."

"What's in a meteortini?" asked Chuck.

Rohi shrugged. "Alcohol, I hope." She slumped back into the booth. "You did well back there with Mr. Brondo. Coming up with that task force idea . . . good thinking."

Chuck scratched the back of his neck. "Yeah, thanks. I've always had a bit of a knack for bullshitting."

Rohi's face screwed up in confused disgust. "For *what*?"

"For bullshitting. What's that look for? Oh! Never mind, it's just an Earth term for, like, making up stuff off the top of your head."

Rohi's face relaxed. "Ohhhh. Okay, it's like piss-mouthing."

"Um, sure."

Their waitress returned with the drinks. Chuck received another frosty bottle, and Rohi was given some fluorescent blue concoction. He held his up. "Cheers?"

"I don't hear any cheers," said a perplexed Rohi.

Chuck smiled. "No, it's an Earth thing. We clink our glasses together. It's supposed to bring good luck or something." He furrowed his brow. "Now that I think about it, I have no idea why we do it."

Rohi smiled. "Well, here's to your strange Earth customs." She slammed her glass into Chuck's bottle. He was surprised neither one cracked.

"Youse two make such a cute couple. Youse reminds me of me an' my Zonny, back when we was first datin'."

Chuck and Rohi turned to the waitress, who was leaning against the table. Before they could correct her, she patted the table and said, "Enjoy them drinks, okay? Let me know iffin youse need anything else."

The next few moments passed awkwardly, with Chuck drumming his fingers on the table and Rohi studying her beverage intently. Finally, Chuck couldn't bear the silence. "So, uh, Mr. Brondo is an interesting guy."

"You could say that."

"What'd you call him a minute ago? Eccentric psychopath? I mean, he's weird . . . but I got a pretty harmless vibe from him."

Rohi raised an eyebrow. "Then you need to fix whatever part of your anatomy senses these *vibes*. Mr. Brondo is a remorseless killer."

"Then why are you friends with him?"

"I'm not his fucking friend. I know this whole thing is still new to you, but try to fathom what it entails to run an agency responsible for protecting hundreds of billions of beings. Order is our greatest ally and chaos is our worst fear. Mr. Brondo is a not a good guy, but there is an order to the way in which he conducts his business. Now don't get me wrong. I would love to book him an extended visit in Helon Prison. The guy's probably had over a hundred people dusted, but every single one was 'of the criminal element,' so to speak."

"So you're fine letting a mass murderer run wild?"

"As long as he sticks to killing his fellow scrogbags, you're damn right I'm fine with it. I've saved a lot of civilian lives with intel from him. I have no problem sleeping at night, so you can keep your judgments to yourself."

Chuck leaned in. "Holy shit, that's why you're really here."

"What are you talking about?"

"You think your aunt . . . er . . . the vice director might have been doing the same thing: only pretending to be crooked."

Rohi's expression hardened. "So what if I am? She was family, my mentor, my idol. So what if I want to know for sure what happened to her?"

Chuck was saved from having to respond to that by the arrival of the Herbling bodyguard. He jerked a leafy thumb, indicating they should follow him.

***

They were back in Mr. Brondo's office, where he was enjoying something from a glass chalice. It was filled with a dull orange liquid with tendrils of smoke crawling over the rim. He took a long, loud sip from a straw before pushing it aside. "So, my new Earth fwend, did you enjoy the Moon Bar's wibations?"

"Uh, yes . . . yes, I did. Thank you very much."

Mr. Brondo waved a hand dismissively. "'Twas nothing." He indicated the drink on his desk. "Have you ever twied a Wugnum Twist? We extwact the juices from onwy the fweshest wugnum egg sacs."

Chuck tried not to gag. Rohi interjected, "Mr. Brondo, while we have greatly appreciated your hospitality, we need to move on to business. Were your sources able to tell you anything helpful?"

He made a show of turning his head to face her. "My sources ahways pwovide helpful information."

He took what Chuck felt was a wholly unnecessary pause before saying, "Wocating a single ship in the whole of the universe is essentiawy impossible, even for my extensive sources."

Chuck's face fell. Rohi narrowed her eyes skeptically. Mr. Brondo continued, "Tell me, Division Officer Kahpanova, what do you know of Pa Tahae?"

She raised an eyebrow skeptically. "Pa Tahae? It's a myth."

Mr. Brondo giggled. "I assure you, Pa Tahae is vewy weal."

"And that's where they are?"

Mr. Brondo showed his palms. "I cannot say whether they are there or not. I can onwy say that wecentwy there was something of a stir in one of the marketpwaces. My wocal contact spoke with the vendors in this marketpwace. They say the twouble was caused by a Yobwon and a Dwonwa, both wearing white pwison scwubs. Intewesting, no?"

Chuck was on his feet. "We have to go."

Mr. Brondo held a hand up. "Not so fast, my wittle swice of Earth cake." He turned back to Rohi. "Weveawing the wocation of Pa Tahae to a Universal Waw Enforcement agent could be vewy wisky for me. If I give you the coordinates, the scales will have tipped in my favor. Are you agweeable to this?"

Rohi gave Chuck a hard stare and then looked at Mr. Brondo. "Agreed." She stood up next to Chuck.

"How are you pwanning to get there?" Mr. Brondo asked.

"We have a ship," answered Rohi.

He giggled again. "You cannot go to Pa Tahae in a Universal Waw Enforcement ship. And you certainwy cannot walk awound dwessed like that."

"What did you have in mind?" she asked apprehensively.

Mr. Brondo answered in the form of an extended giggling fit.

TEXT UNIT 0042

Chuck looked with awe at the makeshift medley that comprised . . . his outfit. The cuffs of his baggy mustard-colored pants were tucked into clunky magenta boots with thick jagged soles. An oversized buckle shaped like the skull of some unfamiliar alien fastened the belt that held up his pants. His matching mustard-yellow T-shirt fit much tighter than the pants. His jacket made him feel like he should be riding a Harley instead of a spaceship. It was a shade of gold so dark it was almost brown, and the trim matched the bright magenta of his boots. He scratched at the freshly shaven sides of his scalp. Chuck had always wanted a mohawk but had been too insecure to try it out.

We must certainwy do something about that scwuffy-wooking hair, Mr. Brondo had said.

Who's scruffy looking?! a grinning Chuck had replied, amusing no one.

Mr. Brondo had been downright obsessive about the way Chuck and Rohi looked before deigning to give them the coordinates. *It is cwitical that no one knows you are affiwiated with Universal Waw Enforcement,* he had said.

Chuck didn't mind. In fact, he thought he looked pretty cool. Rohi, on the other hand, had been visibly annoyed through the whole process. He glanced over at her as she flew them into Roqua's atmosphere. Her boots were similar to his, except they were a brilliant shade of green. Chuck had dated an art major briefly in college; she would have called the color something like harlequin or chartreuse. Stemming from the boots was a pair of black leggings that looked almost painted on. They flowed seamlessly into a tight black sleeveless shirt. The matching jacket rested on the empty seat to her left. It was Mr. Brondo's idea for her hair that had really pissed Rohi off. But Chuck admired the streaks of bright green that ran through her sea of black locks.

She caught Chuck's stare and snapped, "What are you looking at?"

Chuck quickly looked away. "Oh, uh, nothing. . . . I'm just . . . disoriented from the anomaly jump." He wasn't. In fact, he was starting to enjoy the odd sensation the jumps brought on. It was like going over a big drop on a roller coaster; the first few times, that sinking feeling you get in your stomach is terrifying. Then, after you get over the fear, you start to enjoy the rush.

Chuck avoided her glare by studying the interior of the cockpit. A fine layer of dust coated every surface of their borrowed ship's interior.

At least the outside has some character, thought Chuck. The ship had, at one time, been quite nice. That was before some, to quote Rohi, *wannabe gangster punk* had decided to "customize" it by attaching a few dozen frivolous spikes and slathering five different hues of red paint to the exterior. The ship had found its way into Mr. Brondo's possession when the aforementioned punk had gotten in too deep at the gaming tables.

Rohi brought the ship in at a low angle and skimmed along the water. The white light of the local sun made the surface of Roqua's ocean look like a field of blue diamonds. Chuck played with the console in front of him, scrolling through the various viewscreen angles: nothing but blue ocean to the front, blue ocean to the right, blue ocean to the left, blue ocean to the rear. . . .

"What the hell is that?" he mused aloud. It looked as if five small objects were trailing them, cutting through the water in a perfect *v* formation.

"What the hell is what?" asked Rohi.

"Check the rear view," answered Chuck.

She tapped a couple of icons on her own console to bring up the screen. Chuck continued to stare as the five objects began to slowly rise out of the water. The objects were tall, very narrow, and seemed to curve slightly backward, which was allowing them to slice through the water quite rapidly. Chuck saw a large oblong shadow rising underneath the objects.

"Oh, shit," muttered Rohi.

"What is it?" asked Chuck, but she ignored him. He looked back to his console in time to catch light glinting off the objects. More specifically, he caught light glinting off the pink scales of the objects.

"Oh, shit!" shouted Chuck as Rohi slammed the accelerator forward, simultaneously pulling the ship upward. They moved just in time to avoid the snapping jaws of a cruise-liner-sized fish. Chuck gawked as its five dorsal fins passed underneath them and it crashed back into the surf.

"M—maybe we should stay a little higher up from the water," he stammered in between gasps for air.

"Yeah, great idea!"

Chuck couldn't tell if she was being sarcastic. It didn't matter because his attention was then pulled by the appearance of a brown dot on the horizon. When they got a little closer, he saw that the brown dot was actually a titanic mountain piercing the ocean's otherwise pristine surface.

Fifteen minutes later, Rohi was setting the ship down on a platform that jutted out from a rocky cliff face. They got up from their chairs, and Rohi grabbed her jacket. "Remember, we're smugglers trying to find our comrades."

"I got it," replied Chuck.

They exited the ship and gazed up at the wall-clinging mishmash that was Pa Tahae. Chuck made the mistake of glancing over the platform's edge at the crashing waves far below. Dizziness had begun to overtake him when Rohi's firm grip pulled him back from the edge.

"You all right?" There was legitimate concern in her voice.

"Yeah, yeah, I'll be . . ." He paused when his eyes fell on the approaching individuals. One was a tall and lean Soreshi. The only clothing he wore was a pair of brown pants, a matching pair of boots, and a circular gold medallion that bounced against the bare green scales on his chest. He carried a double-barreled rifle.

The other was a Puzuru, whose camouflage-patterned skin ranged across various hues of cream and off-white. He wore a dark tan robe, and as if to complete the stereotypical "monk" look, his head was clean-shaven. He looked at them with piercing blue eyes and said, "I hear there's a nasty comet storm on the system's edge."

Rohi responded confidently, "Only Law Cogs and tourists worry about the weather."

The Puzuru smiled and nodded to the Soreshi, who then slung the rifle casually over his shoulder. The Puzuru gave them a slight bow. "Welcome to Pa Tahae. I know the password system is antiquated, but it still works for the most part. Allow me to introduce myself: my name is Tyrei. Mr. Brondo told me you'd be coming."

He turned to head back to the city. Rohi and Chuck had begun to follow when the Soreshi hissed, "It be twenty pecks to park at LeGatt's pier."

Tyrei turned around. "I hope you two brought Tahlians. The last people to stiff LeGatt here received an in-depth tour of the ocean floor."

Rohi eyed the smirking Puzuru as she dug into her jacket pocket. She pulled out a few white cards and handed them to LeGatt. He snatched the Tahlians and gave them a fang-filled grin as he stuffed them in his pocket. The Puzuru "monk," Tyrei, started walking back toward the city. Rohi and Chuck hurried to catch up.

"I thought you were supposed to help us out," quipped Rohi once they'd fallen in beside him. Tyrei walked deliberately yet casually; his hands clasped behind his back.

"I am here to help you navigate the city, not foot your bill," he replied. He then eyed Chuck. "I don't believe I am acquainted with your species. Where do you hail from?"

Chuck glanced at Rohi, who nodded. "I'm from Earth," he answered.

Tyrei raised his nonexistent eyebrows. "Intriguing. When did Earth join the Sentient Coalition?"

Chuck froze. His brain whirred. *What should I say? I pulled that secret undercover story out of my ass back at Mr. Brondo's. It won't work here. Think, Chuck, think! What would Han Solo do? What would Rick Deckard do? Time to channel your inner Harrison Ford . . .*

He took a step forward, looked Tyrei dead in the eye, and said, "I don't need the Coalition to tell me how to make my own way. Now, are you here to learn our life stories or to help us navigate the city?" It took everything he had not to look away from that cold blue stare. Tyrei held his gaze steady before finally blinking.

He smiled. "I meant no offense." They continued walking as Tyrei said, "I think you will find yourself right at home here, friend. Pa Tahae is a city built on the principle that every being has the right to make their own way, free from the shackles of the Coalition and the ULE oppressors."

Chuck could feel Rohi bristle. He took the lead. "So tell us about this incident in the marketplace."

"There is not much to tell. A violent confrontation broke out between some of our local freelancers and a pair of escaped inmates: a Yoblon and a Dronla, both male. Violence is a tool of the trade for many who call Pa Tahae home, though we try to minimize confrontations between our citizens. Ordinarily I'd be happy to broker a meeting between you and the freelancers, but I understand they departed earlier today."

"Do you have any idea where they went?" asked Rohi, a little too eagerly.

Tyrei gave her a dismissive look. "Citizens of Pa Tahae do not concern themselves with affairs not their own."

Chuck was afraid she might punch him and jumped back in. "What about the escaped inmates? What happened to them?"

Tyrei spread his hands. "Our fair city has plenty of Yoblon, not so many Dronla, and virtually no instances of a Yoblon and Dronla associating with each other . . . except for some recent whispers originating from the pub district of Level Two."

"Great! How do we get to Level Two?"

Tyrei began to walk again. He led them between some buildings, then around a couple twists and turns, until they found themselves on a ledge looking out at the ocean. For a moment Chuck and Rohi got lost in the view. The sound of

Tyrei clearing his throat shook them out of it. They looked to the left and saw him standing next to a wide tube of metal scaffolding. A cage big enough to fit six or seven average humanoids hung inside the tube. Chuck leaned his head our over the ledge. The scaffolding tube ran vertically, and Chuck could see its bottom end, a few hundred yards below them. Looking up, he couldn't see its top end.

Chuck felt fear grip his chest when he saw the other individual. The being's skin was orange. Its face had no nose, and its right eye was a vertical slit. Rohi's hand on his arm pulled Chuck back from the edge of panic, and he saw that this being was too scrawny to be the marauder captain. The Ochrean teenager didn't seem to notice them. He was too busy reclining against the cage and flicking pebbles over the ledge.

Tyrei gestured to him. "Paani's lift runs through all thirteen levels of the city. I wish you the best of luck in locating your associates."

"That's it? You're leaving us?" asked Chuck.

Tyrei folded his hands in front of him. "You know everything I do."

"What happened to *I'm here to help you navigate the city*?" shot Rohi.

He waved a hand at the lift. "I navigated you here. The only law in Pa Tahae is the law of commerce. If you want me to chaperone you through Level Two, I will require due compensation in the form of five hundred Tahlians . . . per hour."

Rohi looked at Chuck. "Do you have anything?"

Chuck shook his head.

"So, what, I'm just supposed to bankroll everything?"

"Well excuse me for not rolling in cash only one day after getting out of prison!"

"Where you'd still be rotting if it wasn't for me! And you're welcome, by the way."

They were interrupted by a loud cough and turned to see Tyrei staring at them dumbly.

Paani, having apparently lost interest in his pebbles, finally spoke. "So you two be like . . . you know . . ." He was bobbing his head suggestively.

"No," snapped Rohi and Chuck in unison.

"Tops," he replied with a wink in Rohi's direction.

She ignored him, collected herself, and forced a smile. "Thank you, Tyrei, but we'll take it from here."

The Puzuru bowed slightly, turned, and then strolled casually back the way they'd come. Chuck could have sworn he heard him humming a tune. They approached the Ochrean.

"What level ya need?" asked Paani in a wholly uninterested manner.

"Level Two," answered Rohi.

"Please," added Chuck, earning him an annoyed glance.

Paani shrugged. "Piece o' jubla. We on six now, an' it five pecks per level."

Rohi huffed and dug into her jacket, pulling out twenty Tahlians. Paani swiped them from her hand, holding them close to his one vertical eye, as if verifying their authenticity. When he was satisfied, he shoved them in his pocket and swung the lift gate open.

He beamed at Rohi. "Afta you."

She stepped past him into the cage. The youth gave little thought to discretion as he studied her backside. He grinned at Chuck, who rolled his eyes and followed. Paani pulled the lift gate shut behind them, locked it, and pushed a lever. The gears creaked, and they began to descend slowly through the tube of metal scaffolding. The mesh floor of the cage offered a crisscross view of the churning waves below. Chuck gripped the cage nervously, focusing on not looking down.

Paani grinned. "Don' worry, mon. Paani's lift very strong. Once carried a trio o' Aviapes all da way up to thirteen."

Chuck glanced over his shoulder, where the ocean stretched forever. The city-facing view through Levels Five and Four was nothing but rough concrete, save for two sealed doors. The view opened up when they reached Level Three. They found themselves looking over some kind of outside factory floor. A hundred beings scurried around wearing burned and blackened welding gear. Sparks shot up from various workstations.

"Dis where dey fix da ships," explained Paani.

Chuck saw a pair of short, stocky workers straddling a giant turbine. If their animated hand movements were any indication, they were involved in quite the heated discussion. One apparently had had enough, and he slapped the other in his helmeted face; he then retaliated with a shove. There was a brief skirmish of slaps and shoves, and then one decided to clock the other with a wide mallet, sending him toppling off the turbine. Chuck's mouth fell open. Paani must have been watching, too, because he started laughing uncontrollably.

"Did you see that?" Chuck asked Rohi.

"See what?" she replied, but they were already passing into Level Two, which also had something of an open-air layout. Chuck saw two rows of tightly packed buildings separated by a dusty stone road and running parallel to the cliff face. Alleys cut between the buildings, across the road to a narrow lane that ran along the outer edge of the level. Paani brought the lift to a stop along this outer lane.

He pushed the gate open. "Level Two."

He gave another wink to Rohi and a nod to Chuck as they stepped out of the lift cage. He closed the door behind them and said, "Keep a good grip on ya moneys, mon."

With that he swung the lever up, and the lift began to rise. Chuck and Rohi watched him ascend for a few moments before turning around toward the buildings. Upon closer inspection, *shacks* was a much more appropriate term for the structures they were looking at. At least half of them had been made from wood, or at least a wood-like substance.

"So what now?" asked Chuck.

Rohi shrugged. "I guess we start asking if anyone's seen an overly polite Dronla and an annoying Yoblon, who also happen to be wearing prison scrubs."

They cut through an alley and turned onto the one road of Level Two. The sun was going down, and lights started coming on in the windows of the bordering buildings. Despite the occasional use of concrete and metal, the area gave Chuck a real "old west" kind of vibe. It took at least ten minutes before they saw another being. Sitting on the porch of a dilapidated two-story house was an elderly alien, of a race unfamiliar to Chuck. He only assumed the alien was old because of its long, dirty, white beard. Dark circles hung under the alien's tired eyes. Deep wrinkles ran along the alien's face, and its head was covered in a shoulder-length mop of eggshell-colored hair. Its skin was a sickly shade of green, and everything from the neck down was covered in a dark blue muumuu.

"Look, there's someone. Excuse me, sir?" asked Chuck. The alien ignored him.

Rohi pawed at his arm. "Um, Chuck?"

He brushed her off and trotted ahead. "Hello? Sir?" Still no acknowledgment from the old alien.

"Chuck?"

He stepped right in front of the alien. "Hello, sir. My name is—"

The alien popped to its feet and began shouting at Chuck in a string of unintelligible syllables. Rohi tugged him away from the ranting alien, who continued to shout after them as they moved on.

"What the hell was that?"

"Never startle an old Bogtek woman," responded Rohi.

"That was a woman? She had a beard!"

"Well yeah, the Bogtek home world is really damp and cold. The women grow long beards to keep their newborns warm while nursing."

"Wait . . . what?!"

"Yeah, they wrap the baby up in the hair."

"You're fucking with me, aren't you?"

Rohi didn't answer. She was busy staring apprehensively at the trio of aliens that had appeared in front of them. Chuck noted the sun had gone down with surprising speed. A floodlight affixed to a nearby shack illuminated the part of the street they were standing on. The three beings standing across from them were all new species to Chuck. The two flanking individuals stood at average height with unremarkably humanoid bodies, except for their heads. Their scales were a dazzling hue of aquamarine. They had very high foreheads ending in blue fins. They had no visible noses, and their circular, black eyes were very close to their wide mouths, which were constantly opening and closing. Thin vent-like openings accented the sides of their necks.

Fish people, thought Chuck. *Of course there'd be fish people.*

The one in the center stood well over six feet. Her sand-colored skin was rough, almost stone-like. It stretched tightly over a pair of broad shoulders. Sprouting from those shoulders was a thick neck that led up to a square jaw. Her coffee-tinted hair was pulled back into a braid that fell to her waist. Two features in particular were vying for Chuck's attention: The first was her considerably well-endowed chest, which is what led him to assume she was a she, although the recent Bogtek incident was giving him doubts. The second was the additional pair of arms that stemmed from her rib cage.

She peered at them with dark eyes, an unsettling grin spreading across her wide face. "Good evening. My name is Zinzi." She spread her four hands out. "We're the Level Two welcoming committee."

Chuck shifted nervously. Rohi's voice was firm as she said, "Can we help you?"

Somehow, the grin got wider. "Oh, no, it *us* who can help *you*," she replied. "You see, Level Two can be very dangerous. It's important to have protection. Otherwise bad things can happen."

Rohi was unflinching. "Let me guess. You'd like to offer us that protection . . . for a price."

"It's one of the many services we happily provide to our fair city's visitors."

"I'll bet it is. If it's all the same, we're going to continue on alone."

Zinzi looked almost sad. "For your sake, I'm sorry to hear that." She then cracked four sets of knuckles and said to her comrades, "You two take the J'Kari. I'll handle the weird-looking one."

The fish people produced batons that hummed with blue electricity and advanced. Rohi shoved Chuck to the side.

"Run!" she commanded.

Chuck ran to his right and hopped over a railing onto a building's front porch. He spun around to see Zinzi and her four muscle-bound arms bearing down on him. Over her shoulder he caught a glimpse of Rohi and the fish people. The first one took a wide swing that she easily avoided, countering with a kick to his midsection. Chuck didn't see what happened next as he was too busy ducking two of Zinzi's thick hands. He took off down the length of the porch, with her keeping pace on the other side of the railing.

The end of the porch was coming up fast, and Chuck had no idea what he was going to do. Seconds before they hit the end, Zinzi made her move. She eked out a little extra speed, reached the end first, grabbed the corner awning support, and swung herself around to face the oncoming Chuck. With maybe a second to spare before colliding with Zinzi's broad frame, Chuck's Little League instincts kicked in. He dropped to the ground, sliding right between her wide-set legs. He wasted no time in popping to his feet and sprinting back across the street. Zinzi whirled around with a string of curses and continued the chase.

An almost stair-like assortment of stacked boxes caught Chuck's attention, and he made for it. In a maneuver that surprised even himself with its athleticism, Chuck bounded up the boxes and leapt onto a long, flat wooden awning. Zinzi opted to follow along at ground level rather than climb up after him. Chuck realized why when he heard a loud crack and felt the wood awning beneath his feet shudder. She was taking out the awning support beams. Chuck kept running. There was another crack and shudder. Chuck's path became inclined as the awning fell away behind him. There was another crack, and the wooden frame screamed in agony as it gave way. In his last second of firm footing, Chuck launched himself through the window of the building attached to the now-dismantled awning. To his dismay, there was no second-story floor to break his fall, and he plummeted down to the main floor. He crashed into a table laden with gaming cards and drinking mugs, which spilled all over him as the table collapsed.

Chuck lay there on his back, staring up at the ceiling. His vision was blurry, and there was a ringing in his ears, but he felt the presence of a large crowd around him. One voice cut through all the surprised gasps and murmurs. "Holy humpalope shit! I don't believe it!"

A fuzzy yellow orb appeared in Chuck's field of vision. He blinked a few times, and the orb morphed into a face; a yellow face with a wide nose and a shit-eating grin.

"What the phoob are you doing here, Earth ape?" asked Jopp.

TEXT UNIT 0043

"Am I dead?" Chuck asked the yellow face hovering over him.

Jopp snorted. "You're not that lucky."

He reached out a hand, and Chuck took it. The shooting pains that accompanied his attempt to sit up confirmed that he was indeed still alive. He rubbed the dust from his eyes and looked around the room. Dozens of alien beings gawked back at him. There were a few gaming tables similar to the one he'd smashed, and a cheerful tune lilted through the air. Much of the crowd was leaning on a long brass counter that, if the collection of bottles was any indication, was a bar.

It's a saloon, thought Chuck. *Of course I find Jopp in a bar.*

There was a loud splintering of wood, and Chuck turned to see Zinzi shoving her way through the crowd.

"Got you now, you little yok," she shouted, pointing her two right index fingers at Chuck. He was all out of gas at this point, and he calmly awaited his beating.

She was almost to him when Jopp stepped confidently in her path. "Whoa, whoa, whoa. What's the matter, babe?"

Chuck silently mouthed the word *babe* to no one in particular.

Zinzi glared down at Jopp. "This weird-looking freak tried to skip out on the protection fee."

"Ohhhh."

Jopp grabbed her lower left hand with his right, and then patted it comfortingly with his left. "This is just a big misunderstanding. Zinzi, this is my friend Chuck I told you about."

She looked over Jopp to Chuck. "You are the Earth ape known as Chuck?"

Chuck nodded. A bright smile appeared across her face. "Well, why didn't you say so?!" She bounded over and pulled him to his feet as if he weighed nothing. She began dusting him off with her two lower hands. "Are you okay? I'm so sorry about that."

"Uh, it's cool," was all he could muster. Then his eyes went wide. "Where's Rohi?!"

"Right here," called an unseen voice. The crowd parted to reveal Rohi leaning against the door frame.

"Are you all right?" asked Chuck.

"I'm fine," she answered.

"Where are Flibb and Bubbla?" asked Zinzi.

Rohi massaged her knuckles. "They're sleeping it off in the street. Probably going to have some major headaches when they wake up."

Zinzi looked more impressed than upset. "You want to join the welcoming committee?"

Jopp grinned at Rohi. "You couldn't resist my charm, could you?"

Zinzi smacked him upside the head. He grimaced. "Babe, I was only joking. You know I'm not interested in any two-arm trollops. Now give me some sweet."

Chuck watched in abject horror as Zinzi leaned down and planted a sloppy kiss on Jopp's mouth. It was only then that Chuck noticed the bandaged nub where Jopp's left antenna had been.

"Jopp, what happened to your head?!"

Jopp pulled away from his colossal girlfriend and gingerly stroked the nub. "Oh, yeah, that. I guess we got a lot of catching up to do."

"For sure." Chuck had another thought. "Wait, where's Bhanakhana?"

Jopp snapped his fingers. "Oh, yeah!"

He cupped his hand around his mouth and yelled across the room, "Hey, Big Red! Look who it is!"

Chuck watched as the back of a colossal crimson figure rose from a table in the corner. The figure turned around and the recognizable face of Bhanakhana lit up with pleasant surprise.

"Chuck!"

He was across the room in three steps, clasping his giant hands around Chuck's shoulders. "It is so good to see you! I am so glad you have made it to the party!"

The distinct aroma of Flanisi Ale wafted into Chuck's nose. He looked at Jopp. "Is he drunk?"

Jopp chuckled. "Oh, yeah."

"I have imbibed thirty-six units of alcohol! It is a most pleasant sensation!"

"The big guy's a drinking machine."

"Beep boop beep. I am a machine." Bhanakhana began giggling. Jopp joined in, laughing and egging him on. Bhanakhana let go of Chuck and rigidly moved his arms like an android. "Beepity beep boopity boop."

Tears were rolling down Jopp's face. Bhanakhana suddenly froze, his arms held in awkwardly bent positions.

"Need more fuel!" he shouted.

Jopp waved to the barkeep: an exposed brain with two eyes and ten tentacles who slung a bottle across the room. Bhanakhana caught it and removed the cap in one deft motion.

Chuck was startled to see Rohi had walked up next to him. "What the fuck am I looking at?"

Bhanakhana pointed at her. "Aha! Cursing! Jopp has been educating me in the art of profanity! Watch!" He made a show of composing himself before declaring, "You appear as if your face were comprised of dung!" This prompted another giggling fit.

"Believe it or not, he's getting better at it," said Jopp and laughed.

Rohi grabbed Chuck's arm and whispered, "We really don't have time for this."

Chuck nodded and stepped closer to Jopp. "We need to talk, now."

**

Chuck, Jopp, Rohi, and Bhanakhana sat around a table in the corner. Well, Chuck, Jopp, Rohi, and Bhanakhana's lower half were sitting. The big Dronla's upper half was splayed face down across the table. His body heaved rhythmically with each breath. A tiny trickle of drool flowed from his open mouth.

"He'll be fine," Jopp answered in response to the unspoken question. He gave Chuck a sly grin. "So, you devil, how'd you convince Agent Hot Pants here to jump you from the freezer?"

Rohi snarled, "Agent *what*?"

Jopp held his palms up defensively. "It's a compliment!" Then to Chuck he muttered, "Yeesh, so uptight."

Chuck gave Rohi the *calm down* look. Then to Jopp he said, "She believes we didn't kill the vice director."

Jopp glanced at Rohi. "Oh, really? When did that happen? When the Psychotic Best Friends Club kidnapped us after kicking your ass?"

Rohi glared back. Chuck slapped the table. "Hey! She's putting herself on the line here, too, all right? So do me a favor and drop the attitude."

Jopp snarked, "Oh, I'm doing you favors now?"

Chuck was unwavering. "You're damn right, you are. 'Cause if it wasn't for your drunken ass, I'd be back home, blissfully ignorant to all this shit."

Surprisingly Jopp looked contrite. He took a long pull from his bottle, sighed, and held out his hand to Rohi. "Let's start over. Hi, I'm Jopp. I'm sort of the Gorth-brain responsible for this mess."

Rohi leered at him for a moment before relenting. She shook his hand. "Division Officer Rohi Kahpanova. It's a . . . an *experience* to make your acquaintance."

Jopp pulled his hand from Rohi. "Hey! Keep that ULE stuff on the whisper here, okay? They are 'Enemy Number One' around these parts."

When their hands had touched, Chuck saw Zinzi, who'd been eyeing them from the bar, bristle. He nodded in her direction. "So what's up with you and her?"

"Oh"—Jopp turned around to blow Zinzi a kiss—"that's a long story."

"You've only been here a day," commented Rohi.

"That's all the time I need, sweets," replied Jopp. "Make the right moves, and you just might find that out for yourself."

"Ew."

Chuck wasn't paying attention as his eye had been drawn back to Jopp's bandaged nub. "Jopp, what happened to your head?"

Jopp's hand went instinctively to the bandage. "Oh, yeah, I had ol' lefty removed. . . . It's the latest fashion trend."

"Really?"

"Fuck no, not really! Those assholes cut it off during a spirited interrogation session. They wanted us to give them the case."

"And where is the case?"

Jopp shrugged. "They've got it, for all I know." He took another drink. "And good fucking riddance, too."

"They just took it and let you live?"

"They probably think we're dead. See, Big Red here had a shine-bomb stashed next to the case. He sets it off, and we make a run for it while Asshole and Company are all wonky-like. Blada blada blada . . . they chase us through the city, we drop the case, get knocked over the outer ledge, and wham-bam our way down a couple levels until we crash through Sludlut's roof."

"Who the hell is Sludlut?"

"That's Sludlut."

Chuck and Rohi followed Jopp's finger, which pointed to a morbidly obese alien seated at another table. He resembled the old bearded woman who had accosted Chuck earlier.

"Breaking out of a ULE freezer is like a stamp of honor around here. So anyway, Sludlut cracks our wrist shackles, gets us some new clothes, and hooks us up with a sweet bar tab, all in exchange for us telling everyone he was the mastermind behind our escape."

"How is it even possible for someone to be so lucky and unlucky at the same time?" asked Rohi.

Jopp beamed. "My mom says it's because I'm special."

"Listen," snapped Chuck. "We think Quo is involved with all this."

"Really?"

"Yes!"

"Why?"

"Oh, I don't know, maybe because of the totally suspicious way in which he *personally* made sure *everything was in order*."

Realization flooded over Jopp's face. "Oh, yeah. . . . That actually makes total sense." He shrugged. "Oh, well."

"*Oh, well*? That's it? Let's go get him!"

"And then what happens when we get him?" Jopp pointed his finger at nothing in an accusatory manner. "Hey, wealthiest and most powerful person in the universe! We know you're up to something but have no idea what it is! We're here to say . . . stop it!"

"So what do you want to do? Just stay here forever?"

Jopp looked around the room. "Um, I see no problem with that."

"Pa . . .Tahae . . . forever," mumbled the half-snoozing Bhanakhana.

Jopp pointed. "See? And he's the smart one!"

"What about Rohi?" asked Chuck. "Is she just supposed to give up being an agent and stay here, too?"

Jopp gave Rohi the once-over, his gaze lingering a bit too long on her skintight pants. He raised an eyebrow and looked at Chuck. "Again, I see no problem with that."

"Jopp."

He leaned back. "I can see it all now: we'll set up shop as a wily smuggler crew. Big Red will be the brains, Earth man Chuck will handle the menial labor, and I'll be the fearless leader who's caught in a love triangle with Zinzi and Miss Sassy Pants over here."

"Jop—wait . . ." Chuck's face suddenly got excited. "Could I wear a brown overcoat and use the code name Mal?"

"Sure thing, *Mal*," said Jopp.

Chuck barely contained a delighted squeal.

"Chuck!" exclaimed Rohi.

Chuck's face fell. "Rohi's right. We can't stay."

Jopp leaned back. "Suit yourself, buddy."

Chuck stood up from the table. "I don't know how we're going to do it, but we're going to make this right. For what it's worth, I'm glad that you're okay. Let's go, Rohi."

Rohi followed as he started to walk away. They were halfway across the bar when they heard someone shout, "Excuse me, everyone!"

The music cut off and everyone went quiet. Chuck and Rohi turned around to see Jopp standing on the table. He addressed the crowd: "As you all know, we already stuck it to those Yulee tight-asses when we walked right out of their freezer box!"

The crowd cheered.

"My associates have informed me that another servant of the Coalition tyrants: Prime Partners Intergalactic Consortium"—the mention of the company's name elicited a series of boos and hisses—"has concocted a new scheme to continue oppressing our beautiful universe."

More boos.

"But my associates also tell me we can stop this scheme. We have an opportunity to strike a blow for liberty."

The crowd cheered.

"We can bring that menacing monolith of monopoly to its knees!"

More cheers.

"I ask you now, free citizens . . . are you with us?!"

The crowd erupted with an exuberant roar.

TEXT UNIT 0044

Chuck, Rohi, Jopp, Bhanakhana, and no one else sat in the control room of their borrowed ship.

"So much for striking a blow for the free citizens," grumbled Rohi.

"A lot of help your new friends were," quipped Chuck.

"It's not my fault we couldn't afford to pay everyone's *tactical consulting fee*. But hey, at least they gave us these." Jopp held up one of the pulse pistols.

"We had to pay for them!" Chuck shot back.

"There's only one law in Pa Tahae," preached Jopp.

"Yeah, yeah, commerce. We know."

"You're just lucky I still had that currency card we got from ol' what's-his-name."

"Dagwam," corrected Chuck. "Yeah, about that. . . . How did you hide it from the ULE agents when we were arrested?"

"You don't really want to know," answered Jopp.

"Ew," said Chuck and Rohi simultaneously.

"Please do not shout," begged Bhanakhana. He was slumped forward in his chair, holding his tiny head in his giant hands.

"Aw," said Jopp. "Someone's riding the vomit comet."

"On Earth, it's called a hangover," added Chuck.

"Why's it called *a hangover*?" asked Rohi.

"You know . . . I don't know," he replied.

Bhanakhana groaned. "Can we please not be here anymore?"

Rohi pressed a couple of buttons, and the ship rumbled to life. Nothing happened after that. She stared at the console with a furrowed brow.

"We're still gravi-docked."

They heard a banging at the ship's side hatch. Chuck and Jopp went back to open the door and found the serpentine face of LeGatt staring back at them. He was still shirtless and still had the rifle slung over his shoulder, but he was wearing a new medallion.

"Nice flash," commented Jopp.

LeGatt responded with a nod and a polite hiss. Then to Chuck he said, "Ya still owe me. Settle up and I release the gravi-dock."

"We already paid you!" protested Chuck.

"It be twenty pecks to *park* at LeGatt's pier." He gave them a wide, fang-filled grin. "It be fifty pecks to *leave* LeGatt's pier."

"Not cool, LeGatt."

He shrugged. "'Tis what 'tis."

Chuck sighed and turned to Jopp. "Pay the man."

Jopp grumbled as he rummaged through his pockets for the currency card.

***

Fifteen minutes later they were exiting Roqua's atmosphere.

"So, do we have anything slightly resembling a plan?" wondered Jopp.

"Uh, catch them in the act?"

"Oh, sure, yeah, catch them in the act . . . the act of doing the thing . . . the thing we have no idea about. How are we supposed to catch them in the act if we have no idea what the act is?"

Chuck threw his hands up. "I don't know! I'm brainstorming!"

"I think there's headache medication in the back if you need it," commented Rohi.

"No, *brainstorming* means—ever mind," Chuck huffed.

"You possess medicinal remedies to alleviate the unpleasantness in my cranium?! Why was this information not imparted to me at an earlier time?!" Bhanakhana rushed to the back of the ship.

Rohi kept the conversation moving. "We need to get some kind of proof that Quo is involved with the marauders."

"Also known as pirates," added Chuck. She shot him a look, to which he responded, "If I go down, I want to say I went down fighting space pirates. It sounds cooler."

Rohi inhaled and continued, "Fine, whatever. So I figure we locate Quo and discreetly monitor him until the *pirates* show themselves."

Chuck nodded. "Great. Now we just need to find Quo."

"He's in Takutai, at the Grand Papai resort."

Both Rohi and Chuck turned around to Jopp. He was playing with the holographic screen from a data bracelet.

He looked up at them. "What?"

"How do you know that?"

"*The Waxing Whisper.*"

"The trashy gossip feed?" asked Rohi.

"You mean the legitimate news feed," corrected Jopp.

"Sure it is."

"See for yourself." Jopp spun the holographic screen around, giving Chuck and Rohi a great view of two young Yoblon women in something of a compromising position. Rohi's face screwed up in revulsion.

Chuck chuckled, "Um . . . Jopp . . ."

"What's wrong?" asked Jopp. He glanced at the image. "Whoops! Wrong view panel! That's, uh, research! I'm helping the big guy with his next study." He swiped his fingers across the display and then spun it back toward them.

"Here you go!"

Chuck and Rohi saw a wide shot of a gorgeous beachside resort. The architecture looked like a series of bright blue bubbles stacked on top of each other to form a building. The headline read, "Irony in Action: Top Industry Execs Hold Efficiency Summit at 99 Star Resort." Below that was a list of notable attendees, and the very first one was Quo Agban Delanius Zarvinston XXIX, executive regent for Prime Partners Intergalactic Consortium.

Chuck nodded. "Well, okay then. How far away is Takutai?"

"About a day," answered Rohi.

A deep groan signaled Bhanakhana's return to the room. He leaned against the wall with one hand while holding the other to his stomach.

"How you holding up, Big Red?" asked Jopp.

"The med bay is now out of cranial pain alleviators, and I would highly advise against use of the lavatory for at least thirty-five minutes, or perhaps forty-five minutes."

TEXT UNIT 0045

Chuck scanned the desolate sea of endless white rock. "This is a little underwhelming. I thought Takutai was supposed to be this crazy-opulent beach resort planet."

"It is," said Jopp. "We're just not at that part of it yet."

"But I thought, like, the whole planet would be one big beach."

"Why would you assume that?"

"George Lucas."

"What?"

"Never mind."

Another few seconds passed quietly before Chuck spoke again. "You know, you never did get around to telling me how you wound up on Earth in the first place. Or how you lost an entire cargo ship."

"Oh, that," muttered Jopp. "It was a girl."

Chuck snorted. "Big surprise."

"You want to hear this story or not?"

Chuck nodded.

Jopp kept his eyes fixed on the horizon. "I thought we were in love. I mean, we hadn't known each other that long, but still . . . it felt real. Like really real. Like I'd found my other half. Don't get me wrong; she wasn't some innocent angel or anything. I knew she'd had something of a troubled past, but it seemed like that shit was well behind her. Then I get the big one, the big contract. Prime Partners wanted me to run Tier 9 cargo. It meant I'd be transporting some of the most valuable goods in the universe. It was against protocol, but the girl came with me. The job was going to take almost two weeks to complete, and you know your ol' pal Jopp wasn't going to go two weeks without a little lovin'. So she came with me, and for a few days it was great. One evening we were hitting the drink a little harder than usual. I, predictably, passed out. When I woke up again, I was in the transport ship's escape pod. The viewport told me I was floating in space; the transport ship was nowhere in sight. On the floor of the escape pod was a case of Flanisi Ale and a note."

"Shit," said Chuck with a sigh.

"Shit is right."

"I'm sorry, Jopp. That really sucks."

"Like our new pal LeGatt says, *It is what it is, Earth man*."

They stopped talking while a huge freighter cruised overhead, its loud turbines preventing any reasonable conversation. The sounds of the freighter were soon replaced by awkward silence.

Chuck couldn't help himself. "So, is that why you're such a dick?"

Jopp turned angrily, but then saw Chuck's wry smile. Jopp's expression softened to a mischievous grin. "Nope. I've always been this awesome."

"Hey, get over here, you two," called Rohi. They turned around and trotted across the platform known as Takutai Way

Station 38. It was a flat circle of pressed concrete alloy, about a half mile in diameter, with six dozen evenly spaced fueling depots. At the center was a small structure where travelers could purchase an assortment of convenience items.

Rohi and Bhanakhana were standing next to the *Vindicator*, which is what Jopp had taken to calling their borrowed ship. They were staring intently at projected images from Rohi's data bracelet, which was resting on a makeshift table made from a discarded battery cell.

"What's up?" asked Jopp, as he and Chuck approached.

Rohi glared at him. "Please don't use my DB for your smut. Or at least erase your view logs when you're done. I turned this thing on and got treated to the business end of a Venovan woman."

"Hey, it's not smut. It's art." Jopp patted Bhanakhana on the arm. "How you feeling, Bee-Three?"

"Why do you persist in the use of monikers which are not my proper name?" asked Bhanakhana Bhen Bhindo.

"I say them with the utmost respect and affection."

Bhanakhana eyed Jopp skeptically. "In answer to your question, my well-being has improved significantly, though I believe I will undergo an extended hiatus from the consumption of alcohol."

"You're a better man than me."

Bhanakhana smirked. "Of that, I am certain."

Chuck jumped in. "So, what's the plan?"

Rohi indicated the screen. "The Grand Papai is one of the largest and most exclusive resorts on the planet. It's essentially a city in itself."

"Eh, it's not that all that special," said Jopp, scoffing.

"You've been to the Grand Papai?" asked an incredulous Rohi.

"Oh, yeah," replied Jopp. "I, uh, once dated the heiress to the Lantaki Turbine empire."

Rohi rolled her eyes. "Forget it. I don't want to know. Anyway, the summit officially starts tomorrow morning. There's a private welcoming event for the guests tonight."

"So how we sneaking in, huh?" Jopp asked. "Steal some uniforms and pretend to work there? Oooo . . . or we could pose as reporters covering the event! No! Wait! Let's be executives from an up-and-coming company that's revolutionizing the industry! I'll be the executive premier, of course, and you can all be my entourage. Now, what would we call the company. . . ." He snapped his fingers. "Jopp Corp!"

Three sets of unamused eyes peered back at him.

"Well, excuse me for trying to have a little fun before we die or go to prison forever."

Rohi sighed. "Yeah, well, we could do all that, or we can just walk right in. Like normal people."

Jopp folded his arms. "And what makes you think they'll let us in?"

"It's a resort, not a fortress. There aren't any black hole moats to cross or laser walls to scale. Like I said, we walk right in."

Jopp put his hands on his hips. "I know places like this; only registered guests are allowed on the property."

"Which is why Bhanakhana just made us a reservation."

Jopp eyed Bhanakhana. "How'd you manage that?"

Bhanakhana smiled. "I used the application known as Galaxy Trotter. They made securing a reservation fast and easy."

"Wow, I guess they really are the universe's number one travel service!" Jopp ended the statement with a toothy grin to no one in particular.*

* *This message brought to you by Galaxy Trotter: for all your space travel needs.*

TEXT UNIT 0046

Chuck would have liked to describe the beaches at the Grand Papai as beautiful, stunning, or breathtaking, but those words just felt inadequate. The sands were teal, turquoise, cyan . . . every imaginable combination of blue and green. The grains were so fine the beach could have easily been confused for the ocean. Speaking of the water, it was as clear as glass. There were no real waves, just the minimal ebb and flow that comes with the tide. It was as if the sun had turned this sea into its own personal vanity mirror. Plants that resembled the mutated older brothers of palm trees dotted the shore. Their pearl trunks were four to five times wider than palm trees. Plum-purple leaves stretched fifteen feet in every direction.

Then there was the resort itself. Papai did indeed look as if a god had built a toy castle out of bubbles. However, the picture from the article hardly did it justice. The blue of the exterior was so bright and so reflective it looked as if the complex was coated in sapphire.

"Daaaaaamn . . ." was all Chuck could muster.

Even Jopp was speechless as they flew past it all, heading straight for the stark white cliffs that acted as a backdrop for the rich colors of the beach. A square opening appeared in the cliff face, and Rohi piloted them through, into the hollowed-out mountain that served as the docking bay.

Jopp scoffed, "Can't have any tacky ship lots sullying the majestic profile of the Grand Papai, now, can we?"

Once they landed, Rohi hopped up. "Okay. We all remember the plan?"

"Yup," responded Chuck.

"Affirmative," responded Bhanakhana.

An agitated huffing and puffing was the only response from Jopp.

"Oh, get over it. It's not a big deal," Chuck said.

"Then switch parts with me," countered Jopp.

Chuck smirked. "Hell no."

Rohi snapped her fingers. "Hey! Stick to the plan. And for your information, Jopp, you can't have Chuck's role because I'm just not that good an actor."

"Daaaaaamn . . ."

"Oh, shut up," grumbled Jopp. "Let's just get this over with."

They exited the ship and found themselves looking up at the bellhop. He was a Tahl, and despite his youth his long lilac-tinted frame stretched just shy of seven feet. He looked from the four arriving guests to the one dirty duffel bag sitting next to them.

"Uh, is that all your luggage?" he asked.

Rohi brought that red-hot smile back. "Unfortunately we're not staying very long. Could you be a darling and take us to the reception desk?"

As the bellhop lifted the duffel bag, they heard a metal clacking sound.

"Uh . . . right this way." He led them out of the docking bay. The duffel bag swayed and bounced with each step.

Rohi fell back and pulled Jopp in tight to whisper in his ear. "You remembered to set the pistols to sleep mode, right?"

Jopp nodded in a wholly unconvincing manner. Rohi grimaced and kept walking. Chuck gawked at the dazzling images that bordered their path. From floor to ceiling, viewscreen panels covered both walls of this hallway. Each panel played a looping video of the many activities and amenities available at the resort. The passed the spa screen, and Chuck wondered what a "Goulap massage" consisted of. He thought the fish from the underwater-viewing tour looked equally beautiful and terrifying. He thought of those same two adjectives again when he saw the featured entrees for the resort restaurants.

The hallway ended at a pair of blue crystal double doors. They slowly swung inward as the group approached, revealing the stunning reception lobby. Natural light poured in from the blue glass roof, illuminating the lobby's centerpiece: a tower of white rock and purple vegetation encircled by a moat of crystal-clear water. Blue-silver desks ran along the edge of the circular room. The bellhop led them to one of these counters, where a uniformed Tahl woman was waiting. She put on the kind of smile you only see from people whose jobs require said smile.

"Welcome to the Grand Papai!" she boomed. "Are you checking in today?"

Rohi leaned on the counter. "Yes, and not a moment too soon. We're the Bhindo reservation. As you can see from our appearance, we've had a bit of a rough trip."

The reception clerk laughed in that noncommittal way, which says, *I agree you look like shit but am too polite to say so.* She tapped a few keys on her console and beamed. "Yes, here we are. I see you've reserved a pair of rooms. What brings you to the Grand Papai?"

Rohi beamed and put her arm through Chuck's. "Well, my lifemate and I wanted to have a little celebratory vacation with our friends." She gestured to Jopp and Bhanakhana. "They're going to become fathers."

The clerk clasped her hands together and squealed, "Oh, how wonderful! You must be so excited!"

Bhanakhana nodded. "Thank you. It is a most joyous experience." He put his hand around Jopp's shoulder. "Would you not say so?"

Jopp forced a smile. "Oh, yeah . . . best time of my life."

"Well, I just think that's great!" fawned the clerk. Then to Rohi: "Now, as I am sure you are aware, we require the first night's payment at the time of check-in."

Rohi grinned. "Of course." She handed the currency card to the clerk, who scanned it. Chuck thought he saw a tear in Jopp's eye as he watched his last five thousand Tahlians disappear.

The clerk slid two envelopes across the counter. "Your rooms are ready. Feel free to clean up before you join us at one of our famous Imperial Class restaurants."

Rohi took the envelopes. "About that. Getting here has been a real nightmare. We had to find a rental ship because our original shuttle broke down going through an asteroid dust storm. And on top of that, the ship carrying our luggage missed its anomaly coordinates. Right now, our things are in the outer reaches of Hyok. Could you please send a pair of clothiers to our rooms?"

The clerk smiled. "I can arrange that, and I'm so sorry to hear your vacation got off to such a rough start. I'm going to send up some complimentary plates of tuatahi kai as well as a bottle of waina."

"Oh, that would be so wonderful, thank you."

The clerk bowed her head. "It's my pleasure. I hope you enjoy your time here at the Grand Papai."

***

Ten minutes later, Chuck and Rohi opened the door to their hotel room. Waiting for them on the table was a tall black bottle and a large plate of rainbow-colored discs. Rohi scooped up a handful and stepped further into the villa. She popped them in her mouth, chewing casually as she inspected the room.

"What do they taste like?" asked Chuck.

She spun her head around. "You've never had tuatahi kai?"

Chuck pointed to his face. "Earth man, remember?"

She nodded to the plate. "Just try one."

He grabbed one of the colorful discs and took a small bite. It was salty and savory. Chuck decided it reminded him of sushi. He tossed the rest of the disc into his mouth and picked up the bottle. "What's this?"

Just then there was a knock at the door. Chuck opened it to find Jopp. He had an identical black bottle in his hand. The top was off, and his lips were stained red.

"Dude! This is some tops waina!"

TEXT UNIT 0047

Chuck took a sip from his glass of waina and stared out at the sun setting over the ocean. He set the glass down and brushed a hair off his brand-new suit. It was black with a subtle check pattern. His polished black shoes were like mirrors. His white shirt was crisp, and it clung to his skin in a not unpleasant manner. The clothier had been at a loss for what to do with the unruly streak of brown hair Mr. Brondo had left him. In the end they'd cropped it close, forming a clean mohawk, about a quarter inch in length. The cut under his right eye had finally closed up. Apparently, Herblings secrete a mildly toxic enzyme when agitated. Chuck had that enzyme to thank for the scar that would be left behind.

"You want to pour me a glass of that?"

Chuck turned around and hoped his jaw wouldn't need stitches after hitting the floor. He immediately decided that all the awesome, beautiful, daunting, terrifying, and magnificent things he'd seen had nothing on Rohi in her new black dress. She noticed Chuck's expression and arched an eyebrow. "I hope that's a compliment."

Chuck closed his mouth and shook himself out of his daze. "Er, yeah, sorry."

He fumbled for the bottle and poured some of the red libation into an empty glass. He gave it to her, and she started to take a drink but paused.

"*Cheers*, was it?"

Chuck laughed. "Yeah." He grabbed his own glass and gently clinked it to hers. "Cheers." He took a sip while she drained her glass.

She held it out. "Hit me again."

"You sure?"

She sighed. "Well, seeing as tonight is likely going to end with us either dead or in jail, I figure I might as well enjoy a drink or two."

Chuck smirked as he filled her glass. "I wonder where you got that idea." He topped off his own drink before holding up his glass. "Here's to the most insane"—he looked at Rohi—"yet most amazing couple of days of my life."

She mimicked his motion, and they held eye contact as they drank. Chuck put his glass down. "Rohi, there's something I've been—" He was interrupted by a loud knocking.

They walked through the room and swung the door open. Jopp and Bhanakhana wore similar black suits and each had a new black duffel bag slung over their shoulders. Jopp held a tray that was half full of something resembling miniature quiches. He had crumbs on his red-stained lips.

"You two rea—" Jopp stopped speaking when he saw Rohi. He wiped his face with his sleeve. "Damn, girl. Looking tops!"

She rolled her eyes. Jopp popped another of the quiche things in his mouth. Chuck indicated the tray. "Jopp, what is that?"

Jopp shrugged. "You can credit stuff to the room. I figure since we'll probably end up dead or in jail, I might as well live it up." He punctuated the thought with a deep belch.

Bhanakhana sighed. "That is his third tray of food. At this point, I am less disgusted and more fascinated with his stomach capacity."

Jopp patted his gut. "It's like I got a tiny anomaly in my tummy."

"That would be most improbable."

Rohi pinched the bridge of her nose. "If you all are done, can we get on with this incredibly dumb thing we're about to do?"

TEXT UNIT 0048

The sun was still peeking over the watery horizon as Chuck and Rohi walked arm in arm over the bridge that connected the two halves of the resort. Viewscape Point, as the staff had referred to it, was suspended three stories in the air and earned its name by providing a sweeping panorama of the beach.

They crossed the bridge and passed through a pair of glass doors, leaving the cool sea breeze behind them. Once inside, a digital sign indicated that the Efficiency Summit welcoming gala was to the right in the Sandfish Ballroom.

They came to a pair of blue-and-silver doors. Chuck could only assume the multifinned monstrosity painted above them was a sandfish. Perched on a stool next to the doors was a Tahl in a hotel security uniform.

"Here we go," Rohi muttered under her breath.

They approached the Tahl, who beamed and stood up. "Hello! May I please see your invitation?"

Rohi confidently held out her ULE badge.

"What's this about?" asked the doorman.

"Oh, they didn't tell you?"

"Tell me what?"

Rohi gave an exasperated sigh. "Ugh . . . High Command didn't send word? What's new, right?"

The doorman was visibly confused.

She leaned in and said quietly, "We're the undercover security detail. You know how these executives are. They treat the agency like we're their own personal bodyguards. Of course High Command goes along with it because they love those corporate contributions. Meanwhile, it's working-stiff Law Cogs like me and my partner here who end up having to babysit their spoiled asses."

The doorman nodded. "I get it. They got the whole resort staff running around like crazy. You'd think the old kings of Regattalatta were here." He held the door open. "Good luck in there, agent."

She treated him to one of her scalding-hot smiles. Chuck didn't even need to look to know where the doorman's eyes were focused as they walked past. In all fairness to him, Rohi's dress was a little on the snug side, not that Chuck was complaining.

The doors opened into an opulent ballroom. On the far end of the room rose a dais. Three dozen round tables populated the space in front of the dais. Between them and the tables were what Chuck guessed to be at least three hundred beings milling about. Waiters scurried around carrying trays of exotic foods and glowing drinks. The inscrutable chatter of a hundred conversations permeated the air.

Chuck and Rohi circumnavigated the crowd to a relatively quiet corner. Chuck snatched two bubbly pink drinks off a passing waiter's tray. He handed one to Rohi. "So we look more natural."

She took it. "You sure it's not because you're nervous?"

He chuckled. "Nervous? I'm terrified. But it looks weird to stand in the corner by ourselves without a drink."

Rohi eyed him as she took a sip. Chuck tucked his chin in tight and spoke into his collar. "Jopp—"

***

"*Jopp—can you hear me? We made it inside the gala,*" said the near-invisible receiver stuck to Jopp's right antenna.

Jopp replied into his collar, "I hear ya. Any hot little solar flares running around the party?"

"*Jopp.*"

"Yeah, yeah. We're in position." Jopp and Bhanakhana were lounging at the lobby bar. Bhanakhana sat facing the entrance while Jopp had his back to it. Jopp continued the conversation with his collar. "Executive Regent Dickhead hasn't shown up yet." Then to Bhanakhana he said, "What is it about pompous scrogbags that makes them always have to show up late to everything?"

Bhanakhana shrugged. "Perhaps they feel it is a sign of power to make people wait for them."

"The only power that gives them is the power to make me want to punch them in the yub nubs." Jopp noticed Bhanakhana fidgeting. "What's wrong?"

Bhanakhana patted his chest. "I am not accustomed to wearing a weapon. It is not a very comfortable feeling."

Jopp started to make a wisecrack but paused when he saw Bhanakhana's eyes widen. He nodded slowly and deliberately. Jopp risked a quick glance over his shoulder. He spoke into the collar again. "Quo's here. Checking in now. And he brought his entire scrogbag entourage."

"*I don't suppose you see either the case or the pirates near him?*"

With a huff Jopp said, "I wish it was that easy. We're not that lucky, remember?"

Bhanakhana gave the table three firm taps.

"All right," said Jopp, "they're heading to the room. You two enjoy your party while we do the dangerous part."

"*I don't think they allow lemonheads in here, anyway.*"

***

"*Oh, that really stings coming from a hairless Earth ape,*" said the receiver in Chuck's ear.

"Be careful," Chuck replied to his collar.

"*Yeah, yeah . . .*"

Chuck nodded to Rohi. "He's here."

She tossed back her drink and set the glass on the tray of a passing waiter.

"Maybe you should slow down," Chuck suggested.

"Listen." She put a hand on her hip. "For one, I can handle my liquor. And two, unless you want to be the one to sidle up next to Quo . . ."

The look on Chuck's face made her turn around. She found herself face-to-face with an elderly Puzuru holding two flutes of the bubbly pink liquid. His jigsaw-patterned skin looked like it had once ranged across multiple vibrant shades of orange, but was now a more muted canvas of pale peach tones. There were bags under his eyes, a wattle of skin hung under his jaw-line, and his thinning auburn hair was brushed into an obvious comb-over. Two strands of facial hair hung from the sides of his mouth.

He handed Rohi one of the flutes. "A beautiful lady such as yourself should never be without a beverage." Then to Chuck: "Shame on you, young man."

"Um, sorry?"

The Puruzu held his now-free hand out to Rohi. "Hello, my dear. My name is Durei Durnsteen, of the Puznadia Durnsteens."

She graciously took his hand. "It's so nice to meet you. My name is Rohi, and this—"

She turned to introduce Chuck, but he wasn't paying attention. He was busy staring at the woman who'd just joined them. She was a good foot taller than Rohi's new friend and maybe half an inch taller than Chuck. Her hair was platinum blonde with streaks of silver. Her skin, of which much was on display, was powder blue. If Rohi's dress was snug, than hers was shrink-wrapped over her voluptuous figure. Her face was young and attractive yet seemed like it existed in a perpetual expression of disinterest.

"Pardon me," said the elderly Puzuru. "This is my wife, Vay."

Vay raised her glass halfheartedly and gave the slightest hint of a smile.

"Vay, these are my new friends, Rohi and . . . what was your name again, son?"

"Chuck." He held his hand out to no one in particular.

Durei gave him a curt but polite nod. "Nice meeting you, Chuck." He immediately turned his full attention back to Rohi. "So, my dear, are you familiar with the history of this resort? Well, the Durnsteens have been coming here for . . ."

Chuck tuned out the old Puzuru's droning and tapped his foot awkwardly on the floor. Vay was staring at him with that disinterested gaze.

"So, like, what are you?" she asked Chuck in a nasally voice.

"Um, I'm from Earth?" Chuck answered, unsure of why his tone was so apologetic.

"Really?" Her face registered the slightest hint of emotion.

"Uh, yep."

"That's so random." She pulled out a pocket-sized tablet from what Chuck guessed was her purse. "I totally need to bleep this." Her thumbs tapped frantically across the screen. She then stepped in close to Chuck and held the tablet out at arm's length. He saw their own mirrored faces looking back at him. A small light flashed, and Vay went back to typing. "This is so totally going to blow up my Bleepline. That skanky bitch Niri is going to be so jealous."

Chuck found himself missing prison.

TEXT UNIT 0049

"This is the dumbest plan ever," mumbled Jopp.

"Shhhh," hissed Bhanakhana as he pulled Jopp behind a corner just in time to avoid being seen.

This process, complete with the commentary, had already repeated itself three times over. They were following Quo and his menagerie through the halls of the Grand Papai's Penthouse Wing. A small red head and a big yellow one risked a peek around the corner. Quo's entourage had stopped at the end of the hall in front of a pair of blue crystal doors. The bellhop used his employee passkey to open the doors, holding them open for the guests to enter. Jopp watched the bellhop slide the passkey casually into a pocket. He pulled himself back behind the corner and started psyching himself up. "Okay, okay . . . here we go . . . think drunk, think drunk . . ."

Bhanakhana smirked. "I would imagine that should be quite easy for you."

"Do you mind? I'm trying to get into character."

"He is coming."

Jopp took a deep breath and then stumbled into the hall, nearly running into the returning bellhop.

"Excuse me, sir," said the bellhop.

Jopp wobbled and squinted back at him. "Fyll! Ish that you, Fyll?"

"Pardon?"

"It ish you! Fyll! What are you doin' here, man?!"

"I'm terribly sorry, sir. I'm not Fyll. Are you feeling all right?"

"What?! I feel phoobin' tops!" Jopp staggered toward the bellhop.

"Can I help you back to you room, sir?"

"Yeah! The room! I got mo' bottles we can drink!" Jopp swung his arm around the bellhop. "Me an' my buddy Fyllllll!"

The bellhop put his arm around Jopp in an attempt to steady him. They took two steps and Jopp tripped, sending all his weight into the bellhop. They both tumbled to the floor.

Bhanakhana came rushing around the corner. "There you are, you shameless drunk! Just look at yourself!"

He reached down and pulled the bellhop to his feet, making a show of brushing him off. "I am so dreadfully sorry about my lifemate. He simply cannot control himself."

Jopp pointed up from the ground. "I handle my booze just fine, dammit!"

Bhanakhana scooped Jopp up off the floor. "Again, I am so sorry."

The bellhop held his hands up. "Really it's no trouble. Do you need any help?"

Jopp pointed at the bellhop, "Look! Ish Fyll!"

Bhanakhana patted Jopp's shoulder. "That is not Fyll, dear." Then to the bellhop, "Thank you so much, but I'm just going to put him to bed."

"Okay, well you two have a nice evening." The bellhop continued on down the hall.

***

Jopp and Bhanakhana were back sitting in a corner of the lobby bar. Jopp rolled the bellhop's passkey through his fingers.

"Would you please put that away?" asked Bhanakhana.

"You know, just 'cause we're pretending to be married doesn't mean you get to nag me all the time."

Bhanakhana gave him a look that prompted Jopp to slide the key into his pocket without further comment. He drummed his yellow fingers on the table. "So you didn't say anything about my performance. Personally, I thought it was Takoto Award–worthy."

Bhanakhana grinned. "Can you call it a performance when you are just acting as yourself?"

"I think I liked you better when you had no sense of humor."

Bhanakhana's smile faded, and he tapped the table two times. Jopp didn't even risk a look, instead opting to lie down along the booth seat, essentially making himself invisible to anyone passing through the lobby. There was the buzz of excited chatter and the clicking of a dozen pairs of fancy shoes as Quo's entourage made their way toward the Viewscape Point bridge.

When they had cleared the lobby, Bhanakhana said, "They're gone."

Jopp sat up and spoke into his collar. "Chuck, the humpalope herd is on its way."

"*The what? Oh, okay, got it,*" sounded Chuck's voice.

Then a different, nasally voice said, "*Shut up, Niri, he's totally a real Earth man!*"

"What the fuck is going on over there?"

PATRICK EDWARDS

"You don't want to know."

Then the nasally voice said, *"Who are you talk—"* The line cut off.

Jopp looked up at Bhanakhana. "Don't ask."

"Very well. Let us commence our next task."

"You can make anything sound lame, can't you?"

"Pardon?"

"Never mind. Let's go."

Five minutes later they were back at Quo's penthouse. Jopp pulled the passkey out of his pocket. He started to reach for the door but hesitated.

"Wait, what if he's got, like, security in there?"

Bhanakhana arched an eyebrow. "What manner of security are you referring to?"

"I don't know, man. Maybe he's got a guard muckdog or something."

"For one thing, I believe this establishment prohibits pets. For another, we followed them here from the lobby and, as such, most certainly would have smelled any accompanying muckdogs."

"It was just an example! We don't know what he might have in there."

"Well, we cannot simply stand here."

"No," growled a low voice from behind them. "You cannot."

They turned around to see Haaga, Ghono, and Jorwei, each wielding a high-powered mecha rifle.

Jopp waved. "Hiiiiiiiiiiiiii."

TEXT UNIT 0050

"Who are you talking to?" Vay asked with an expression Chuck had become all too familiar with back in high school. It was the expression girls made when you were about to cross the line from interesting to weird.

"Er . . . uh . . . it's . . ."

Rohi tugged on his arm. "I need to talk you. It's important."

Oh, thank god, thought Chuck. He gave Vay a polite smile. "It was nice talking with you."

Vay shot Rohi an annoyed glance. "Ugh, whatever."

Chuck followed Rohi off to the side.

"What's wrong?" he asked.

"Nothing. I just couldn't stand listening to him ramble about his *esteemed lineage* any longer."

Chuck laughed. "We could trade. I'm sure you and Vay would have lots to talk about."

She rolled her eyes. "Oh, I'm sure." She tapped his collar. "So, we heard anything yet?"

Chuck's face lit up. "Oh, yeah! He should be here any—"

A swift rise in the volume of the room's chatter caused them to look back at the ballroom entrance. The crowd was making way for Quo and company. Chuck counted about ten or eleven Tahls. He recognized the two next to Quo as the same executives from their first meeting. They headed for the dais, and the crowd's eyes followed. Quo stepped up onto the stage alone and situated himself behind the podium. The crowd went quiet with anticipation.

Quo smiled and leaned into the microphone. "Good evening. My name is Quo Agban Delanius Zarvinston XXIX, executive regent for Prime Partners Intergalactic Consortium. I am honored that you have all taken time from your busy schedules to join us for what is sure to be a monumental event."

The wall behind him transformed into a slowly spinning picture of a star-filled galaxy.

"We are now living in a truly remarkable era. Interplanetary war is at an all-time low. Citizen-on-citizen crime is declining at an exponential rate. The intergalactic economy is booming. We are on the precipice of achieving something no civilization has ever come close to: universal order. Now, there are many entities who deserve credit for the gains we've made: the Sentient Coalition, the Universal Law Enforcement agency, and even those big softies at the Compassion for Life Alliance."

This elicited a rolling chuckle from the audience.

"But there is one group, in particular, I would like to thank. And that is the fine display of accomplished people I see gathered here today. Honestly, it makes all of my hearts swell. I look out across this room, and I see titans of industry, leaders of a generation, the embodiment of achievement. I see the people who have put the well-being of this universe on their backs. I look around this room, and I see the future."

The crowd cheered. Rohi leaned into Chuck. "Someone's been reading a little too much Yad Rann."

Quo made a *settle down* motion with his hands. "Now, things may be good. But as everyone in this room can tell you, they can always be better. You are all standing in this room because you aren't satisfied with 'good enough.' That's what this summit is about: pushing through 'good enough' and reaching greatness. But that all begins tomorrow. For tonight, enjoy the party. I'm told it's another twenty minutes or so until dinner, so please continue to enjoy some drinks and hors d'oeuvres. And for Bjordax sake, relax and have a little fun. You've earned it."

The crowd whistled and clapped as Quo stepped down from the dais. He walked through the crowd, shaking hands and taking pictures with the guests. Rohi moved away from Chuck and positioned herself so as to be in his path. He was just a few yards away, getting his ear talked off by a pair of grizzled old Yoblons. He shook their hands and continued moving in Chuck and Rohi's direction. She nervously downed the remainder of her drink. He was now only a few feet away. She caught his eye and gave him a warm, inviting smile. He was right there. He looked as if he was about to speak when one of his security detail stepped in between them. He whispered something into Quo's ear, causing his eyes to narrow. He nodded to the guard, who stepped back. He gave Rohi a polite nod and began following the guard toward the exit. One of his executive lackeys tried to follow, but Quo waved him off. Chuck didn't see the other one.

Then Rohi was back at his side.

"What happened?"

She threw her hands up. "I don't know. I had him! Then that guy whispered something to him, and he took off."

Chuck's eyes widened with fear. He spoke into his collar. "Jopp! Jopp, can you hear me?"

TEXT UNIT 0051

"Jopp, can you hear me? I think Quo might be heading back to the room," said the almost-invisible receiver stuck to Jopp's right antenna.

Jopp wasn't really listening, as he was too busy concentrating on the barrel of the mecha rifle Jorwei was pointing at his head. He hoped Quo didn't mind stains on his penthouse couch. Bhanakhana sat next to him, also experiencing the sensation of having a weapon that could turn his head into jelly aimed between his eyes.

Haaga folded his arms across his chest and raised an eyebrow. "You two might be the Zuul-damn stupidest rockbrains I've ever had the displeasure of knowing. You were free. You had to have figured we thought you were dead after that fall. All you had to do was lay low in Pa Tahae, a city built for that exact purpose. But for some unfathomable reason, you followed us here . . . and to do what?" He picked up one of the pistols. "Shoot us with your toys?"

"Maybe they're sweet on us," said Jorwei, chuckling.

"Or they got some kind of hero complex," added Ghono. He leaned in close to Bhanakhana. "You fashion yourself some kind of hero, brother?"

Bhanakhana's tone was like ice. "You are no kin of mine."

Ghono smirked.

"It doesn't matter," said Haaga. "Our deal is about to be done. Then I'm going to personally put a mecha bolt in each of your heads."

Jopp looked past Haaga to see the penthouse door crack open. Their captors turned around as Quo and a security guard stepped inside.

Quo looked around the room. "What is going on here?" His eyes fell on Jopp. "And what in the ten hells are you doing here, Mr. Wenslode?"

"We know everything, Quo! You shady scrogbag!" Jopp was silenced by a smack from Jorwei.

"Excuse me?" said Quo.

Haaga stepped forward. "It's nice to meet you in person, old friend."

"Pardon?" said Quo.

Haaga unslung his duffel bag, dropping it on the coffee table. He unfastened the seal and pulled out the black case. He set it on the table and slid it toward Quo. "We'll just take our ten million Tahlians and be on our way."

"What is that? Who the hell are you people?"

"We were told to meet you here."

"I was told there was an issue with my suite."

Jopp felt a slight nudge on his thigh. He glanced over, and Bhanakhana flashed him a quick look at something in his right hand. It was a small black cylinder. Jopp's eyes bugged in surprise. Bhanakhana rested his left hand on his thigh. He extended one finger. Jopp's breathing quickened. He extended a second finger. Jopp's heart started pounding. He extended a third finger. Jopp squeezed his eyes shut and covered his antenna just as the shine-bomb went off. He opened his eyes. The air was sparkling, and there were five bodies on the floor. Bhanakhana was already on his feet and moving. He snatched the case and made for the door. Jopp leapt up after him, grabbing their two pistols off the table as he fled. They raced down the hall, the sound of angry shouts trailing after them.

"This feels familiar!" yelled Jopp.

"Unpleasantly so!" called Bhanakhana.

They ran until they suddenly found themselves back in the lobby. They had arrived in such a flurry that everyone was staring at them. Jopp noticed two individuals, a Soreshi and a thick, orange-skinned Ochrean staring particularly hard. They both had long black bags hanging over their shoulders. In unison they brought their right hands to their ears. They looked at each other, then back at Jopp and Bhanakhana. In an instant, the bags were on the ground, and they were pulling out two more of those lovely mecha rifles.

"Oh, shit!" said Jopp.

"Indeed," concurred Bhanakhana. They sprinted for the bar, diving behind a booth just as the marauders opened fire. The shots turned the top half of the booth into splinters and dust. The other guests screamed and scattered. The barrage continued, tearing chunks off the lobby's beautiful centerpiece.

"I don't suppose you have any more shine-bombs?!" shouted Jopp.

"That was my last one!"

"Of course it was!"

Bhanakhana pointed past the bar to a swinging steel door. "Through the kitchen!"

Jopp hefted a pistol in each hand. "I'll cover you."

"Cover me? You may have watched one too many adventure films."

"Just go when I say go, okay?" Jopp peeked out. "Ready? *Go!*"

He popped up and began firing rounds wildly. The Soreshi and Ochrean dove out of the way. Bhanakhana hopped the bar and plowed through the steel door. Jopp trained his pistols on the prone Ochrean. He was about to fire when he noticed movement to his right.

"Shit stacks!" he yelled, ducking just in time to avoid the Soreshi's countervolley.

Good job getting yourself flanked, you stupid yok! Jopp cursed to himself. The Soreshi had gotten a perfect vantage on the kitchen door. There was no way Jopp was getting there without earning an extra hole or two in his backside. He let off a couple suppressing shots and called out, "B!"

The door cracked slightly, revealing a red face. Jopp grinned and winked before spinning around and firing into the large windowpane that overlooked the pool outside, turning the glass into a spider web of cracks. Bhanakhana called out to Jopp, but he was already in motion. Shots whizzed past Jopp's head as he crashed through the window. A thousand glass shards and a stout yellow Yoblon spilled down into the pool below.

TEXT UNIT 0052

Bhanakhana could only watch as Jopp dove through the window amid a hail of gunfire. He stared at the square of night sky where the window had once been. The distinctive rasp of a Soreshi yelling, "Go after the Yoblon! I'll take the kitchen!" snapped Bhanakhana out of his haze. He pressed his back flat against the wall, right next to the door. He heard the clicking of boots approaching the door and tightened his grip on the black case. The door slowly opened inward. Bhanakhana raised the case high. The barrel of a rifle poked out. Bhanakhana brought the case down hard, knocking the rifle to the ground. He yanked the door wide open and pulled the stunned Soreshi into the kitchen by his scaly neck. An instant later Bhanakhana's fist connected with the Soreshi's face. He dropped the unconscious reptilian and picked the case back up. He then cracked the door and cautiously peeked around the edge. There was no sign of the other shooter, and the lobby was deserted. He was about to step out when he heard a gravelly voice shouting, "Shai! Shai! Can you hear me?! Come in, dammit!"

Bhanakhana caught his breath as Haaga, Ghono, and Jorwei poured into the lobby, their backs to the bar. As quietly and gently as possible, Bhanakhana backed into the kitchen. As he moved away from the door, he frantically scanned the kitchen for another way out. He didn't see the pot sitting on the edge of the counter until his elbow made contact. He gaped in horror as it fell to the floor with a crash. He heard the gravelly voice say, "Ghono, check the kitchen." It was followed by the sound of heavy footsteps coming toward the door. Bhanakhana held his breath. Then a pair of shots rang out. The gravelly voice yelled, "It came from outside! Let's go!"

Bhanakhana listened as the clip-clop of boots headed away from the door. He crept closer, with the intention of peeking to see if the coast was clear. He put his hand on the door and flinched in terror when a deafening barrage of automatic gunfire resonated through the air.

TEXT UNIT 0053

Jopp splashed and floundered, cursing his species' inherent lack of buoyancy. Swimming to the pool's edge would have been a little easier had he been willing to let go of one or both of the pistols. *I'll be damned if I go down unarmed after pulling a stunt like that,* he thought. He reached the ladder and tossed the pistols on the ground next to it. When he'd first hit the water, a dozen or so resort guests had rushed over to help. They'd changed their minds and run away once they'd seen the pistols. He pulled himself out of the water, grabbed his weapons, and pointed them up at the vacant window. He waited for one of the shooters to show his face. Ten seconds passed. Then twenty.

A scream drew his attention to the other side of the pool. The Ochrean marauder had made his way down to the pool level from the lobby. He and Jopp spotted each other at the same moment. Jopp spun his pistols around. The marauder raised his rifle. They both fired. Jopp's right shoulder exploded in pain as a mecha bolt ripped through it, the force of the shot knocking him to the ground. He stared at the stars hanging overhead, waiting to die.

When a few seconds had passed without the arrival of his death, Jopp attempted to sit up. His shoulder screamed with agony, and his right arm hung limp. He pushed himself to his feet. He saw the marauder. The Ochrean was laid out on the ground, and there was nothing but a green stain where the left half of his face should have been.

"Fuuuuuuuck," Jopp said, breathing hard.

He took a step toward the corpse but paused when he heard a gravelly voice yelling from up above, "It came from outside! Let's go!" He turned, saw a door, and made for it as fast as his bleeding shoulder would let him.

TEXT UNIT 0054

A few moments before Jopp's window stunt, Haaga Viim ran down the halls of the resort's penthouse wing with Jorwei and Ghono in tow. His eyes burned with white-hot rage. They came around the bend. The lobby was at the end of the hall. He shouted into his comm, "Shai! Shai! Can you hear me?! Come in, dammit!"

They charged into the lobby, rifles at the ready. The floor was scattered with debris: chunks of decorative rock, leafy vines ripped from their displays, splinters from shredded tables and booths. There was no one in sight. It was utterly silent.

A loud crash echoed from the door behind the lobby bar. Haaga nodded toward it. "Ghono, check the kitchen."

Ghono began to stomp his way toward the door. A two shots rang out, causing him to freeze. He looked back at Haaga, who called, "It came from outside! Let's go!"

Ghono scrutinized the kitchen door for a moment longer before following after Haaga.

As the three of them approached the lobby elevator bank, one of the doors dinged. It slid open, revealing a handful of armed hotel security personnel. The surprise of seeing the marauders caused the guards to hesitate for a second. This second was all Haaga's trio needed. The firefight didn't last long and was decidedly one-sided.

They rode the now-bloodstained elevator down to the pool deck. They opted not to make the same mistake the security detail had and had their weapons ready when the doors opened. The only thing waiting for them, however, was the body of their comrade. Haaga approached cautiously, unflinching at the remaining half of the man's face that stared lifelessly into the sky.

"Sorry, boss," offered Jorwei.

This man, Shuuja, had been one of the first slaves he'd liberated from his home world's oppression. Haaga's face tightened with resolve.

"Over here," called Ghono.

Haaga and Jorwei came around the pool to where Ghono was standing. At his feet was a small purple bloodstain. A trail of purple dots led from the stain to a door.

Ghono sneered. "What's round and yellow and bleeds purple?"

"When this is over," Haaga said to Ghono, "the Yoblon is yours to do whatever with . . . as long as it hurts."

TEXT UNIT 0055

The gala patrons were being led to their tables for dinner while Chuck and Rohi lingered awkwardly by the bar. Rohi was clenching and unclenching her fists compulsively.

Chuck shrugged. "Maybe we should sit down?"

"And do what?" she huffed. "Enjoy a nice romantic dinner? Jopp and Bhanakhana could've gotten jammed. What are we still doing here?"

"Maybe it had nothing to do with Jopp and Bhanakhana."

She scoffed, "Oh, sure, he just happened to get pulled out of here by security at the same time our guys are breaking into his penthouse?"

"So what were we supposed to do? Follow after him? Like that wouldn't have been incredibly conspicuous."

"Well, we can't just sit here and hope everything works out."

Chuck threw his hands up. "I don't—" His ear buzzed. *"Chuck . . . Chuck . . . you there?"*

He yanked his collar up toward his mouth. "Jopp?! Jopp, what's going on?!"

"*The plop glob has hit the acceleran.*"

"What?"

"*Our pirate buddies are here, and they're ripping this place apart. . . . I'm . . . I'm hurt, man.*"

"Where are you?"

"*I don't know. . . . I climbed some stairs. . . . I'm outside now . . . on some . . . like . . . bridge or something.*"

"Keep moving!" Chuck looked up at Rohi. "He's on the bridge. He's hurt."

"Let's get him."

They rushed out of the ballroom, past the security guard, and down the hall. When they were halfway to the bridge, a squat yellow figure stumbled into view.

"Jopp!" they shouted in unison. He looked up and gave them a weak half smile. They raced up to him, and Chuck's face dropped when they got closer. Jopp was pale. A dark purple, almost black, stain ran down his limp right arm. He held a pistol loosely in his left.

"What happened?"

Jopp managed a chuckle. "Oh, it's a marvelous story . . . and I'd be happy to tell it to you in detail . . . but for now you think we could get me some medical attention?"

Chuck helped support him while Rohi took the pistol. They hurried back down the hall toward the ballroom. The door guard stood up and held out one hand. "What the phoob is going on here?"

The guard saw the pistol in Rohi's grip, and he reached for the one strapped to his hip.

"Listen," barked Rohi. "Shit is going down. I don't have time to explain, but you need to get every security guard on the property here. Now!"

"Hold on just a—" The guard was unable to finish his sentence, as his head disappeared in an explosion of pink matter.

They spun around to see Haaga, Ghono, and Jorwei racing toward them. Rohi leveled the pistol and fired off a few rounds, causing them to duck into the hallway alcoves.

"Get inside!" she screamed.

Chuck yanked the door open and hustled Jopp inside. Rohi let off two more suppressing shots and followed. She slammed the door closed behind her and turned around to see every set of eyes in the room staring at them.

Chuck had moved Jopp over to the side and was propping him up against the bar. He yelled at the bartender for water and clean towels.

Rohi ran up to the crowd, some of whom had already gone back to enjoying their dinner. She held up her badge. "Universal Law Enforcement! I need everyone to head for the exits immediately!"

Nobody moved.

They just stared.

A few took sips from their drinks.

"Are you people stupid?! I said *move!*"

As soon as the words left her mouth, the ballroom doors exploded in a flurry of gunfire.

This got the crowd's attention. Three hundred sheltered and pampered beings suddenly realized they were in very real danger. They reacted as one might expect, with abject terror and panic. The throng of crazed gala patrons surged toward the various exits. Rohi hopped up on a chair and saw Haaga, Ghono, and Jorwei come through the shredded remains of the ballroom doors. They were scanning the rioting mass of people and didn't see her. Rohi raised her pistol and took aim. Right as their eyes fell on her, she pulled the trigger.

Nothing happened.

She glanced at the weapon and saw the blinking ammo light.

"Are you fucking serious?!"

The marauders grinned and brought their rifles up. Rohi saw Chuck sprinting toward them from the bar. No way he was going to make it. The barrels steadied. Rohi braced herself for the shot. Her mouth fell open when she saw a black rectangular object suddenly fly in from the ballroom doorway. It connected with Haaga's back and sent him sprawling. She didn't get a chance to process this as the black projectile was immediately followed by the diving frame of Bhanakhana tackling Ghono and Jorwei to the ground. Her eyes went back to Haaga, who had returned to his feet. He seemed uninterested in the three-way wrestling match going on behind him and intent on finishing Rohi. He brought his rifle up again.

Haaga never saw Chuck coming. Chuck lowered his shoulder and drove it into Haaga's stomach. Chuck's momentum was so great he lost his footing, and they both tumbled to the floor. Rohi hopped off her chair and sprinted over.

The tables were turning on Bhanakhana fast. Jorwei took the Dronla's knee out with a well-placed kick. Ghono punched him in the head. Jorwei reared back to deliver another kick, but a chair crashed into his chest and sent him toppling backward. The shock made Ghono pause for a second, and Bhanakhana took advantage. He lunged, wrapped his arms around Ghono's waist, lifted him off the ground, and drove him into a table, which buckled under their combined weight.

Rohi grabbed another chair and swung it at Jorwei. He caught it by the legs and wrenched it out of her grasp. He tossed it aside dismissively and sized her up. "Before we begin, I want you to know: I take no pleasure in beating up women."

Rohi was unfazed. "That's funny . . . 'cause I take a lot of pleasure in beating up scared little puzzlefaces."

That didn't sit well with Jorwei, and he came in with a wild right hook. Rohi ducked and countered with an uppercut. He staggered, and she went for another.

Ghono kicked Bhanakhana off him and jumped to his feet. He pulled his white blade from his belt and grinned. "I'm going to enjoy carving you up."

Haaga tossed Chuck aside with minimal effort. They clambered to their feet, and Chuck swung a fist at Haaga's jaw. It seemed to annoy Haaga more than hurt him. He responded by punching Chuck in the face, reopening the cut under his eye. The force of the blow dropped Chuck to the ground. He scrambled to his hands and knees, and Haaga kicked him in the gut.

Rohi ducked another wild swing from Jorwei. She brought her leg around, connecting her heel with the side of Jorwei's head. He crumpled to the ground. She whipped off his belt and tied his hands behind his back.

Ghono lunged forward. Bhanakhana caught his knife hand by the wrist and jabbed Ghono in the face with his free hand. Ghono tried to wrench his hand free, but Bhanakhana's grip was firm. He then tried to punch with his other hand, but Bhanakhana caught that one, too. They grappled, the blade in Ghono's grip hovering in the air between them.

In an attempt to break the stalemate, Ghono kicked Bhanakhana squarely in the chest. Bhanakhana fell backward, but his grip on Ghono's wrists held strong, and the other Dronla fell with him. They toppled to the ground with a thud.

Ghono let out a pained gasp.

Bhanakhana was on his back, Ghono's limp body draped on top of him. Ghono's eyes, where once so much hatred had lived, now stared lifelessly back at Bhanakhana. He grunted and heaved the body to the floor, rolling it onto its back.

Bhanakhana stood up and stared down at the vibrating white knife buried deeply in Ghono's chest.

Haaga dropped on top of Chuck. He wrapped his thick orange hands around Chuck's neck and squeezed. Chuck clawed and scratched, but it did nothing. He started to feel light-headed. He saw white spots. He thought a nap sounded good right about now. Just before he lost consciousness, he felt something roll against his arm. He touched it and recognized the smooth coldness of a large bottle. His fingers found the neck and gripped it tightly. With every ounce of strength he had left, Chuck smashed the bottle into the side of Haaga's head. The hands relaxed their grip as the unconscious form of Haaga collapsed to the side. Chuck sat up, coughing and rubbing his neck, as Rohi and Bhanakhana rushed over.

"Are you all right?!" they asked in unison.

"I think so," answered Chuck.

"You're welcome," called a familiar voice.

Chuck looked to his right to see Jopp, sitting against the bar. Laying next to him were a half dozen bottles identical to the one Chuck had just clobbered Haaga with.

"Thanks," said Chuck.

Jopp grabbed another of the bottles with his good hand. "And they say alcohol is bad for you."

"Oh, my goodness! Are you all right?!"

The four of them turned to see one of the Prime Partners executives. He was looking quite concerned. Jopp pulled out the robo-cork with his mouth and held the bottle aloft. "Hey, Loq, what's going on? You know your boss is a real yok?"

He took a big gulp.

Loq's expression changed to that of a disappointed parent. "Yes, it is most regrettable. It turns out Quo was in league with these"—he nudged Haaga with his foot—"gutter scum. Rest assured, Quo is currently in the custody of hotel security, and the ULE are on their way."

"Remind me to talk with you later about hazard pay."

Loq nodded. "I assure you, Mr. Wenslode, you will be handsomely compensated for your trouble." He looked to the others. "Due restitution will be made available to each of you for your help in resolving this terrible incident."

"Damn straight!"

"Yes, well . . ." Loq's eyes fell on the black case. "I had better get this to our lab for testing."

Chuck watched as Loq reached down and grabbed the case. His long fingers wrapped delicately around the handle, and he lifted it off the ground. Something felt off to Chuck, but he couldn't put his finger on it. Loq nodded again and turned to leave.

Chuck snapped his fingers and blurted, "Green!"

Rohi, Bhanakhana, and Jopp all looked at him like he'd gone crazy.

"Um, what?"

Chuck pointed at the case. "Green! The lock turned green when he touched it!" He looked at Jopp. "Didn't you say . . ."

Jopp finished the thought. "Only the dick who locked the case could unlock it."

They all turned back to see that Loq had set the black case down. Now he was holding Haaga's mecha rifle.

Chuck pointed. "It was you."

Loq gave a tired sigh. "You just had to say something. You couldn't just let it go."

"What the fuck, Loq?"

"Shut up, Mr. Wenslode. I'm tired of your worthless prattling. Quo should have had you sent to Helon in the first place. Instead he trusted you and a dumb Earth ape to make a transport run! That's just one more way in which I'll be a far superior executive regent once he's been locked up."

Rohi stepped forward. "What about the vice director?"

Loq shrugged. "What about her? Just another bent Law Cog looking for a payday."

"I don't believe you."

He shrugged again. "Believe what you want. It won't matter in a second." He leveled the rifle at them. "It's a shame the marauders killed you before I got here to save the day."

"Wait!" yelled Chuck.

They all stopped and looked at him.

"What was in the case?!" he asked pleadingly.

Loq looked at him dismissively and spat, "Does it even matter at this point?"

"Well . . . yeah! I really want to know."

Loq laughed. "Sorry to disappoint you."

Rohi took a step closer. "I'm going to end you."

Loq smirked. "That would be quite the trick, considering I have the gun."

Rohi returned the smirk. "Well, what are you waiting for? Pull the trigger. Unless you don't have the yub nubs for it."

Loq's expression hardened. He raised the rifle at Rohi and pulled the trigger. No shot fired. The rifle buzzed, and a blue electrical current shot up Loq's arm. He dropped the gun and fell to the ground in a twitching mass.

Rohi strolled up to him. She looked down at his convulsing figure and grinned. "You don't know much about weapons, do you?" She kicked at the rifle. "The Clixx line mecha rifle has a bio-signature security feature. Only the owner can pull the trigger. Anyone else who tries gets treated to fifty thousand stun volts." She crouched down close. "But I'm guessing you figured that last part out by now."

She stood up and looked back at Chuck. He asked, "You get all that?"

She reached into her cleavage and pulled out a small microphone. "We got it."

"Great job, team! Can we get me a phoobing doctor, now?" said Jopp.

TEXT UNIT 0056

"Ow! Are you a doctor?! Or a Grimtak interrogator?!" shouted Jopp.

The lilac-colored Tahl physician rolled her eyes. She checked the sling holding Jopp's right arm one last time before standing up. She looked to Chuck. "He's going to be fine."

"Will I ever play the polytone, doc?"

"Were you capable of playing it before?" asked Bhanakhana.

"No."

The doctor shook her head and added, "Like I said, he's going to be fine."

She headed off to tend to some other guests, leaving Chuck, Jopp, and Bhanakhana sitting on one of the few still-intact lobby couches. The resort was a swirling madhouse of traumatized patrons, hotel staff, and ULE agents. Chuck overheard a manager of some kind screaming into a commline about his "property damage deductible." An older woman was demanding that they leave and never come back to the resort, while her husband was insisting he could turn this situation into a couple of free nights.

They saw Quo making his way toward them. Chuck and Bhanakhana quickly rose to their feet. Jopp stayed put.

"Get up!" Chuck hissed at him.

"No way! After what we've been through? He should be kissing my—"

"Hello, Mr. Wenslode."

Something about Quo's voice always made it seem like he was a principal contemplating how to punish you for cutting class.

Jopp hopped to his feet with a big fake smile.

"There's the boss man! What's happening, Quo?"

Quo sighed deeply.

"I understand I have you all to thank for exposing Loq as the loathsome little flipback that he is, as well as clearing my name from any part in the matter."

Jopp waved dismissively. "Eh, it was nothing. I knew all along you had nothing to do with it. I told these two as much, didn't I?"

Chuck and Bhanakhana could only shrug. Quo forced a smile.

"I'm sure you did. I simply wanted to offer my gratitude."

He gave a little nod and made to leave.

"Wait, that's it?" protested Jopp. "Don't we get some kind of, I don't know, reward or something?"

Quo responded with mild trepidation, "What did you have in mind?"

Jopp rubbed his chin in an attempt at appearing shrewd. "Fifty thousand Tahlians . . . each! And a new ship!"

Quo smiled and clasped his hands behind his back.

"An interesting proposal."

He moved in close to Jopp, bent down to the much shorter Yoblon's eye level, and said, "Here's my counteroffer: I completely absolve you of your massive debt. And in return, you will never . . . ever . . . come anywhere near me or my company again."

Jopp thought for a moment before thrusting his good hand forward. "You got a deal!"

Quo ignored Jopp's hand, nodded to Chuck, and tried to leave again.

"Wait!" said Chuck. "What the hell was in the case?!"

Quo shook his head.

"I am sorry. My legal advocacy team has advised me not to comment on that."

He walked off across the lobby and was mobbed by the recently arrived intergalactic media.

Chuck threw his hands up and shouted, "You have got to be kidding me!"

Bhanakhana rested a hand on Chuck's shoulder. "The universe is an endless font of mystery and wonder."

Chuck turned his head with an annoyed expression.

"Seriously? That's all you got?"

"That was beautiful," mused Jopp.

Chuck wanted to comment, but the approach of Rohi and a cadre of ULE agents pulled his attention. She was back in the all-black uniform, a helmet propped between her side and elbow. She smiled. "Hi, guys. I'd like to introduce you to someone."

An agent almost as tall and broad as Bhanakhana stepped forward. He reached up and pulled off his helmet, revealing himself to be a J'Kari. He had an iron jawline and strong cheekbones. He possessed the distinguished yet grizzled look of someone who'd kept himself in considerably good shape despite his advanced age. His salt-and-pepper quiff was perfectly combed.

"I'd like you all to meet High Admiral Roklar Kahpanova."

Chuck silently mouthed *Kahpanova* to Jopp.

"I would like to thank you three for your assistance in the apprehension of these criminals." The high admiral's voice was gruff but devoid of malice. "I would also like to personally apologize for the false accusations leveled against your persons. The charges have been officially dropped. You are all free citizens."

He gave Bhanakhana's right hand a firm grip and shake. He did the same, albeit slightly more awkwardly, with Jopp's left. When it was Chuck's turn, the high admiral's eyes narrowed, and he gave Chuck a scrutinizing once-over.

"So, Earth man, now that this nonsense is settled, how is it you plan on making your way in our society?"

Chuck's eyes met his. "I'm sure I'll find a way, sir."

Chuck then held out his hand. The high admiral grabbed it with a viselike grip and pulled Chuck in close. Very quietly, so that only Chuck could hear, he said, "You keep yourself out of trouble, you hear me?"

Chuck responded with a wide-eyed nod. The high admiral released his hand after a final squeeze. He looked from Chuck to Rohi and gave her a quick smile before heading off. The rest of his cadre followed, but Rohi lingered behind. She raised her eyebrows expectantly. Jopp got the hint. "Hey, uh, Big Red . . . let's grab a drink."

He tugged a confused Bhanakhana away, leaving Chuck and Rohi alone.

Chuck pointed over her shoulder and asked, "So, was that . . ."

Rohi chuckled. "Yeah, that was my father. This is kind of the family trade."

Chuck nodded. "So you're leaving, then?"

"Yeah, we've got a lot of junk to wade through with all this. My report is going to be light-years long . . . and I'll probably have to deal with a minor judiciary committee. You know, for breaking a suspected murderer out of jail."

"But that's not right."

She waved him off.

"It'll be fine. At the end of the day, I did some real good. Despite all its bureaucracy, the agency is pretty good at seeing the big picture."

Chuck shifted his weight nervously.

"So, will I see you again?"

She smiled coyly. "Possibly. Why?"

Chuck returned the smile. "Well, I don't know about where you come from, but on Earth it's a pretty big deal when a girl introduces a guy to her dad. It usually means she really likes him."

Rohi grabbed his collar and pulled him close.

"Shut up."

Chuck had never considered himself much of a skilled romantic, but he was pretty sure the kiss that followed would have put both Casanova and Don Juan to shame. When Rohi finally pulled away, she giggled at the dumbstruck look on his face.

"Wow" was all Chuck could say.

She smiled and winked.

"See you around, Chuck the Earth man."

He watched as she hurried off to catch up with the other agents. Chuck was frozen in place until he felt a hand slap him in the back.

"Yeeeeaaaaah, buddy!" Jopp said with a wide grin.

"Well done," concurred Bhanakhana.

Chuck shrugged off Jopp's hand. "Okay, okay."

The three of them stood there in awkward silence for a few seconds.

"So, what do we do now?" asked Chuck.

"I would very much like to retrieve my vessel from Pa Tahae," said Bhanakhana.

"Ah damn, that's right," said Jopp.

"Yeah about that," said Chuck. "Bhanakhana, I'm really sorry you got roped into all this."

"Especially since you got nothing to show for it," added Jopp. "I mean, I got my debt cleared, and this guy over here got a girl that's so far out of his league she's in a different dimension."

Chuck feigned like he was going to punch Jopp's bad arm.

He flinched and cried, "Don't joke about that! This shit hurts."

Chuck looked back to Bhanakhana. "So, anyway, I'm really sorry."

Bhanakhana smiled. "Do not trouble yourself. I had a most exhilarating time."

"Can we at least find some way to pay you back for your trouble?"

"That will not be necessary. I am rather well off, financially speaking."

"Um, what?" Jopp's face lit up.

"Occasionally in my travels, I come across very rare and valuable artifacts. I sell them to museums so that all may experience the wonder of other cultures."

"You're a treasure hunter?!"

"Certainly not. I am a sentologist, who occasionally stumbles across these artifacts during my studies. I have no desire to accumulate wealth. It has merely been a side effect of my work."

"No desire to accumulate wealth? I feel like I don't even know you!"

Bhanakhana ignored that. "It occurs to me that, were I to hire a professional pilot and a research assistant, I would have much more time to spend on my actual work. I do not suppose either of you would be interested?"

Chuck and Jopp looked at each other and shrugged. Chuck held his hand out. "You got a deal."

Bhanakhana took his hand and beamed. "Splendid! Let us be away."

The three of them headed off toward the ship hangar. As they walked Bhanakhana turned to Chuck. "I do have a favor to ask of you."

"Sure."

"I am just about finished with my dissertation on Earth. As the first of your kind to experience our intergalactic society, I feel your perspective would make an excellent ending."

Jopp jumped in. "Yeah, what do you think of the *real* universe, Earth man?"

He chuckled. "It's utterly insane"—he looked over his shoulder toward where Rohi was talking with some other agents—"but also amazing"—he looked back at them—"and you know what else? I'd thought there'd be more robots!"

"Oh, yeah," said Jopp. "You don't know about the Automaclysm of '73."

"It was a most troubling time in history," Bhanakhana agreed.

"As it turns out, giving sentience to machines is a really, really, really bad idea," Jopp added as he and Bhanakhana started walking down the hall. "My granddad fought in the war. I remember his stories from when I was a kid. You think I'm a badass? You should have seen my granddad. He was probably the biggest Yoblon anyone had ever seen. One time he knocked out three Fendigs with a single punch. He could drink all night and still fly a battle cruiser through a meteor storm the next morning. Then there was the time he . . ."

Chuck just smiled, shook his head, and followed after them.

The End
... or is it?
Yes ... yes, it is. I don't know why I misled you. I'm sorry.
The End
Thanks for reading.
I really hope you enjoyed it.

AN EXCERPT FROM
SPACE TRIPPING: HOLY HOOCH

"They want to eat your head," said Bhanakhana, translating the words of the Painaporo tribal chief.

"Well, they can't eat my head," Jopp protested. "I'm using my head."

"That's debatable," added Chuck.

"Shut up, Earth ape," snapped the stocky, yellow-skinned Yoblon.

Chuck didn't shut up. "Maybe they like the taste of lemons."

"My head doesn't taste like a lemon!" cried Jopp.

Chuck couldn't help himself. "That's right, it just looks like one."

Jopp turned to Chuck and unloaded a verbal onslaught of truly vile yet surprisingly creative expletives. He paused his tirade when he saw the stunned look on Bhanakhana's face. The hulking, red-hued Dronla cleared his throat. "I hope you are not expecting me to translate all that."

"No!"

"Do the Painaporo even have a word for *squibbling shit-stain*?" asked Chuck.

"As a matter of fact, they do," answered Bhanakhana.

"Excuse me," interjected Jopp. "Can we get back to the matter at hand?"

"Don't you mean matter at *head*?"

"I'm so glad you're enjoying this, Earth ape." Jopp then looked back to Bhanakhana. "I don't care what you tell them. Just know that I plan on shooting anyone who gets too close." His stubby yellow fingers grazed over the pulse pistol at his hip.

Bhanakhana grimaced. "Why must you persist in carrying that *thing*?"

Jopp made a show of glaring at Bhanakhana as he pointed to the top of his own head. Yoblons typically have a pair of three-inch hearing nodes. Jopp had one three-inch node and one inch-long nub that used to be a node. "Lefty" had been cut off during a spirited interrogation session with a homicidal marauder.

"I think you look cool with only one antenna," offered Chuck.

"One and a half!" snapped Jopp.

A series of unintelligible syllables pulled the trio's attention back to the crowd of Painaporo tribesmen. They reminded Chuck of five-foot-tall purple pineapples with arms and legs. He'd mentioned that to Jopp and Bhanakhana when they'd first arrived. The next few minutes had been wasted attempting to explain what a pineapple was.

"What's he saying?" asked Jopp.

"*She* is telling me that outsiders must appease Hoodoo."

"What's a hoodoo?" asked Chuck.

"Hoodoo is their god. He rules over the jungle."

"And Hoodoo wants to eat Jopp's head?"

"Apparently."

"Is there any other way to make an offering that doesn't require me dying?" asked Jopp.

Bhanakhana spoke to the tribal chief. She conferred with her fellow elders for a moment and then gave Bhanakhana a rather long-winded response. Bhanakhana was visibly taken aback, and he kept glancing back and forth between Jopp and the tribe.

"So, what'd she say?"

"Well . . . she has informed me there is indeed another way to make an offering to Hoodoo."

"Okay, what is it?"

"Well . . . the offering to Hoodoo must be a gift of life. Giving yourself over as sustenance is one way of providing life. The other way to give life would be . . ." Bhanakhana stalled.

"Spit it out, already."

"How shall I phrase this? You would have to . . . be *intimate* with the council of tribal matriarchs."

"Wait." Chuck gave them a devilish grin. "So Jopp's choice is either get his head cut off and eaten or he has to get freaky with a bunch of old pineapple ladies?"

"Not the words I would have chosen, but yes, that is correct."

Jopp scratched his chin. "I think I thought of a third choice."

***

"Oh shit oh shit oh shit oh shit oh shit," screamed Chuck and Jopp as they sprinted back to the ship.

"I am most displeased with this turn of events," huffed Bhanakhana as he lumbered alongside them. He glanced back over his massive shoulder, saw the hoard of angry Painaporo chasing after them, and quickened his pace.

"Most displeased indeed."

The trio burst out of the jungle and onto a rocky beach. Their ship, a late-model Estal Cube, rested at the water's edge, green waves lapping gently at its base. A door-shaped hole appeared in the side of the ship's chrome finish, allowing them to hurry inside without having to slow down. Bhanakhana used his data bracelet to power up the engine as they rushed to the bridge. Jopp dove into the pilot's chair and pulled up the navigational interface.

"Ready to leave whenever you are, Big Red," he called over his shoulder.

Bhanakhana glanced at his data bracelet again. "All systems shall be operational in six seconds."

Jopp's hand hovered over the flight console.

Chuck secured his chair's safety restraints.

"Three seconds . . . two seconds . . . proceed."

Jopp slapped the propulsion icon.

Outside, six dozen anthropomorphic pineapples took a break from hurling stone knives at the ship to gawk as the three-story silver cube shot up into the clouds. That night there would be much revelry amongst the Painaporo to celebrate the ousting of the strange intruders. Hoodoo would certainly be pleased.

ACKNOWLEDGMENTS

Disclaimer
There are a lot of people I need to thank. So if pages on pages of heartfelt gratitude doesn't sound interesting, you should skip this.

Still here?

You big softie.

Acknowledgments
To my amazing wife, Katie:

I am so lucky to have you as my partner in this surreal adventure called life. Thank you for pushing me every day to be a little bit better in everything I do. I would not be half the writer, half the man, or half the father without you by my side. This book would not exist without you.

I love you, Katie Rose.

To Mom & Dad:
Thank you for being the kind of parents that most people can only dream of. Thank you for always encouraging me to pursue whatever silly passion happened to hold my interest "that month." Thank you for raising me to believe nothing was unattainable.

To Erin:
Katie may be my "partner in life" but, kid sister, you will always be my "partner in crime." Your razor-sharp and unforgiving wit has been instrumental in me honing my own particular brand of humor. Love you . . .
   . . . you b-word.

To Al:
Take care of my sister . . . or else. That is all.

To Margie & "Big" Pat:
Complaining about your in-laws is one of the most over-used clichés in humor. Fortunately, it doesn't apply to me. I am so very lucky to have you in my life. Thank you for accepting me into your family with such open arms. Thank you for your relentless support of my writing career. Thank you for raising Katie to be such a tremendous woman.

To Kristie:
You're an awesome sister-in-law. But more importantly, you're an awesome sister to my wife. Thank you for being there for Katie whenever she's needed you.

To Tony:
Me encanta tomar cerveza contigo. Gracias por ser un gran cuñado.

To "the Cousins":
Most families have "that one weird cousin." Well in our family, we're all "that one weird cousin." I must have done something pretty great in a past life to earn such an amazing support system of wonderful weirdos. Thank you all so very much.

To Ryan:
Thank you for always being the type of guy I could feel good about looking up to.

To the Bishop & Snyder families:
We don't share any DNA . . . and I'm pretty sure there are no legal ties between us (none that I'm allowed to speak about publicly anyway), but make no mistake about it: I consider you all my family. Except for Paul . . . it's best we not discuss Paul.

To Paul *(damn, couldn't help myself)*:
Thanks for being my brother through everything.

To the Cincinnati Writer's Project:
I owe a lot to you all. You turned me from a wiseass goofball who could occasionally string a sentence together into a wiseass goofball who can actually write. Thank you so very much.

To the knuckleheads of the "Hurricane Ditka" League:
Can I be real with you all for a second? Fantasy Football is kind of a silly game. But you know what? Playing that silly game with you all and forcing myself to write those beautifully insightful and devastatingly funny weekly articles laid the foundation for me thinking I could make a go of this writing thing. Thanks, you big dumb jerks.

To Chris Hardwick:

Chris, you have no idea who I am . . . except for that one time you responded to a tweet I sent about a comic I made about one of your shows. . . . That was freakin' awesome. Anyway . . . I can't thank you enough for being such an inspiration to me during this process. Hearing your voice on the *Nerdist* podcast constantly encouraging people to stop waiting for permission and to just "make your thing" was instrumental in me resolving to finish this book. If you ever come across this, Chris, please know just how much you've inspired people to go after what they really want. From the bottom of my heart, thank you.

ABOUT THE AUTHOR

Patrick Edwards was born and raised in Chicago, Illinois, and currently lives in Cincinnati, Ohio, with his newborn daughter, Gabriella Rose, and his wife, Katie Rose, whom he married at Disney World because they both just refuse to grow up. *Space Tripping* is his first novel.

LIST OF PATRONS

Avalon Marissa Radys

Al Warpinski

Dan Zurawski

Edward J. Edwards

Jerry Snyder

Katie Rose Gough Edwards

Mason Cole

Mike Paukstis

Tyler Brundage

INKSHARES